RED THORNS

Red Thorns

A DARK COLLEGE BULLY ROMANCE

REBEL HART

1

DANI

"I still don't know about this dorm room situation," Mom said.

"Honey, she made her choice. We agreed to let her make her own decision," Dad murmured.

"But the apartments we saw were beautiful. And she'd have her privacy."

"Rena, stop it."

"Just try to talk to her, Peter. Please?"

I sighed. "I can hear you two, you know."

Mom smiled at me hesitantly and Dad shook his head. As I rolled my last suitcase out the front door of our beautiful two-story home, I didn't let their conversation dampen my spirits. I was excited to be rooming with my best friend, Hannah. I'd met her during orientation last year when we were both freshmen. And we seemed to latch on to one another. She was peppy and loud, with a boisterous laugh and curves that made every available boy on campus come over and talk to us just to get in good with her. She loved big costume jewelry and clothes that were a size too small. And through it all, we helped one another get through the tumultuous insanity that was freshman year of college.

I was lucky to be rooming with her again for our sophomore year.

"There she is, my future human resources professional. I'm proud of you, princess."

I smiled. "Hi, Daddy."

I set my suitcase beside him and leapt into his open arms. I'd taken general studies courses all throughout last year before I ended up declaring a human resources degree. And while it wasn't the sparkling medical degree or business degree my parents wanted for me, they supported me nonetheless.

Kind of.

"Well, just know you can change that major at any time," Mom said.

"Rena," Dad murmured.

I patted his back. "It's okay. Really. I promise."

"So we have a surprise for you!"

Dad held me by the shoulders and gave me that 'oh, shit' look he always got whenever Mom sprang something on him.

"We do?" Dad asked.

"Yes. We do. We're going to campus to help you unpack!"

I nodded slowly. "Thank you, Mom. I really appreciate it."

She placed her hand against my car. "Oh, you

don't have to thank us for something like that. Plus, I've been dying to know how this car drives."

"I think your mother wants to drive it herself," Dad murmured.

"Well, can you blame me? I mean, look at it. Sure, it's not the newest model. A few years old. But the pearl white paint is pristine and the leather seats are heated. Heated, sweetheart. Oh, this Range Rover is a dream."

I giggled. "At least you know what to get her for Christmas, Daddy."

He cleared his throat. "All right. Let's heave this last suitcase into the back and get on the road, then."

"Oh, can we stop by that coffee place just out of town? I never get over there and they have the best iced mochas in West Bloomfield!"

I looked over at Dad. "Yeah, Daddy. Best iced mochas ever."

He grimaced. "Why would anyone put coffee and chocolate together?"

"Come on, you two! Quit dragging!"

"Shouldn't I be the one to make this dri--?"

Mom snatched the keys from my hand and bounced her way into the driver's seat. I'd never seen her so peppy before. Or happy. And I knew the worse it got, the more worried she was growing. I still didn't know why me living in the dorms again made her so nervous. But I didn't question it. For Dad's sake, and my own.

"Let's get you to campus, then," he said.

The ten-hour drive to Ann Arbor was excruciating.

But it didn't squelch my excitement over the new year. I had a major, specialized classes to take, and with a lot of my required classes out of the way that meant I could really dig into my studies. Really focus. And if I played my cards right with some summer courses, I'd be able to graduate a semester early.

Something I knew my father would take pride in, since he'd done it himself during his own college years.

"So, how's Hannah?" Dad asked.

"Oh, please tell me you're rooming with her. I don't know if I can take you rooming with another stranger like that," Mom said.

I smiled. "Yep. She's my roomie. I'm really excited, too. We already know how we want to set up our dorm room."

"Oh? Have you already seen your room?" Mom asked.

"Yep. We requested the dorm building we were in last year because of its central location on campus."

Mom paused. "The really rundown building?"

Dad took her hand. "Honey, take a breath. She's our college girl now. She's not in pigtails anymore."

Mom ripped her hand away. "I know that."

I leaned forward and kissed Mom on her cheek. While I was a Daddy's girl, I knew Mom was struggling more with this than most. I knew it was a culture thing, too. With my father being Korean, he understood the value of letting children go when it came to their education. Being thankful for their grown-up state and encouraging them to reach for the stars. It's what his parents wanted for him, and that was how he was raised.

My mother, on the other hand, was a typical American helicopter parent.

"Take before and after pictures for your mother. You know she'll like that," Dad said.

I smiled. "I wouldn't have it any other way. You can give us some design tips, Mom."

"Oh! That would be lovely. Are you allowed to paint the walls?" she asked.

"Oh, boy," Dad murmured.

I snickered. "I don't think we can paint the walls, no."

"What about pictures? Can you hang pictures?"

"I think the walls are painted cement blocks. So that might be hard."

Mom's eyes bulged. "Cement blocks. Okay. Great."

I threw my head back in laughter as the smile plastered on her face slid slowly into an expression of disgust. With my mother being the forefront interior designer of our town, I could only imagine the horrors rushing through her head right now.

"Hey, it could be worse," Dad said.

"Don't you say it," Mom glowered.

"She could have shiplap scuffed up underneath some molded carpet."

"You said it! Why would you say it!? You monster."

I laughed until tears crested my eyes as my parents kissed in the front seat.

I took naps in the back seat until we finally made it to campus. I mean, we didn't get there until almost nine o'clock at night. But we made it and we were alive. Most everyone else had already shooed their parents away so they could go do other things on campus. I texted Hannah as we pulled onto campus. I heard music coming from one of the dorm buildings and groups of students were rushing around in packs to and from the cafeteria. The University of Michigan firmly welcomed me back with its newly-installed lit-up sign and directional arrows pointing me to my dorm.

As if I didn't already know where to go.

"Finally!" Hannah squealed.

I threw the Range Rover door open and leapt into my best friend's arms.

"Oh, I missed you so much over the summer," I murmured.

"We have to drop your stuff and get dinner. I want to tell you all about Europe," she said.

The revving of an engine caught my attention and I pulled away from Hannah. As the two of us held hands, I felt someone wrap their arm around my shoulder. I looked up at my father as we all stared out toward the main road, watching as a couple of lamp posts flickered with the need for a new bulb.

"What's that racket?" Mom asked.

"Motorcycles, I think," Dad said.

The rumbling got louder. Bigger. Stronger. I felt my ribcage shaking as a motorcycle peeled around the corner. There was a group of them. A large group of them. I counted four. Five. Seven. Eleven.

"How many of them are there?" Hannah murmured.

My eyes slid over their bikes. Some were stark black. Others had red racing stripes. It was intriguing, too, how their eyes raked over campus. There was a man at the front and a man at the back. Almost like a pack of wolves. And as my eyes slid along their leather jackets and torn-up denim, my curiosity piqued.

Not that it mattered.

"Well, don't I feel better," Mom said.

"Honey, don't," Dad said.

"Let's get you upstairs, shall we? We're on the top level with a great view. And a corner room, so there's a little extra space," Hannah said.

"Yes," I hissed.

"Goodie," Mom said flatly.

"Are there elevators?" Dad asked.

"Actually, yes. There is one. Though it takes a while for it to come downstairs sometimes. Since there's only one elevator servicing the whole building," Hannah said.

"I don't mind the wait," Mom said.

"I'll wait with your mother. You girls take up the lighter things," Dad said.

The engines continued revving off in the distance as Hannah and I hauled things out of the car. I had all sorts of things to take upstairs. Snacks I packed. Outfits I wanted to hang up instead of pack away in my dresser. Decorations for my desk and sheets for my bed. Hannah helped me get everything up to the top floor while Mom and Dad stayed downstairs with my four small suitcases.

And when I walked into the dorm room, it felt like home.

"Wow, this is bigger," I said.

"See? Told you. Now, let's put these snacks in the little pantry I've got made up. I already stacked my mini-fridge with sodas and cold coffees. So we should be good to go for the first week or so," Hannah said.

She helped me make up my bed and rearrange my things. I wanted my desk in the corner near the window, because she was right. The view was outstanding. As I gazed out the window, I saw those bikers come back down the street, revving their engines as if they were trying to alert campus to their presence.

The guy at the front of the pack pulled off to the side.

Huh.

"We're here!" Mom chimed in.

"We made it. You weren't kidding about that elevator," Dad said.

I pulled away from the window and took the suitcases from them. I saw Mom looking around the room with a wary eye as Dad rubbed her back. And when my stomach growled out loud, Hannah giggled.

"Do you want us to get a hotel room and come help you tomorrow?" Mom asked.

"Honey, she's got it from here," Dad said.

"I mean, we could grocery shop for you."

"Rena."

"Pick up a few things."

"Reen."

"I could pick up some decora--"

I threw my arms around my mother's neck and held her tightly. And when she wrapped her arms around me, I felt her sniffle. She shook with the force it took to hold back her tears, and I stroked her back lovingly. I knew she was going to miss me.

Just like I'd miss her.

"I love you so much," she whispered.

"I love you too, Mom."

"We are going to get a hotel for the night and rent a car to get home, so if you need us, call. Otherwise, you girls have a fantastic start to your semester," Dad said.

Then he pulled Mom away from me and softly guided her to the door and down the hallway to the elevator, where they finally disappeared.

"Is that car downstairs yours for the semester?" Hannah asked.

I grinned. "We should go find a parking spot for it. I've already secured a pass."

"Holy shit. This is going to be awesome!"

"I got it in the mail two weeks ago. Let's go!"

With Hannah's hand in mine, we raced down the stairs. With my parents nowhere in sight, we rushed over to the pearl white SUV and pulled the doors open. I felt the hairs on the nape of my neck prickle and turned around, leaning my back against the open door. When my gaze wandered across the street, I saw him.

In his leather jacket. And his black denim jeans. With his boots, and those long legs straddling his puttering motorcycle. A cigarette dangled from his lips.

"You coming?" Hannah asked.

It was dark, but I could've sworn he was staring at me from beyond the puffs of cigarette smoke. Underneath the flickering lamp light, I caught flashes of him. Flashes of tan skin and broad shoulders. Brown hair. Or was it black?

"Come on, the cafeteria closes in an hour," Hannah implored.

Maybe he's a student?

The more the man stared at me, the more I felt myself blushing. My cheeks burned and my neck heated. Even my hands began to tremble a bit. I cleared my throat as the soft smell of cigarette smoke finally graced my nose. But it wasn't until Hannah stepped in front of me that it snapped me from my trance.

"Hello? Earth to Dani? We need to go park," she said.

I cleared my throat. "Yes. Sorry. I'm coming."

The rumbling of motorcycles started up again as I turned my back. And for some reason, the rattling of my ribcage knocked me off balance. I felt my knees weaken as I reached for the inside of the door, trying to catch myself. As the sound grew, my legs turned to jello and I fell to my ass on the pavement of the parking lot. Above the roaring of the bikes' engines came a sound more intimidating. More infuriating. More embarrassing than ever.

The sound of men laughing at me as I sat there beside the SUV.

2

MAX

The girl was… strange. Dark brown hair. Slanted eyes. Tan skin, but not tan enough to protect her from the sun. She looked almost Asian. Except for those pinched, full lips.

Must've been her parents with her.

As the men roared with laughter, I put the kickstand down on my bike. With the engine still running, I tucked my cigarette into the side of my lips and started across the road. I kept my eyes on her, watching as she scrambled to her feet. She had on a white T-shirt and skinny jeans that accented her legs. Short and petite, rounding out into a set of hips that dipped softly into a waist.

Her waist.

I like waists.

My boots charging across the pavement sounded in my ears. My men quickly stopped laughing as they watched me approach her. She scrambled to her feet, clinging to that car of hers for dear life. It was a nice car. Big. Probably a gas-guzzler. I preferred my bike. The open road. Feeling the wind and the elements against my skin.

And it didn't guzzle gas.

"Need help?" I asked.

The girl whipped around in her tennis shoes and her wallet flew out of her pocket, along with her phone. Something in a small tube, too. Possibly lip gloss. She crouched back down to try and collect the rolling tube as it threatened to hide underneath the massive white car.

I stopped it with my boot.

"There," I said.

Her fingers reached out for it and I noticed how delicate they were. They looked soft, like feathers on a duck's back. I drew in another long pull from my cigarette before she gripped that little tube. And when she stood back up, she started coughing as her head shot straight into the cloud of smoke wafting away from my face.

"I don't need help, thanks."

Her voice was soft. Her eyes didn't quite meet mine. I bent down anyway and picked up her wallet while she scrambled for her phone. A phone that wouldn't stop buzzing. No doubt her parents, who I had seen leave only minutes before she emerged from her dorm room.

I peeked into the car and saw another girl staring at me with a grin on her face.

"Hey there, handsome," she said.

I nodded, but didn't say anything.

The girl with the tree trunk hair waved her hand in her face before she coughed again. My eyes slowly slid down her body, drinking in her languid movements. Her neck, straight and graceful. Her arms, softly toned. Her T-shirt, clinging softly to her chest and slipping to the top of her jeans. Where it was haphazardly tucked in before her legs took over the show.

I liked her legs.

Which meant I'd like her ass, too.

"This your dorm?" I asked.

"Sure is, bucko," the girl in the car said.

I ignored her as my eyes met the bright brown eyes of the girl in front of me. And as they met my green ones, she nodded.

But she didn't speak.

"Need anything else taken upstairs?" I asked.

"No," she finally said.

"Actually, there is one more suitcase back here," the girl in the car said.

"Hannah, shut up. No, I don't need your help."

"It's a big one, too. I don't think I can carry it."

"I can. I'll get it upstairs."

"We really could use your--"

"We don't need your help," the girl said curtly.

I sucked on my cigarette, inhaling the smoke as it filled my lungs. Then I let the butt fall from my mouth before I blew the smoke into the air. The girl in front of me waved her hand around, coughing and sputtering as she backed up. And it gave me enough time to reach for the door beside me and rip it open.

"Hey! I don't need your help," she said.

I looked into the back seat and saw a small suitcase sitting on the floorboard. Hell, it looked more like a toiletry bag than anything else. I quirked an eyebrow at this Hannah girl. The one with the big jewelry and the thick cheeks that peaked like apples the broader she smiled.

"See? Suitcase," she said.

"I've got it," the girl behind me insisted.

"I'll carry it up," I said.

"Oh, wonderful," Hannah said.

"It's just my shampoo and stuff. It's fine."

I scooped it up and closed the car door before I turned back to my guys. I waved my hand at them, signaling that I'd be right back. And when I did, their damn catcalling started up. Whistles filled the air and a couple of the guys gave me a thumbs-up. Then the comments began.

"We give you five minutes with that one!"

"I think you got ten in ya!"

"Pics, or it didn't happen, Max!"

The guys burst into laughter as I snickered, shaking my head at those asshats. But when I felt someone tugging at the bag in my hand, I looked down to see the dark-haired girl fighting me for the damn thing.

"Give it. I've got it," she said.

The bright pink of her face and the worried furrow of her brow told me everything I needed to know. She was embarrassed. And for some reason, that mattered. I held my hand up toward the guys again and made a fist, telling them they needed to

shut the fuck up. And they did, too. Almost immediately.

Causing the girl to look up at me with those bright
brown eyes of hers again.

"I've got it," I said.

Her eyes darted back across the road, coming back
to mine before she slowly turned to her friend in the
car. I waited for her hand to drop and those delicate
fingers of hers to pull back. All she had to do was let
me help. Let me get the rest of her stuff to her room so
I knew where to find her if I wanted to see her again.

And I knew I wanted to see her again.

"There's always the pizza joint that stays open until
midnight," Hannah said.

The girl sighed. "Fine. There are a couple of other
things I need to grab really quickly, though."

"Toss them my way."

She walked around to the back of her car and
opened the trunk. The plastic bags she pulled out
looked as if they were filled with nothing but snacks,
sweets, and junk. Oh, yeah. They were college girls, all
right. I walked over and took the bags from her, giving
her the breadth and ability to close the trunk. I heard
the guys snickering and laughing to themselves across
the street. The warm summer breeze that kicked up
carried their sounds as the girl led me to the dorm
doors. I heard one last guy whistle at me just before we
breached the threshold, and I promised to figure out
who it was and put him on janitorial duty for an entire
fucking week.

But it still made me chuckle to myself.

I ducked through the entrance and was led to an elevator. Where I had to duck once again just to get in. I stood by the small girl as we rode all the way to the top floor in silence. And since she insisted on standing in front of me, I checked out her assets.

Oh, yeah. I really like her ass.

"It's just down the hall. At the corner," she said.

The doors opened and I ducked again. I watched as some of the other college kids peeked their heads out to yell at someone down the hallway. But when they saw me coming, they shut up. People always shut up when I arrived on the scene. Whether it was the smell of cigarettes on my leather jacket or the sheer size of my body, I wasn't sure. I enjoyed it, though.

They stared at me as the two of us made our way to her dorm room.

"I can take it from here," she said.

"Open the door," I said.

"I can take--"

"I said open the door."

She stared at me for a long time. But finally, she caved. They always caved, too. That was the best part. No matter how strong of a front they put up, eventually they no longer resisted me. I grinned as she unlocked the door. She swung it open and walked inside, then held out her arms. She looked exasperated. Tired of my shit. And as I looked back down the hallway, I saw a few girls standing near their own doors with their eyes sliding up and down my body.

A flash of jealousy ignited within me, too.

I can't believe my cousin gets to spend his year surrounded by so many babes.

Benji had the smarts of the family. Book smarts, anyway. Which is why I always encouraged him to get his degree instead of putzing around with the crew. He had potential, you know? Not like the rest of us. He could stay out of trouble with that brain of his.

I wish I had this kind of free time to fuck around.

"All right, now give me my things."

The girl's voice ripped me from my trance. She had spunk, I'd give her that. Even though she still wouldn't quite look me in the eye. Not unless I demanded it. Then again, I knew how scary I looked. I knew how I came off to people. And while it was intentional most of the time, it wasn't intentional right now.

Still, when I tried to walk through the door, she stopped me.

"No. Hand me my things."

I grinned. "But I came up all this way."

She snickered. "And I can take it from here."

"Cute."

"Nothing personal. Just how it is."

"I understand. Daddy taught you not to trust strangers, didn't he?"

"It's not like that."

I passed off the bags. "Sure it's not."

"No, really. It's not."

I grinned. "See you around, Daddy's girl."

I winked at her before I backtracked down the hallway. Now all I had to do was wait. With everyone's eyes on me and the girls practically licking their lips at my patched leather jacket, I slid my hand into my jeans pocket.

Three. Two. One…

"My name is Danika!"

Her voice echoed down the hallway in sweet, sweet release. Victory was mine once again. Girls were so easy to figure out. A full-blown smile crossed my face as I jammed my finger into the elevator button and listened to the gears groan as I turned around. I saw her standing at the other end of the hallway, her hands balled into fists. Her cheeks were brighter than ever, her eyes glaring at me in frustration I wanted to devour with my own two lips.

"Good to know, Daddy's girl!"

The elevator opened and I ducked down, backing my way in. I felt people scurrying around me, trying to get off before they were crushed by my massive form. I kept my eyes on the girl as the doors closed, and for a split second I thought she might come after me. Beat those delicate fists against my chest to try and 'show me a thing or two.'

But she didn't.

Good for her.

"That quick, huh?"

Hannah's voice ripped me from my trance as the elevator doors opened again.

"Oh, come on. Do you really think I don't know your game?" she asked.

I stepped off the elevator. "Good night, Hannah."

"At least you picked up my name. Kudos to you!"

I lifted my hand to wave at her over my shoulder. I

heard her giggling as the elevator doors closed off her sound, and I made my way back out into the night. I always felt more comfortable at night. As if I were shrouded from the world. It worked with the reputation I had in town. Hell, with the reputation of my entire crew. I took great pride in cleaning up the Red Thorns. Especially after the chaos my father plunged us into for a while. But it wasn't easy. Ann Arbor was still scared of us after all these years. And rightfully so.

A little bit of fear never hurt anyone.

"Seven minutes, forty-two seconds!"

"A new record for limp dick over here!"

I shook my head as I crossed the road, making my way back to my bike.

"So you got pictures?"

"Oh, I bet he's got lots of pictures."

"Max always has the best ones. Which shots did you get this time?"

I ignored their statements as I hiked my leg back over my bike. I kicked up the stand and revved my engine, checking my fuel levels. I needed a fucking gas station. Then a nice cold shower.

"Oh, shit. That her in the window?"

Rupert's voice caught my ear and I slowly lifted my eyes. As I sat there with my legs straddling my bike, I pulled out another cigarette and slipped it between my lips as one of the guys held up a light for me. I puffed and pulled, until it was lit and burning at the end with that relaxing sizzle I always enjoyed.

With Danika staring at me from her dorm room window.

"Yep. That's her," I said.

"Oh, you've got her on your hook, Max."

"When you coming back for round two?"

I didn't answer the question. I just kept staring at her until the curtain fell between the two of us and separated our worlds once more.

I'll be back for you.

That I was sure of.

3

DANI

"Ho-lee-shit," Hannah said.

The curtain dropped from my hand as I quickly whipped around.

"And you're still flushed! Did he kiss you? Did he hold you close? Tell me what those muscles felt like. Because that's a big boy with some big muscles underneath those clothes."

I blinked. "What?"

"Girl, you don't even have your voice! He did something, didn't he? Oh, you have to tell me all the juicy details. What's his name? Where's he from? What do those lips of his feel like?"

I paused. What was his name? I should have asked.

"You kissed a guy and you don't even know his name?" Hannah asked.

"We didn't kiss," I blurted out.

"Then why are you so flushed right now?"

Because he's the sexiest man I've ever seen.

"I just--he wanted to come into the room. Is that normal?" I asked.

"You didn't let him in?" Hannah asked.

I shook my head. "No."

"Girl, why the hell didn't you let him in!? I would've given you privacy. Come back with a pizza to help you refuel."

I wrinkled my nose. "I'm not going to sleep with a guy whose name I don't know."

"That's half the fun, Dani. That's what college is all about. Making friends, getting good grades, going to parties, and making lovely mistakes like that."

"Your definition of fun and my definition of fun are very different. And besides, I haven't even had--"

I stopped myself as Hannah drew in a breath. "You've never had sex?"

I rolled my eyes. "Thanks for blurting that out everywhere."

"Holy. Fuck. You've never had sex!"

"I hate you."

She gripped my upper arms. "This is perfect."

I furrowed my brow. "What is?"

"This. All of this. I now know what my goal for this year is."

I quirked an eyebrow. "Getting good grades?"

"No. We're going to get you laid."

"Uh, no."

"Yes."

"I said no. Why doesn't anyone like that word?"

"We're going to find you a guy to lose your virginity to."

"Isn't that supposed to be something I dictate?"

She grinned wildly. "We could work on Mr. Motorcycle, if you want."

"No, thank you."

"Oh, come on, Dani."

"Seriously, Hannah. When I'm ready, it'll happen. But it won't happen until I'm ready. End of story."

She playfully sighed. "Fine, fine. Be a party pooper."

"Sorry I won't let you dictate who I have sex with and when."

She rolled her eyes. "Such a drama queen."

She smiled brightly at me. "Ready for that pizza joint?"

"Is it bad that I kind of just want to unpack?"

She shrugged. "That's fine. They deliver, and Mom gave me mounds of pizza money before she left this morning. It's on me."

I nodded. "Sounds like a plan."

I hoisted my first suitcase onto my bed and unzipped it. All of my jeans. Wonderful. Easy enough. I didn't even own a pair of shorts. Jeans were much too comfortable. I had my pajama pants and my jeans packed away in the same suitcase. Along with three professional pencil skirts Mom insisted she buy me before the start of the year.

"Wow, those are nice. Are those new?" Hannah asked.

I nodded. "Mom insisted I have them just in case anything came up."

"Like having sex?"

I chewed on the inside of my cheek. "Drop it."

"Consider it dropped."

I knew better than that, though.

"What do you want on your pizza, Dani? I'm about to order online."

I shrugged. "The usual's fine. Pepperoni and mushroom with olives."

"Oh, do you have any of that honey sauce?"

I smiled. "I brought four of them with me this time instead of just two."

"I fucking love you."

"That stuff is really good, isn't it? Also, random fact. It goes really well in coffee."

"Wait, what?"

"Yeah, I know that sounds weird. But a few days ago I made myself a mug of coffee and didn't have any sugar. Without thinking, I reached for what I thought was the honey to sweeten it. But it was that hot honey stuff. If you don't mind a little spice in your coffee, it's *really* good."

"I'll have to try that tomorrow."

I started placing my clothes in the small dresser I had put in my corner closet. Then I hung up my good shirts, my pencil skirts, and the couple of nicer long-sleeve shirts that I didn't want to get wrinkled and tossed my chucks into the bottom of the closet. I decorated my desk with all my little trinkets. And just as I got all of my chargers for my side of the room set up, someone knocked at the door.

"Pizza's here!" Hannah exclaimed.

"Wow, that was fast."

She snickered. "Dani, you've been unpacking for over an hour now."

I paused. "I have?"

"Yep! And I think you've been thinking about Mr. Hunk of ManMeat a little too much, too."

I rolled my eyes. "You would think that."

"Tell me you weren't."

I shook my head. "No, actually, I wasn't. Because the last thing I need is distractions."

"I mean, you could have a good time with him and then he wouldn't be a distraction any longer."

"You know good and well that man only wants one thing from me. And it's not something I'm willing to give to him. Whether I knew him or not."

"Now you're just being dramatic."

I stored my suitcase under my bed. "No, Hannah. I'm being serious. I'm still a virgin, okay? There's nothing wrong with that. I'm sure as hell not sharing my body with a man I don't know who is only going to take what he wants before leaving. Got it?"

Her eyebrows rose. "Wow, you cursed."

"Because I'm serious, and I want you to drop the topic."

She placed the pizza on her bed. "Consider it dropped."

"Now, if you want to have something to go with this pizza, help me with that red suitcase of mine."

"Why? What's in it?"

"Why don't you hand it to me and we can see?"

She shrugged as she set the pizza down, then walked over to the suitcase leaning against the wall.

The second she picked it up, her eyes ignited. I smiled brightly as she carried it over to me. I carefully unzipped the hardened case and flipped open the top. My pride and joy from last year. A present my father got me specifically for dorm living.

"You brought the TV back," Hannah said.

I nodded. "I brought the TV back."

"Here, we can use my dresser as a little mount since it's already over on this side of the room."

"That's what I was thinking. Because putting its back toward the window won't cast that awful glare we had last year."

"I'll shove the dresser over and you hook it up. I'm terrible with shit like that."

I nodded. "Sounds good. I need to dig out all the cables, anyway."

Hannah groaned. "Do we have the DVD player, too?"

I pulled out the Roku stick. "Oh, no. We've got something much better."

"I fucking love your parents. And the fact that you're an only child."

I shrugged. Sure, maybe my parents did spoil me. Between my mother's successful interior design business and my father's pharmaceutical work, they were more than comfortable. But I didn't consider myself spoiled. Sure, they treated me to things every now and again. I didn't let that get in the way of the important things, though. Like school, and making very good grades. Studying for tests was always a priority, and I had a life plan laid out that didn't include any sort of money my parents always talked about throwing at me once I graduated.

Hannah sighed. "All right. Ready when you are."

"When I tell you to, I need you to rattle off the password for this wifi so I can make sure everything hooks up well."

"I can do that."

I heaved the television up. "Good."

I heard Hannah munching on pizza as the smell of that hot honey filled the air. It was very distracting, but it only made me work quicker. I got the television hooked up with power and slipped the Roku stick into the HDMI port. I checked to make sure the power worked, and before I knew it the Roku was prompting me to sign into the wifi.

"All right. Password time."

Hannah swallowed hard before she cleared her throat.

"Capital U-lowercase o-Capital M, 9-3-4-1, under-score-lowercase c-Capital O-lowercase m."

I typed it in. "Well, that was complex. Let's see if it works."

I watched the loading screen as the Roku did its thinking. I'd brought the DVD player just in case we needed it. But I hoped the internet was strong enough for something like this. I murmured to myself, saying a little prayer for our pizza and movie night. And when the home screen for the Roku popped up, I threw my fists into the air.

"Victory is ours!"

Hannah clapped her hands. "Now get over here

and help me eat this food. And grab me a soda, would you?"

I tossed her the remote. "Find something you want to watch."

"Just not a chick flick. I want something funny tonight. Something that'll make us laugh so hard we're scared of throwing our pizza back up."

I opened the fridge. "I hear Trevor Noah's new standup is hysterical."

"Oh, Trevor Noah it is, then."

I plucked us both a soda from the mini-fridge, then hopped onto Hannah's bed. And as I poured that hot honey over my first slice of pizza, I drew in a deep breath. This was it. We had a week before classes started, then we'd be well on our way to tackling our second year of college. It felt good, no longer being a freshman, a stranger on campus, always questioning things. Registration had been easier this time around. Moving in had been a breeze. Sort of. And now, I got to spend quality time with my best friend for an entire week before classes dragged us to opposite ends of campus.

Hannah guffawed. "Oh, my God. My stomach. It hurts."

I had to stop eating pizza in order to take deep breaths. My gosh, this standup special really was hysterical. It almost made it hard to eat.

Almost.

We stuffed ourselves stupid with pizza as the comedy show wound down. And just as we started throwing things into our small trash cans, I heard loud music rolling down the hallway. The walls thudded. Lights went off. And as I saw the soft glow of ethereal colors from underneath the doorway, my eyes slid over to Hannah.

"You know what that means," I said.

She grinned. "Yep. It means decorating is going to be left until tomorrow. Because the first dorm party of the semester is already under way!"

She raced for her closet and started sifting through her clothes. The music grew closer. And closer. Until the loud music was all my brain registered. I had just enough time to put up a few music posters to offset the twinkling lights Hannah had already strung up on her end. Then I changed my pizza-covered T-shirt and slipped out of my tennis shoes. Hannah changed her outfit four separate times, giving me even more time to unpack the rest of my shirts and jam my underwear into a drawer in my dresser.

After she was done, she swung our room door open.

"Welcome to campus, guys. Woo hoo!"

A random voice filled our room before a string of fake flowers descended around my head.

"These. Are so. Cute," Hannah yelled.

"Whenever you're ready, there's drinks and some snacks. Come enjoy yourselves!"

I nodded. "Thanks!"

I walked over to the window and peeked down. I saw students piling into the dorm as music started pulsing below us. Each floor of the dorm was gearing up for their own party, hosting a level-by-level concoction of drinks, snacks, dancing, and decorations. Strobe lights quickly filled the room. I peeked out into the hallway and saw Hannah with her hands in the air, already dancing with a drink in her hand, enjoying her 'not freshman' status.

"Come on! What are you waiting for!?" she yelled.

Rearranging the flowers around my neck, I started for the hallway, ready to make a new memory, usher in the new college year, and hopefully shake that massive brute of a man from my mind long enough to get some sleep tonight.

4

MAX

"Hey, got a smoke?"

I rolled my eyes as Benji rode up on his rust bucket of a bike.

"No, I don't."

"Ah, come on, Max. You always have a pack on you."

"And I'm not giving you a single one."

Benji snickered as he parked his bike next to me. Most men didn't dare do that. Not when I was at the helm. But he was my cousin, and he was an idiot. Booksmart, sure. But certainly not street smart. He didn't understand how this game worked. How things were played. And as the guys smoked their cigarettes and shot the shit, I gazed across the street. At that damn dorm building.

For the second day in a row.

"He's already rubbing shoulders with some girl, you know."

Rupert's voice piped up behind me and Benji snickered.

"Shouldn't shock me one bit. What floor is she on?"

I licked my lips. "Top floor."

"Wanna know a secret?"

"No."

"You're really going to like this secret, though."

"No."

Rupert smacked my upper arm with his hand. "Listen to the boy for once."

Benji snickered. "I'm not a damn boy. I'm older than you guys were when you pledged this damn crew."

I gritted my teeth. "Watch your mouth."

Benji shrugged. "Whatever. That's my dorm, too."

Rupert barked with laughter. "Of course it is."

I slowly looked over at Benji as a sly smile crossed his face.

"That's your what?"

He grinned. "That's my dorm. I'm on the third floor."

I pointed to the girl's building. "That one."

He nodded. "Yep."

"You're in that dorm."

"Uh huh."

"On the third floor."

He grinned. "Yes, siree. And you don't know what you're missing, either. College girls are where it's at. They know how to have a good time, they know how to keep their feelings in check, and they're always wanting to try new things."

Rupert elbowed me. "You hear that? New things."

"And biker guys are always new things to girls like them."

I sighed. "You're not a biker guy."

Benji waved his hand in the air. "When I graduate, I will be. I'll be so fraught with knowledge on business and shit like that you'll have no choice."

Rupert paused. "The fuck is 'fraught'?"

I rolled my eyes. "Shut up, you two."

I felt the guys staring at me as I watched across the road. All night I'd thought of that girl. Those eyes of hers kept me awake. That ass of hers kept my finger-tips tingling. I didn't know what it was about her. Possibly her clumsiness. Possibly the innocence in her eyes. I could almost smell virgins. They had it written all over their faces. And it was cute when one pretended to be tough.

Even cuter when they pretended not to be inter-ested in me.

Daddy's girl.

The waver of her voice as she called out her name yesterday stuck with me. How nervous she had been, yet the fight she put up. It was admirable. The strength she thought she possessed made me grin. I pulled my pack of cigarettes out from the inside pocket of my leather jacket and slipped one out of the sleeve. I heard someone already strike up a match to hold to my face when Benji's voice piped up.

And his complaining blew out the flame in front of me.

"The fuck? I knew you had cigs on you. Give me one."

I glared at him. "No."

"Dude."

"Benj."

"I'll just go get my own, then."

I nodded. "You do that."

Another match struck up and I stuck the cigarette between my lips. I sucked on it until the damn thing lit, staring Benji down the entire time. No way I'd let this fucker pledge us. He had better things coming with his life. He was destined for more than we were. He deserved a nicer life than this one provided.

I mean, I could only clean up a motorcycle gang so much.

"Whatever," Benji murmured.

Rupert nudged me. "Can I get one of those?"

I handed him the pack and my cousin scoffed.

"Yeah. Great. Rub it in my face, you little fucker."

I blew smoke his way. "You wanna try that again?"

He waved his hand in his face and the guys chuckled at him.

"Can't handle the smoke? Don't ask for the cigarette."

"College is where you're needed, boy. Not here."

"That rust bucket can't keep up with us anyway."

"You get laid with that rust bucket over there?"

Benji grumbled. "I hate you all."

Rupert puffed on his cigarette. "So tell us more about these college girls you meet up with."

Benji glared at him. "Why should I?"

"Because the man asked you a question," I said.

All eyes were on me as my cousin shook his head.

"Girls like them, they don't have sexual boundaries. They know how to have a good time. And there's practically a party every damn night on campus somewhere. We had a party in our dorm last night. Multilevel. There's been talk of another one striking up around nine. But I don't know much about that."

Rupert snickered. "Why not?"

Benji paused. "Because I've been walking around campus to familiarize myself with what my route is."

Good for you. "Find out more about this party for me."

"I'm not part of this crew, remember? You don't get to give me orders."

My eyes slowly fell to his and I narrowed them.

"Get me more information on this party I'm going to attend."

My cousin grinned. "Trying to get some ass?"

"Just go," Rupert said.

"All I'm saying is, this is the place to get it. Want me to check up on your girl for you?"

I puffed smoke in his face. "Just go."

"Fine, whatever."

Benji pushed off the sidewalk with the sputtering old rust bucket I'd told him not to buy. I told him it would suck down more money than it was worth and it still wouldn't ride like he wanted it to. But my cousin was always determined to prove me wrong. I told him he couldn't pledge this crew, but no matter what I did, he always tried. Showed up randomly and tried to ride with us. Tried getting himself into trouble just to show us he was capable of defending himself. I'd had to bail that asshole out of more bullshit in his life than I had the rest of this fucking crew. I used that mindset against him, though.

I told him he'd never get the grades in high school to go to college, and he did.

I told him he'd never get into a university, and he did.

I told him he'd never have the guts to do something no one else in this crew had done, and he did. He was the first one of us to go to school. To declare a degree. To make something of himself.

And if that's what got him away from this place, I'd keep challenging him until it got him as far away from this family as possible.

"So you coming back for the party?" Rupert's voice pulled me from my trance.

"Don't know."

"Oh, come on. You know you're going to come back."

I shrugged. "Got shit to do."

"What kind of shit? Better than getting laid?"

The guys behind me agreed with him as I puffed at the last of my cigarette.

"We'll see," I said.

I let the butt fall from my lips before I smashed it into the ground with my boot.

"Oh, come on. You can tell us. You're coming back, aren't you?"

I slowly looked over at Rupert and blew the last of the smoke I had in my lungs in his face.

"Shut up, Roop."

He snickered. "I love pissing you off."

I revved my engine before I sped off, watching Benji putter his way to his dorm with that awkward bike of his. He was a bit too big for it. Those wheels were a bit too flat. But even so, I saw how girls stared at him, licking their lips and running their eyes over him. To them, he was a prized treasure wrapped in leather, black denim, and cockiness. Which they seemed to enjoy.

Interesting.

No matter. There were other things to focus on before that party. And collecting our next job was one of those things. I rode down toward the main highway with the guys following me. And when our first opening came, we sped in the direction we needed to go. We turned onto the highway and weaved in and out of traffic. Horns honking. People cursing. Lights flashing.

It made me smile, feeling the wind wrapping around my body as the people of Ann Arbor cursed at us.

I thrust my hand into the air as we sped down the road. I twirled it around once, then gave the signal. I held up the number 'two' with my fingers, instructing the men to disperse, to go carry on with their days so I could do what needed to be done. It was time for us to get paid again. Time for us to bow down to the darkness we sold our souls to. I heard men darting to my left and right. I saw Rupert speed ahead of me and pop a wheelie before cruising past a police officer that flashed his lights.

"Better run, boy," I murmured.

I settled in for the ride as I slowed down. I wanted to take this drive slowly, drink in the world around me. Because every job came with a risk I knew I had to take. As president of the Red Thorns motorcycle gang, it was my job to see to it that my men always went home. That they always came out of things alive. Even if it meant my own life in the process.

It came with the territory.

And it was a risk I was always willing to shoulder.

The Red Thorns had been through some shit in their history. My father had established the crew after parting ways with a particularly nasty gang that used to roam these parts. He was the only man in gang history to successfully leave. Before he left, he had to endure a serious amount of ridicule and physical pain, as they burned the crew tattoo right off his back with a brand from a bonfire.

I shivered every time I saw those scars on my father's back.

He'd established the crew I headed up now. But he wasn't a fan of me trying to clean them up. My father was a ruthless man. Angry at what his former crew did to him. What they put him through. What they'd expected of him. They'd turned him into a dark man, and the irony was that he thought he was doing this world a great deal of good. He had become the kind of man he'd tried to get away from, and he didn't even realize it.

I saw it, though.

And so did my older brother.

I need to check on him soon.

I darted down an alleyway and drew in a deep breath. I knew where I was going to pick up this job. The same place I always went. When my father had finally stepped away from the crew, he passed it onto my brother, who was three years older than me, and not very good at standing up to our father. My brother was a pushover. As strong as he was physically, Dad had a grip on him mentally. Which dove this crew into some shady shit for a very long time. But after my brother's accident, after having the only thing he loved ripped away from him, he finally saw the light.

Like I had years before.

That's how the club got passed down to me. From my father, to my older brother, to me. Family lineage, just like tradition stated. But my father didn't like me having control of the Red Thorns. I wasn't as much of a pushover. I always questioned him as well as his motives, something he never enjoyed about me. It had been easier to manipulate my brother than it was me. But with my brother no longer being able to ride due to his injuries, I was the only thing the crew had.

Since Dad was enjoying his wealth too much.

My lungs longed for another cigarette. I pulled over and ripped my helmet off. I always needed a cigarette before going to see my father, who doled out not only our jobs, but our paychecks. Despite not being the president any longer, he still owned us. All of us. We depended on him for jobs, getting paid, and generally keeping our noses clean with the police in the area. Which was why dealing with my father was always a delicate balance. A ballet of tension and release. Pleasure and pain. My father was the ultimate sadist, and I was a dominant in waiting. Accepting my punishment before popping up and showing my father exactly who ran this show.

I struck a match and inhaled deeply, pulling the smoke into my lungs. I felt the nicotine spread through my veins, relaxing me as I sat on the side of the road. Cars whizzed by at lightning speed. Eighty miles an hour wasn't enough on this highway sometimes. And as my eyes looked toward the horizon, I saw it. Up on the hill. With the sun dipping below it, signaling the end of the day.

Our owner's mansion in the middle of his estate. Stationed on a hill for all of Ann Arbor to see.

Like a beacon of darkness that taunted the world to come get him.

5

DANI

I groaned as I lay in bed. Holy mackerel, I shouldn't have done that party. As I lay there staring at the ceiling, I fell in and out of sleep. Instead of getting up and walking campus, or decorating the rest of my side of the room, or generally organizing things, I dozed. The smell of pizza and booze still hung in the air. The beating of the music still thudded in my ears. I rolled over and pulled the covers over my head, determined to go back to sleep. Determined to not let that morning sun wake me up since I hadn't gone to bed until three in the morning.

"Rise and shine, beautiful. It's past lunchtime."

I paused. "What?"

Hannah pulled the comforter off me and the smell of coffee and hot honey perked me right up. I groaned as I sat upright in bed, twisting so my back leaned against the wall. She smiled at me as she handed me the mug of coffee. It even had my name on it.

I cleared my throat. "Cute."

She smiled. "You think? Mom got them for me. You can write on them with markers and erase them later. I kind of wanted to draw a dick on mine."

"Mature."

"Hey, get that coffee in you so you're on my level. I'm already into my third cup, and you're right. This hot honey stuff is amazing. We're definitely going to need more."

I closed my eyes and took my first long pull of that glorious drink. If we had to buy more bottles, then so be it. I was practically addicted to the stuff at this point. And I was glad I finally had someone on my bandwagon. Mom didn't like spicy things and Dad wasn't a honey fan. He didn't like anything that was overly sweet in the first place. Unless, of course, he was talking about the cheesy way my mom went about romance.

I rolled my eyes at the thought.

"So guess what I heard this morning?"

I took another long pull. "I'm surprised you were up this morning."

She snickered. "By morning, I mean an hour ago."

"That sounds better."

"Apparently, there's going to be another party tonight."

I paused. "Another one?"

"Yep. Just for the top three levels, though. Not the entire dorm, like last night."

I blinked. "Yay?"

"Oh, come on. You know you had fun last night.

And I saw you watching out for that hunk of meat the entire time."

"I wasn't watching out for him. I was watching out for myself. There were way too many people stacked on this floor last night."

"Trust me, I know a wandering set of eyes when I see them. And you were definitely hunting him down."

I rolled my eyes. "Whatever. I need more coffee for this."

Hannah snickered. "Anyway, this one is to celebrate. Last night was, like, a campus-wide 'yay semester' party. This one is just for this dorm to celebrate the craziness. No random people coming in and out. Just for us, you know? There shouldn't be a lot of people piled in like last night. You'll enjoy this one better."

"And if I don't enjoy it at all?"

"Quit being a party pooper and drink your coffee. I know how you are when you're tired."

"Then hush so I can drink."

Hannah giggled at me as I drained my drink. And, like the wonderful friend she had become, she got me another mug. She stirred the hot honey in before it filled my nostrils, and the only thing I thought about was how to get out of this party. Where I could go on campus in order to have an excuse to get away from it all.

The sound of bikes outside pulled me from my trance.

Hannah rushed to the window. "Nuh. Uh."

I furrowed my brow. "Are they back out there?"

She grinned. "Why don't you come take a look for yourself?"

The sound of a roaring engine split the air again and I slipped off my bed. With my coffee held tightly in my hands, I walked over to the window and peeked out, hoping and praying the sound wasn't them. I didn't like how those guys made me feel. Just sitting across from campus. Not quite on it, and not quite in it. Hovering, like the creepy guys they were.

But once my eyes fell on the guy who'd helped me with my stuff, a shiver slid down my spine.

And not a cold one, either.

"Where's that one going?"

I followed Hannah's pointing finger and saw where the revving engine was coming from. One of the bikers with a rusted-up bike was riding it onto campus. Over the curb, down the sidewalk, and straight for the dorm. My eyebrows rose as he disappeared underneath the awning of the building. I sipped my coffee and lifted my eyes, gazing back over the street.

Just before the sound of roaring engines kicked up again.

"Where do you think they're going?"

Hannah's voice pulled me from my trance and I backed away from the window.

"Don't know. Don't care."

She snickered. "Oh, come on. You know you care a little bit."

I shrugged. "I care about coffee. Does that count?"

"Well, from the looks of it, we might be seeing more of them this semester."

I frowned. "I don't like the sound of that."

She giggled. "I'm not complaining one bit. I mean, they're pretty hot."

"If you're into that kind of thing."

"You mean bikes and leather and muscles? Hell yeah, I'm into that kind of thing."

"Well, I'm not."

"You talking in your sleep last night told me otherwise."

I paused. "What?"

She laughed. "Yep. Your dreams tell me a different story."

"What are you talking about?"

Hannah started mocking me. "Oh, Troy. Yes. That's it, Troy. I need more things carried up here."

I narrowed my eyes. "I don't even know the man's name. I never got it. Jerk."

She sighed. "Ah well, worth a shot to get you to blush even more than you already were."

My hand flew to my face. "What?"

She threw her head back in laughter. "Works every time."

I groaned as I turned my back to her. I walked over to my desk, preparing myself for the busy afternoon. I sat down and turned on my laptop, pulling up my schedule as I reached for a book. And as I sat it open in my lap, I started plotting out my course around campus for my upcoming weeks as well as finishing up my summer reading for English.

"What are you doing?" Hannah asked.

I licked my lips. "Reading. I didn't quite finish my English stuff this summer."

She ripped the book off my lap. "I don't think so."

"Hey!"

She tossed it to the side. "You and I are going to get ready for this party. You're going to put on something that isn't jeans and a long-sleeve shirt, you're going to have fun, and you're going to join us in that hallway tonight."

I gritted my teeth. "It's two in the afternoon. We've got plenty of time."

"You've got ten minutes. I'm going to go on the prowl to find out more information about this thing tonight. And when I get back, we're going to clean you up. I mean, a good cleaning, too. We're going to trim up your hair, maybe give you some bangs--"

I pointed at her. "You're not cutting my hair."

"Then we'll go to a salon. When's the last time you had it cut?"

"No one's cutting my hair!"

"Then I need to try out some makeup looks on you."

I sighed hotly. "No."

"We're getting you ready for this party and you're going to look stunning. What you're not going to do is spend your last few days of freedom doing something you should've done over the summer. You didn't finish? Tough shit. Time to have some fun before our lives get sucked away with school. Got it?"

I watched with tired eyes as she flounced out of the room. How Hannah always walked with grace and poise was beyond me. Her blunt-cut blond hair swished along her shoulders as she disappeared into the hallway, leaving me to my own devices. I got up and retrieved my book from the floor and dusted it off before I sat back down at my desk.

I cracked the book back open to the last few pages. I only had thirty more pages to finish, and then I'd be able to plot my route around campus. I knew Hannah would be gone longer than ten minutes, too. Which meant I had plenty of time to get this done. But as I read, I kept focusing on my jeans. The ones I had fallen asleep in. I kept focusing on my mismatched socks and the long-sleeved shirt I had on.

What's wrong with this outfit?

It grew hard to concentrate. I mean, I'd never been a self-conscious person. But was it not enough for me to go to a party like this simply by myself? That didn't sit right with me. I didn't like wearing skirts and dresses and makeup and jewelry like Hannah did. Was that not okay? My head spun with all sorts of things she might make me do for this party. So much so that I barely got through the last pages of my required reading for the semester.

And just as I set my book off to the side, my door flew open.

"Hi! Sorry. Hiding from someone."

I whipped my head over toward the door and saw someone barreling in. A guy dressed in all black, with black boots and a scuffed black leather jacket and…

The guy on the rusty motorcycle?

"Uh, hi," I said.

He waved before he closed my door. "This okay? Hope it's okay. Just need a few minutes."

He walked over and helped himself to Hannah's desk chair.

"So what's your name?"

I blinked. "Get out."

He snickered. "Interesting name. I'm Benji."

"Hi, Benji. Get out."

"Just a couple more minutes. I'm sure I'll be good by then."

"I give you none of those. Now, out."

He snickered. "You're a hard one, aren't you?"

"What does that mean?"

"Usually, women don't complain when I barge into their room."

My voice flattened. "You're not my type."

He nodded. "Good to know."

But he still didn't move.

I studied him as he sat there, listening intently to the hallway. He was tall, with long, lanky legs and arms. In fact, the kid was pretty lanky all over, with messy dark brown hair and imposing eyes.

"Making enemies before the semester even starts?" I asked.

He grinned. "Fuck yeah. It's better than what you're doing, sitting in here by yourself."

"Do you even know what I'm doing?"

His eyes fell to my desk. "Studying? Or plotting out your course around campus?"

Well. "What if I told you neither?"

He snickered. "I wouldn't believe you one bit.

You're one of *those* girls. I can already tell."

"One of those girls? What does that mean?"

He shrugged. "The kind of girls that have already cracked open their books and smelled them."

"What's wrong with something like that? Maybe people like the way a fresh book smells."

He chuckled. "Exactly. You're one of those girls."

"And I'd like to know exactly *what* that means, and why it's such a bad thing."

He stood up. "Oh, you know. The goody two shoes. Always getting As. Figures she'd disappoint Daddy with a B. A Daddy's girl, you know? Gotta cross her T's and dot her I's. Hell, I bet you dot I's with a little heart, don't you sweetheart?"

I stood up quickly. "Get out."

"Hold on, I'm almost done."

I strode toward him. "I said get out of my dorm room. Now."

I heard the doorknob turning and the guy in front of me lunged. For the door, that is. He slammed his shoulder against it, holding it closed as the person on the other end fought against it. Holy mackerel, I was trapped with a crazy man. A lanky, disheveled, crazy man with a bike.

"I'm serious. I want you out," I said.

I heard Hannah's voice. "Hey! Let me in! The hell are you doing?"

The guy in the leather coat paused. "Who's that?"

I glared at him. "My roommate. Let her in and see yourself out."

The guy opened the door and Hannah's face fell. I

looked over at her and she peered at me, not wanting to fully take her eyes off the guy. I knew she recognized him. That leather coat and those black jeans. She furrowed her brow slowly before coming into the room, then gripped him by his coat.

"Hey. Wai--what are you--?"

Hannah looked at me. "Any point to him?"

I shook my head. "He said he's hiding from someone. He let himself in and hasn't left yet."

The boy growled. "Let go of me."

Hannah shrugged. "Suit yourself. Go hide somewhere else."

She shoved him out the door and he stumbled into the wall across the hallway. He whipped around with wide, shocked eyes, and I wiggled my fingertips at him. Hannah giggled as she slammed the door closed, then flipped the lock for good measure.

"See? That's what happens when you study unnecessarily and don't pay attention to a damn thing I ask you to do."

I blinked. "Really? You're doing that right now?"

She grinned. "Really, really. Now that we're done with that loser, ready for the details of this party?"

"I'm not going to any party if it's not good enough to go as myself."

"Girl, I'm not dressing you up in my clothes. You're going in yours. You just have such reserved clothing. I mean, look at you! It's August, and you're wearing jeans and a long-sleeved shirt. Aren't you hot?"

"Not really. I stay cold all the time like Mom."

"Well, we're going to at least find you a cute little

short-sleeved shirt in your dresser that you can put on. Maybe something that shows off your assets a bit."

I blinked. "I don't have those like you do, Hannah."

"Oh, come on. I'd kill for your legs."

"And I'd kill for your curves."

She rolled her eyes. "Come on. We don't have that loser distracting you and making you feel weird anymore. So let's find you an outfit for tonight."

I pointed to my laptop. "I really should be--"

Hannah took my hand. "No. I won't let you go another semester without making a friend."

"You're my friend."

"Someone other than me. Dani, you can't go an entire college career and not make any friends. That isn't healthy. College is enjoyed with people. Yes, studies are important, but so are connections. I'm sure even your parents would back that up."

Actually, they already had.

"Fine, okay. We'll do this. Under one condition."

Hannah smiled. "Name it."

I pointed at her. "No. Makeup."

She sighed. "Not even lip gloss?"

"Nope."

"Or a bit of mascara?"

"Nope."

"Or some blush!?"

"Not a bit of it."

She rolled her eyes. "Fine. But that means I get more liberties with your outfit. And jewelry. Come on. Let's get you dolled up for the evening."

6

MAX

I sat at the wrought iron gate of the sprawling property and sighed. I hated coming to this place. It always forecast terrible, awful things to come. The spic-and-span white house always threw people off. Good people lived in white houses. But the blood red shutters told a much different story. It boasted of the blood on the hands of the man that lived here. It boasted of the lives this man had taken when he was the president of our crew. Dread filled my gut. It always did just before I pressed the red button on the intercom. The kind of red that matched the shutters, complemented the wrought iron gates, and always reminded me of exactly whose presence I was about to be graced with.

But, every single time, I pressed that button.

Because we needed jobs, and we needed to get paid.

"Yes?"

"It's Max. Let me up."

"Of course, sir. Right away."

The Australian accent filled my ears as the intercom turned off. And when the wrought iron gates started moving in front of me, I revved my engine, letting Ashton know I was coming. I sped up the driveway, taking in the smell of the apple trees that lined the concrete pathway on either side. It was the only refreshing thing about this property. Picking a sweet, fresh apple off one of those trees was one of the small treasures of life. Its crisp, sweet juice was ready for my tongue as I rode off into the sunset.

After meetings with this man, of course.

Ashton would probably have my head if he knew I was actually picking fruit from his apple trees.

I pulled up to the bottom of the porch steps and killed the engine of my bike. With the kickstand down and my leg swung over, I started up the steps to the white wraparound porch. Such an innocent design to this house. And yet, it had held so many tortures over the years. I knew there was a basement to this property, but I didn't dare go into it. Or ask to see it. Lord only knew the kinds of things Ashton kept down in that place. Especially out here. In the middle of nowhere.

No one could hear you scream in that basement.

The cherry mahogany door greeted me. But I didn't have a chance to use the wrought iron knocker on it. The second I stood in front of it, the door eased itself open. It creaked to life, sending another cold chill down my spine. And as the man attached to that

Australian accent ushered me into the massive foyer, I slid my hands into my leather jacket pockets.

I had easy access to my brass knuckles, just in case.

"Mr. Ryddle will be down soon," the man said.

I nodded. "Thank you."

Ashton insisted the man not have a name. Every time I tried to introduce myself, or get his name, Ashton butted in. As if his personal staff wasn't allowed to have an identity behind these walls. It made me sick. Sure, Ashton paid his staff well. Hell, he paid all of us well. But that payment came at a price.

For his staff, it was their identity.

For us? It was our souls.

"Max."

I slowly looked up toward the top of the steps, watching as he walked down them, his hand lingering on the shining, wooden banister. His footsteps were even and silent. His eyes burrowed into me as an emotionless smile slipped across his cheeks.

"Dad," I said.

"Walk with me. I have a contract for you and your boys."

He motioned for me to follow him and I looked over at the man in the suit. The Australian. The man with no name, and probably no soul, either. He had his hands locked behind him and stared straight ahead. Right by the door, in case anyone else showed up. I wondered if he ever moved from that position. If he ever flinched when my father dragged a hopeless soul through those doors. I wondered about all the atrocities he had seen at my father's hands. Ashton's.

Damn it, I hated calling that man my father.

"Max!"

"Coming."

My eyes diverted away from the Australian and I jogged after him. My father's swift footsteps didn't so much as click across the floor. I caught up with him down the hallway, where pictures of empty eyes and empty smiles hung on the walls. Not family pictures, of course. We didn't have those growing up. There wasn't a picture of myself, nor Josh, nor our father on these walls. Nope. My father bought the frames at exorbitant prices, then put other family pictures in them. People I didn't recognize. People I'd never seen during my life. At first, I thought maybe they were the stock photos that came with the picture frames themselves. Random people in color as well as black and white. But, over time, I had come to a new theory.

These were the families my father had destroyed with his disgusting ways.

Fucking hell.

"Thirsty?"

I watched Ashton pour us each a drink into a crystal glass. I walked into the lounge and the door closed behind me, almost automatically, as if it had been waiting for me to cross over. I didn't turn around, though I wanted to. This entire place gave me the fucking creeps. And I had been to some shady places and done some very shady things in my life for the kind of money Ashton doled out to us.

"Here. You look like you could use one."

I took the glass from him. "Thanks."

He sipped his amber liquid and eyed me carefully. My father did that with everyone. Even when my brother had been in the hospital a few years back, fighting for his life, Ashton studied him as if he were a project. As if my brother wasn't the fruit of his own loins. Ashton was one of the many reasons I had sworn off ever having a family of my own. I didn't want to bring anyone else into the world who could possibly be related to this man. To this terror. To the insanity my father brought to this earth.

I kept my ears peeled for anything shifty as I kept my eyes locked on Ashton.

My father.

And, quite possibly, the devil himself.

"I have a friend coming into town on some business."

I nodded as I sipped my drink, but I didn't dare interrupt him.

"He's a high level businessman, like myself. And he has a tendency to draw the attention of unsavory characters whenever he goes."

I nodded. But again, I didn't interrupt.

"He's a big deal, Max. I need you and your boys on his six when he moves. No matter where he moves. I want your best on this, because there's big money to be had in this job. I need this business relationship untarnished. So no fucking it up."

I sipped my drink. "We can handle it. We always do."

"Not with the last job that happened."

"You know what happened with that last job. We

gave that man explicit instructions and he stepped outside of the lines."

"You're supposed to have contingencies for everything. Men like my friends don't listen to what's good for them. They're powerful. They make their own rules. Have contingency plans for when the rules break."

I nodded. "We will have this one handled without incident."

Ashton narrowed his eyes at me. "You sure about that?"

"Yes."

"Because I don't need you guys fucking this one up. This crew hasn't been what it was underneath myself, or even your brother, since you took up position as president."

I paused. "You mean your son?"

"Yes. Your brother."

I held back the snicker wanting to work its way up my throat.

"It will be handled, Dad. You have my word."

He pointed at me. "I don't just want it handled. I want it perfect. This crew is known for providing not just services, but impeccable services. No matter the cost asked, or the life taken. You willing to do that? *Can you do that, Max?*"

I nodded. "Yes."

"All right. Here's the deal. The client is driving in. Not flying. The last time he attempted to fly, someone tried taking his plane down. He's driving in and heading straight to his hotel. He's staying at La

Grenvan Rouge on the other side of town. Top floor. There's a private elevator he is to always take. He wants you and the boys taking it as well. He arrives in two days. When you and your boys get into the lobby, you go to the front desk and say, 'We're here for Mr. Penthouse'."

Is he fucking kidding me? "Got it."

"You say that, and the front desk will know what to do. They'll let you up, you collect the client, and you follow him wherever he goes while he's in town."

"How long is he in town for?"

Ashton shrugged. "He says a week. Which, in my world, means at least ten days. Maybe more. But the longer you're employed, the more you get paid. A week upfront quoted, plus extra tacked on for the days after that. You know how it goes."

I finished my drink. "Yep."

"Don't bring all of your men for this, either. Just the ones you trust to handle their shit out there. I don't need any of your no-good prospects doing this just to prove themselves. This is a 'seasoned veteran only' kind of job. You hear me?"

"I hear you loud and clear."

"Good. You can see yourself out."

I paused. "Risk factor?"

Ashton narrowed his eyes. "What about it?"

"We haven't discussed risk factor yet."

"And?"

"That comes with these meetings. I need a risk factor."

My father walked over to me and plucked the

empty glass from my fingertips. And as he held both of those crystal glasses in his hands, he gazed directly into my eyes. I didn't know if my father was trying to intimidate me or warn me. I didn't know what the purpose was of him being so close. But I dug my heels in and refused to move. Because the worst thing anyone could do in the presence of Ashton Ryddle was show fear.

"Risk factor," I said.

His nostrils flared. "Do you trust me, son?"

I cracked my neck. "It's standard for us to talk about this."

"Do you. Trust me?"

I rolled my shoulders back. "Fine. I accept the job."

"Good. Two days' time. La Grenvan Rouge. He will be arriving promptly at three in the afternoon. Be there at three thirty. He's got business the first night he's here."

"Noted."

My father finally backed away and waved at me. As if I were a pesky fly he wanted out of his presence. And I was more than glad to leave. I turned in my boots and charged out of the room, angrier than hell at my fucking father. What the ever-blessed fuck was he thinking? Did he even give a shit about our well-being? I snickered at the thought. Of course he didn't. He showed me that after Josh's accident. How little he cared regarding the fact that a crew he used to head up lost good men that day.

Hell, he didn't seem to give a shit that he almost lost his eldest son that day, either.

"Good evening, sir."

The Australian's accent filled my ears as he swung the door open. I didn't bother responding to him, though. I leapt down to my bike, swung my leg over the seat, and cranked up the engine. I needed to get the hell out of here before I did or said something I knew I'd regret. I revved my engine, signaling to my father that I was headed out, then I kicked up burnt rubber peeling out of that damn driveway. I knew he'd have a cow over the dark marks left behind. I didn't care.

All I cared about was getting back home. To Josh. Getting dinner on the stove and pouring us both a drink. I reached my hand up as I rode down the driveway, plucking every apple my hand touched and tucking them into my pockets. I'd gotten about seven of them before the wrought iron gates at the bottom of the hill rolled slowly open for me.

Releasing me from this temporary prison.

7

DANI

I sighed as the party raging just outside the door kept beckoning to me. I didn't like the shirt Hannah had settled on. It was much too tight. My jeans were already tight enough. Why the tight shirt? And why could I see my bra through the white material?

"This is such crap," I murmured.

Hannah poked her head in. "Hey! You coming or what?"

I waved her away. "In a second. I'm… trying to fix something."

I tugged at the white shirt before it *thwaped* right back into place, making Hannah giggle.

"Come on, time's a'wastin', hot stuff."

I rolled my eyes. "Never. Again."

I felt my roommate grab my hand before we stumbled out into the hallway. With the music pumping and the strobe lights going again, it felt as if I had stepped out onto another planet. I squinted as someone shoved a drink in my free hand. I had on my only pair of heels, which somehow kept throwing me off balance. Maybe it was the effects of the light, or the fact that Hannah practically tipped the cup to my lips. But the more beer I chugged down, the looser I felt.

"Need another?" she asked.

I grimaced as the taste of lukewarm beer filled my throat. I forced myself to get it down, but I sure didn't want another one. I tossed the red cup into the nearest trash can before Hannah started bopping around, dancing to the thumping music and reaching for yet another drink.

One of many I presumed she'd already had.

I looked up and down the hallway. Weren't there resident assistants for this kind of thing? I walked down the hallway, eyeing the doors. Waiting for that familiar red sticker to come into view.

"Gotcha," I whispered.

I threw open the RA's door. But instead of being greeted by the boy who had the sign on his door, I was greeted with the back of his ass.

As he plowed his way between the legs of a girl who was much louder than she needed to be.

"Oh, fuck!"

"That's it. Take it. You know you want to."

My eyes bulged as I quickly closed the door, and I suddenly wanted another beer.

You know, to pour into my eyeballs in order to wash that scene from the back of my eyelids.

I peeked over my shoulder and saw Hannah getting comfortable with some guy I didn't recognize. Then again, I didn't recognize anyone. I felt more uncomfortable than I ever had in my entire life. I decided to keep walking down the hallway. I jutted into the small alcove that connected one hallway with another. Opposite sides of the dorm room building that almost felt like different worlds.

Because this hallway didn't have music. Or strobe lights. Or drunk RA's screwing around with their flavor of the night.

At the end of the hallway was a couple making out. The girl straddled his lap, moaning so loud I heard her on the opposite end. I sighed as I made my way for the steps. I walked down a level, leaving one set of music behind for another. And when I pushed myself through the door of the level below my room, I was met with colored lights that twinkled. Drinks that smelled like pineapple and coconut.

I decided to stick around there for a while.

Someone shoved a drink into my hand, but I didn't drink it. I kept it around because it smelled nice and had a quaint little umbrella in it. But that was it. The drink was a nice decoy, too. No one else pushed any other alcohol on me since I carried a full drink around. Which meant I could use it as a disguise. I was more intrigued with exploring the different levels of the party than with actually partying myself.

So I kept making my way down.

Each level had a different theme. A different set of lights, and drinks, and people. Some floors did nothing but dance. Some floors did nothing but make out. One of the floors sounded more like a brothel than an actual party. Which meant I didn't have any issues quickly bypassing that one.

Then, I came to the third floor. Which was really the bottom level of the dorm rooms, since the ground level held nothing but the kitchen and a large pool room and the second floor held a massive soundproof study hall.

There wasn't much of a party going on with this floor, either.

I pushed through the door and the smell of cigarettes filled the air. I wrinkled up my nose as music played haphazardly from some sort of a speaker system in the corner. The music was swiftly overpowered by the thumping of the bass notes above my head. I didn't see anyone doling out alcohol, making out or having sex in any of the rooms or the corners of the hallway. I mean, the place looked almost abandoned.

Until I heard voices.

"Dude, come on. At least blow it out the damn window."

"He's right, Max. Benji here could get into trouble."

"Rupert, shut up."

"Watch your tone."

I froze at that voice. I recognized that voice. I furrowed my brow as I peeked around the corner, taking in the three men standing by the open dorm room window. Cigarette smoke hovered around them, the air thickening with its scent. And the more I watched, the more I recognized. There was that tall, lanky boy again. The one that had barged into my dorm room and refused to leave. There was one with stark red hair sticking out from underneath a beanie. But the tall one—I couldn't take my eyes off the tall one.

Because it was the man who'd helped me with my things up to my room the other day.

His brow was furrowed deeply as he sucked on his cigarette. I watched the thing burn down to almost nothing as he expanded his broad chest. He flicked the entire thing into a wastebasket at his feet before blowing it out the screen window through a small hole in his lips. I couldn't take my eyes off him. The movement was mesmerizing.

The worry in his voice made my spine sizzle, though.

I couldn't tell what they were murmuring about, but I knew it wasn't good. He talked low, with a rumbling voice that weakened my knees. The other two paid close attention to him. And even the lanky guy grew worried. I hated that I didn't know any of their names. I needed to get into a better habit of actually asking for names.

"Are you spying on me, Daddy's girl?"

Oh, no. No, no, no, no.

The drawl ripped me from my trance. And when I gazed into the brooding eyes of the tall one, a wolfish smile took over his face. I wanted to run. I wanted to drop my drink, race back for the door, and get away from them all. That's what my gut told me to do. That's what my brain told me to do.

But my heart told me not to be such a pushover.

"Danika," I said.

The man shrugged. "Whatever. You're a curious one, aren't you?"

I shook my head. "No."

He chuckled. "Said that pretty quick, didn't ya?"

"Maybe I just talk this quickly."

I stepped into the doorway with my drink clutched tightly in my hand. His eyes fell to it before that wolfish smile of his grew into something akin to the Cheshire cat. It unnerved me, how his smile didn't quite reach his eyes. How his stare still inquired what I was doing, even though I claimed to be doing nothing. His eyes locked with mine as he walked forward, towering over me with his shadow as the smell of cigarette smoke hung between us.

As he came to close to me, I caught a whiff of his cologne. Or his aftershave.

Whatever it was, it had my head spinning.

I felt my grip weakening around my drink. My knees trembled as he stood in front of me. My eyes slowly slid up to his, drinking him in as he looked down at me. There was indifference in his eyes. Worry in his brow. And confusion in the turned-up corners of his lips. He was easy to read. At least, up close he was.

He bent toward my ear, gracing my skin with the heat of his breath.

"Liar," he growled.

I flinched at the sound before another chuckle fell from his lips. Then he stepped around me, pushing me against the doorway as he walked past. I let out the breath I had been holding. I watched as the man with the beanie and the red hair walked by me. His eyes fell down my body, as if he were studying me. And not too far behind was the lanky guy who didn't understand personal space.

"You're a terrible spy," he said, almost giggling.

"Benji. Shut up."

I nodded. "Benji."

He winked. "Danika."

I grimaced at him as he slipped beside me, his hand running along my thigh. I jumped at his touch, and not in a good way. And as the three of them walked down the hallway, I whipped around to take them in. Benji was much shorter than the other two. Younger, as well. They all lumbered down the hallway with rolled-back shoulders and leather jackets. Probably thought they looked cool, too.

Idiots.

"Girls," the leader said.

How in the world did I still not know his name?

The giggling of girls came from the other hallway before they dashed out. Two girls with lanky legs and hair down to their waists jumped out from the alcove that connected one hallway to another. I tossed my drink mindlessly into the hallway trash can. I watched as the confusing, intimidating man draped his arms around both girls, pulling them close as he slid his hands down to their waists.

He peered over his shoulder at me.

Disgusting.

The man chuckled before he turned his head forward. Together, the hoard of them stormed through the door, making their way down the stairs. Something swirled in my gut as I stood there, rooted to my place. Something unfamiliar. Something that made me sick.

Something that made me resent those girls.

You need sleep.

Being near that man made me feel as if I were standing on the edge of a cliff, ready to fall off at a moment's notice. And yet, there was something about him that made me think he'd be the one to catch me instead of push me. How could a man so intimidating and so angry-looking also be the man to save someone? He didn't look like a hero at all, with his leather jacket and his cigarette breath and his predatory grin.

Still, it didn't stop me from seeing him that way.

I sighed as I forced myself to move. I took one step. Then another. Soon I was in the stairwell, overwhelmed by the scent of cigarettes, leather, and cologne. Yes, that smell was definitely cologne. What kind of man who rode a bike and chain-smoked also wore cologne? The dichotomy was overwhelming. It grew hard to walk up the steps. All the way back to the top floor.

But it was better than taking the chance that someone was screwing around in the elevator.

The thudding of music as I made my way back to my dorm room made me long for the silence of the third floor. Part of me wanted to go back down there and sit, just enjoy it. But the rest of me wanted to get some sleep. I found my way back to the top floor of the dorm building, with Hannah nowhere in sight. And while I had half a mind to go find her, I also knew she was a big girl.

She could take care of herself.

Sleep. Sleep is good.

I refused the drinks people tried to hand me. I held my arms up as I slipped between people so my hands didn't get misplaced. I did everything I could to keep myself as innocent as possible. Even though hands kept falling on my hips. My thighs. My butt cheeks. Boys wanted to dance. Girls wanted to do shots. The music became more intense, until the thudding of the bass matched the strobing of the lights. It was darn near disorienting. I hated the sensation. And as I teetered my way into my dorm room, I closed the door behind me, breathing a sigh of relief as I shut the chaos out.

Even though my mind still spun on its axis.

Why did those girls make me so upset?

I sat down at my desk and pulled off my heels. I massaged my feet before ripping that stupid white shirt off my body. I changed from my party clothes into my pajamas and eased myself into bed. Tomorrow was another day, and I'd try again. I'd try to be a good student. I'd try to get the rest of my summer reading done. And I'd try to avoid, at all costs, anything that could get me in trouble.

Especially Benji and those lumbering brutes.

8

MAX

I lay there for an hour with a girl sleeping on each side of me. A typical Sunday morning for a man like myself. But neither of them were my cup of tea. I drew in a deep breath as the need for a cigarette nagged at me. The girl to my left, with the thick brown hair, kept snoring in my damn ear all night. And the redhead to my right kept moving her knee a bit too close to the boys. One wrong move and I'd be out of the game for at least a week. Because a woman's legs were never to be messed with in bed.

That much I'd learned the hard way.

"All right. That's enough," I groaned.

I sat up in bed and the girls shifted around. One of them yawned while the other whimpered. I didn't know who did what, and I didn't care. I slid down to the edge of the bed and slipped my feet into my slippers. I stood, stretching my arms over my head and cracking my back from my tailbone all the way up to my shoulders.

"Oh, yeah. That's the stuff," I grunted.

"Hush," one of the girls mumbled.

"Coffee?" another asked.

I ignored them.

I had to check on my brother first.

I picked my shirt off the floor and slipped it on, then shuffled my way out of my bedroom. I knew the girls would go back to sleep. They always did. I invested a hell of a lot of money in a prime place to sleep, especially after moving in with my older brother. I made my way down the hallway, all the way to the back of the house. When I saw his bedroom door hanging wide open, I sighed.

"How's the coffee?" I called out.

"Better hush. You'll wake your company."

I grinned. "Hope we didn't wake you."

"Hope you weren't trying. Because if you were, you lost."

I chuckled as I made my way back down the hall-way. I peeked my head back into my bedroom and, sure enough, the girls were already fast asleep again. I closed my door to let them sleep and cleared my throat. The smell of coffee finally penetrated my senses, leading me to the kitchen, where my brother sat, his cane between his legs, nursing a mug.

"Second cup?" I asked.

"Nope. First."

I nodded. "New pain medication working, then?"

"Seems to be."

I walked over to the coffee pot and reached for my mug. Which was really a small bowl. I never could get enough coffee in my system first thing in the morning. I poured out the straight black liquid and went to sit by my brother, who was having a hell of a time keeping his mug from trembling every time he lifted it or set it down.

"Need help?" I asked.

He snickered. "I should ask you that same question."

"The hell does that mean?"

He nodded toward the hallway. "They asleep again?"

"Yep."

"Must be lazy asses, then. Didn't hear a damn peep from any of you."

I chuckled. "Oh, ho ho. I see how it is, Mr. Can't Get It Up."

"Hey, those are the pain meds talking. I get it up when it counts."

"I'm sure you and Lefty are very happy together."

He snickered. "So do I dare ask?"

I took a long pull from my coffee. "I know you will."

He nodded. "How'd things go with Dad yesterday? He have a job for you? Or paychecks?"

"Both. Checked my account half an hour ago. Payments hit."

"Good. Because the mortgage is due."

"How many more payments do we have on the thing?"

"Seven more. The end is in sight."

I sighed. "Fucking finally."

"What was the job?"

I shot him a look. "You know we're not supposed to talk about that kind of shit."

He shrugged. "We do anyway. What makes this different?"

And when I didn't respond, John drew in a deep breath.

"What's wrong with this one?" he asked.

I shook my head. "You know how my gut is."

"You don't know what's wrong, you just know something is."

"Yep."

"Well, maybe I can help."

"Nope."

"Oh, come on, Max."

"I said no."

He poked me with his cane. "That's going in your groin if you don't start talking."

I grinned. "Cute."

He poised the cane between my legs. "Bad move, coming out here without jeans on."

My face fell. "Fine. Whatever. We have a new contract, yeah. Dad's expressed a need to keep it on the down low as well as use my finest guys. As in, no prospects."

"Oh, boy."

"Yep. Got a client coming into town tomorrow. Name's Mr. Dean."

"Which is probably fake."

"Damn right it is. We're supposed to meet him at the 'La Rogue-a-Grand' or some shit like that in the afternoon after lunch."

He paused. "La Grenvan Rouge?"

I pointed at him. "That place."

"That's a hell of a hotel. Even their dinky rooms cost upwards of a thousand bucks a night to stay."

"Apparently, it pays a pretty penny."

"How long are you guys guarding him?"

"Dad said a week. Ten days, tops."

He paused. "So at least two weeks."

I sipped my coffee. "Yep. At least that."

"Jesus."

"Mm-hmm."

"Did he give you anything other than that? At all?"

I shook my head. "Nope."

"I don't like the sound of this one, Max. I've heard Dad talk about a 'Dean' before."

"You think it's the same one?"

He nodded. "Absolutely. You know Dad. He doesn't keep company much. So you know he's gotten in with them somehow. And if they work for or with Dad...?"

"They're shit news."

"Yeah."

I growled. "Fuck."

"And it's not a good sign that he wants your best men. That means this man is already in some deep shit as it is."

"You think I don't know that?"

He held up his hands. "Just making sure you do. I'd rather talk your ear off about it than you go in blind."

"I never go in blind."

He grinned. "Except when it comes to your women."

I rolled my eyes. "So what else is new?"

He chuckled. "I'm serious, though. The way I've heard Dad talk about this 'Dean' guy? If that's even his name? It's big. He's big, and he's bad. Much bigger fish than the Red Thorns have ever gotten tied up with."

"What have you heard Dad say about this character?"

"It's not what I've heard him say, it's when I've heard him say his name. Remember the first job I ever took as president?"

I blinked. "The Whitecast job."

"The one that went bad. During the cleanup of that job, he kept talking about how 'Dean' would take care of the back end of things."

"Uh huh."

"And that Grouper setup?"

I paused. "Are you kidding me?"

He shook his head. "Nope. Again, one of those instances where he supposedly cashed in a favor with this guy to clean up the back end. Whatever the fuck that means."

"Anything else?"

"Not really. Just a few mentions here and there. Offhanded things."

"Like…?"

He sighed. "Remember when I was in the hospital?"

I bristled. "I'll never forget it."

"I'm pretty sure that Dean guy was in the room with me and Dad at one point."

I narrowed my eyes. "And...?"

"And nothing. I came out of my pain medication stupor long enough to hear Dad say, 'I appreciate it, Dean,' then I was right back out."

"So this guy is really entangled with Dad."

"I'd say he's the closest thing to a friend Dad's got. Which is why I'm wondering why he doesn't travel with his own damn security detail. Because anyone with ties to Dad is always gonna be in some deep-ass shit."

I shrugged. "Beats me. All I know is the money's good, and our boys are overdue for a damn good payday."

"You promise me you'll stay safe."

I nodded. "You know me. I always play it smart. It's why Dad hates the fact that I'm head of this crew now."

He sighed. "Just--don't do anything stupid. We don't need both of us crippled for life."

"Trust me to handle this. We'll get it done, and everything will be fine."

"If you say so, Max."

9

DANI

Note to self: Get to class earlier to get a better seat.

"While I know the first couple days back during the semester are boring syllabus days, I still want you to heed the title of our next lecture on Wednesday: What is Conflict Management? It might seem like an easy question, until you try to answer it yourself. You will find, more likely than not, that your answer brings on more conflict to manage, as does most natural events throughout the course of your day. The point of this course is to work on your negotiation skills. How to manage conflict that comes with every word you say and every sentence you toss out into the world. These are the basics that separate you from everyone else. These are the things that keep you safe. And these are the basics that catapult you into a completely different subset of human interaction."

'Negotiation and Conflict Management' was one of my elective courses. And the more the professor talked, the more excited I was for the class. This settled my debate class requirement as well as opened the door for some of my more advanced courses I'd have to take next year. I was excited to knock two things out at once while having a bit of fun in the process.

As nerdy as that might have sounded.

I didn't like being in the back row, though. It came with a stereotype I didn't want to be attached to. I looked to my right, watching as the boy at the end of the row picked his nose. He had a friend practically snoring on his shoulder. And the girl next to me was slumped so far down into her seat I thought she might slide onto the floor. I turned to my left and gazed at the open chair next to me.

Then the door of the classroom burst open.

"Sorry. Don't mind me. Doctor's note."

The professor stopped talking as my jaw dropped open.

Benji, with a crooked grin on his face and the same black outfit I'd seen him wear twice now, walked over and slapped a piece of paper onto the professor's desk. He gazed out among the class, looking up the tiers we all sat on. And when his eyes met mine, I wanted to melt to the floor like the girl sitting next to me.

"The next time you're this late, don't bother showing up," the professor said. "And this is college. Doctor's notes don't work here, Mr.--"

He made his way for me. "Just call me Benji."

"Next time you're this late, don't bother coming," the professor repeated.

I watched in horror as he dropped down into the

seat next to me. In the back row. And I saw the look of judgment on the professor's face.

Yes, definitely arrive early Wednesday morning for class.

"Well hey there, sweetheart. Long time no see."

I tried my best to ignore him as I glued my eyes to the whiteboard at the front of the class.

"Well, you're looking more uptight than you did yesterday. Where's your bonnet?"

I shifted in my seat, scooting as far away from Benji as I could. He snickered at me before he tossed his books to the floor, making as much noise as possible. I wanted to strangle him. I squinted my eyes in an effort to focus my hearing. But the more Benji rustled around, the more distracted I became.

"Are you serious right now?" I hissed.

He grinned. "What? Can't concentrate? Sounds like a personal problem."

"Is there an issue back there?"

The professor's voice caught my ear and I shook my head.

"No, sir. I'm very sorry," I said.

"Uh huh," he said.

"Uh huh," Benji mocked.

"Shut up," I murmured.

"What was that?" the professor asked.

"She told you to shut up," Benji said.

"What!? I did not!" I exclaimed.

"Are the two of you going to become a problem? Because I have no issues throwing you out of my class."

I glared at Benji, who only smiled back at me

before he plugged his ears with his headphones. After being forty-five minutes late to class in the first place.

"No, sir. I'm sorry. I don't even know this guy," I said.

"We're in the same dorm!" Benji yelled over his music.

"I really don't know him," I insisted.

"She was spying on me last night talking with my guys. I think she's got a crush."

The class giggled and I wanted to die. Right then and there.

"Uh huh. Well, keep your emotions out of this class. They won't do you very well unless you know how to channel them," the professor said.

"Oh, she can channel them all right," Benji said.

"I'm going to kill you," I murmured.

"Sweetheart, you don't have the balls."

He held up his phone before pressing the 'play' button. And as the professor went back to lecturing, it was all I could do to tune out the blaring rock music I heard pouring from the outside of those stupid, cheap ear-plug-music-headphone things. I gripped my pencil so tightly I thought it might break. I shifted around, trying to get comfortable as the snoring to my right mounted with a mighty roar. The girl directly next to me slipped down a little further. The copper of her jeans scraped against the plastic chair.

It took so much energy to focus on the professor that I didn't have enough to keep taking notes.

It's going to be a long semester.

I couldn't pack my things up quickly enough when

the professor finally wound things down. And with an hour before I had to be in my next lecture, the one thing I needed was coffee. I wanted to douse myself in coffee. No, no, I wanted to sink an I.V. directly into my vein and fill it with coffee.

Right after I apologized to my professor.

"Sir, if I could--?"

He held up his hand, stopping me in my tracks.

"What's your name?" he asked.

I swallowed hard. "Danika, sir."

"Miss Danika, first impressions are everything."

"I'm so sorry about what--"

"Let me finish."

I nodded. "I'm sorry. Of course."

He sighed. "They're everything. But they're also up to interpretation by the person who is receiving said first impression. Your words created more conflict than necessary in my class. One could argue it would've been in your benefit to simply stay quiet. You chose not to, which came with consequences. Consequences you couldn't talk yourself out of. That's what my class is all about."

"Yes, sir."

"With that said, it was clear to me you didn't incite what happened. It's not a reflection on you, it's a reflection on him. You have nothing to worry about."

I sighed with relief. "Thank you, Professor."

"No thanks needed. You'll learn a lot more about this as the semester progresses. Just make sure to get here a few minutes before class if you don't want to be in the back."

I nodded. "Already noted and I'll adjust my alarm as necessary."

He smiled. "Good to hear. I'll see you Wednesday morning."

"See you then."

I tossed my backpack over my shoulder and headed out of class. I felt good about things again. Good enough to not want to drown myself in coffee.

"Now, how'd I know you'd throw me under the bus like that?"

Scratch that. I wanted to drown a painful death in my coffee.

"Benji, leave me alone," I said.

I whipped around and watched as he slithered away from the wall like the snake he really was.

"You could've defended me, you know. I'm hurt. I thought we were friends."

I scoffed. "I'm late for my next class."

"Here. I'll walk with you."

I hurried away from him. "No, thanks."

I walked as quickly as I could, but I heard him hot on my heels. Taunting me. Calling me 'Daddy's girl' and 'bonnet lady.' I think I heard 'tightwad' and 'snitch' at some point in time in there as well. I tried not to pay attention. All I wanted was to get away from him. As far away from him as I could.

"Why are you running, Daddy's girl? I thought we could get to know one another!"

I charged out the front doors of the building before running into something hard. Something stiff. Something tall. I fell to the concrete steps and stared at a set of legs and knees.

"I'm sorry. I'm so, so sorry. Are you okay? Are you hur--?"

A hand dipped down into my vision, giving me pause. I blinked as my gaze slid along the leather jacket. Up the proud chest. Over the broad shoulders and up the thick neck to the eyes of that man I kept coming into contact with. I heard Benji laughing behind me as he pushed out the front doors. But, when he saw who was standing there, he stopped. Almost instantly.

"Max? What the hell are you doing here?"

His name is Max?

I stood up straight as his hand fell back to his side. He quirked an eyebrow at me, his stare slowly dropping down my body. I shivered in my tennis shoes, my breath quickening as my cheeks reddened. I didn't even realize I had dropped my backpack until he dipped down and picked it up for me.

Holding it out for me to take.

"Thanks," I said softly.

He nodded, but he didn't say anything. He simply stared at me, his eyes unwilling to let me go.

"You here to make sure I go to class or something?" Benji asked.

"No. I'm here to tell you about the new job."

"Oh, shit, Max. This is gonna be awesome. I knew you'd finally give me a chance. A real chance. Come on. There's this place that has the best fucking coffee. You'll love it, dude."

Max.

The hot guy finally had a name. A name I could call him by the next time I saw him. Because if our lives were any indication, I'd be seeing him sooner than I figured. His stare finally pulled away from me and directed itself over my shoulder, landing on the excited boy behind me. I wanted to take the wins as I could get them, even though I wasn't sure why I thought getting the man's name was a win.

Either way, I wanted to treat myself to some celebratory coffee. Specifically, at the coffeehouse they wouldn't be at. So I stepped around Max's body and started for the sidewalk.

Then I felt someone's hand around my wrist.

10

MAX

"What's your name again, sweetheart?"

I didn't like the way Benji was touching her.

"Danika, you twit."

I watched her cheeks flush deeper as her eyes fell to her feet. It was cute, in a way. If I squinted hard enough.

"Please move. I have to get to my next class," she said softly.

I snickered. "Yeah, Benj."

Benji giggled. "Hey, I'm just trying to make friends with my classmate."

He pulled her back until the two of us were standing in front of her.

"I'm serious. I have to get to class," she said.

Benji shook his head. "You're so skittish. Like a baby deer. Isn't she like a baby deer, Max?"

Her doe eyes cast their way up to mine and I stood

there, rooted in place. She implored me with her eyes, begging me to answer. To save her from the boy who wouldn't let her go. She had been pretty in the dark. But in the sunlight, there was something about her stare that caught my attention. The way her long black hair poured down her back in a low ponytail called to my hand. My entire fist. I suddenly wanted to wrap my hand around it and drag her off to her class just to get her away from Benji. Away from his prying eyes.

Mine.

"You're right, Benj. She is kind of like a baby deer."

She snickered. "Great. You too."

Benji licked his lips. "Yep. Him, too."

Her imploring eyes grew angry, and I found myself paying attention to the details. How thick her black eyelashes were. How her eyes sparkled the angrier she grew. She had strength behind those eyes. There was a wildness to their color that was accentuated by the way her eyes slanted softly upwards, with her eyelids completely invisible beneath the deep ridge of her brow. The angular structure of her face was softened by the roundness of her cheeks. Especially since they were now flushed with red.

Angry, furious red.

This girl has no idea who she's staring at.

The idea was almost laughable.

"What are you looking at?" she asked.

I nodded. "You."

"And why is that?"

Benji scoffed. "Maybe because that's his right as a man."

"Well, don't let those hands get any ideas."

I licked my lips. "And if they do?"

She paused. "Then keep them for the two girls from the hallway. I'm sure they'd enjoy it more than me."

Benji snickered. "Is that jealousy I hear?"

Her eyes widened. "What?"

"Holy shit. You're jealous."

"Jealous of what?"

I grinned as Benji stepped between her and me.

"You're jealous of the girls Maxy-boy here had at the party."

Benji slapped his hand against my chest and I caught his wrist.

"Easy there," I warned.

He giggled nervously. "Doesn't change the fact that you're jealous."

Daddy's girl shook her head. "Nope. Not even a little bit."

"Face it. You like Max, don't you?"

"Nope."

"Oh, then maybe you like me."

I shook my head. "Nope."

Benji sighed. "Well, she's obviously jealous. And that's kind of cute, don't you think?"

Daddy's girl glared at us. "I'm. Not. Jealous. I could never be jealous of a couple of college girls with no standards."

"What did you just say?"

I placed my hand onto Benji's shoulder. The boy was always much too fired up. Always ready to prove his worth. Always ready to jump down someone's throat to prove he belonged somewhere he didn't. It was entertaining for a while. Until it became too much.

Like now.

Benji leaned his head toward her still. Creating a friction against my hand that made me fist his coat. Even still, though, his arms slid out of the jacket, inching him even closer to the girl who had gone from timid, to jealous, to angry, to frightened.

I didn't like the fact that Benji was scaring her.

"Where's your mommy, Bambi?" he whispered.

My nostrils flared. "Enough."

"Huh? Yeah? You like being called Bambi, Little Miss Jealous?"

I growled. "I said, that's enough."

I pulled Benji back to my side as his jacket fell down his back. I watched her jerk away, clutching her backpack to her chest as she rushed off. Her feet carried her away from us as quickly as she could move. And as I stood there, forcing Benji to stay at my side, I wanted nothing more than to twist the little fucker's head off.

Especially since he was laughing.

"Oh, wow. Chicks like her are too easy of a target. Man. She needs a damn backbone, don't you think?"

He looked up at me and I glared at him. Ready to rip him to shreds and cast him to all the corners of the globe. Benji didn't know the first thing about being a Red Thorn. Or a decent-enough human being. He thought being in the crew was all big talk, sex, cigarettes, and fast bikes. He didn't understand the world we delved into. He didn't understand the price we all paid. The devil we had sold our souls to in exchange for a small slice of heaven every once in a while.

In the form of money in our pockets.

"The hell's that look for?" he asked.

My hand gripped the back of his neck. "Follow me."

"Ouch. Hey. Max. Fuck--ah, dude. Seriously?"

I pushed him back up the concrete steps and into the building. We tore through the foyer. I walked down the hallway straight in front of us. And the first empty classroom we came to, I shoved him in. After looking both ways over my shoulder, I slipped into the classroom as well. I closed the door behind me, then checked the corners. Just to make sure there were no cameras that might be recording us. Or listening in. Or focused on us in any way.

Privacy was always key when it came to these kinds of jobs.

"What the actual fuck, man?" he asked.

I narrowed my eyes. "Time to focus on the job and less on the goodie two shoes you go to class with. All right?"

He adjusted his leather jacket. "Yeah. Yeah, I got it. You got a job you're finally gonna let me do?"

"There's a job in the works, yes. Not sure if I'll need your help much. But you're looking for a way to prove yourself and I'm looking for my best guys to help out with this."

"Well, you know I'm good at what I do when you actually let me do it."

I growled. "Don't test me."

He held up his hands. "You call the shots, boss. I'm just a willing participant. Glad to finally get a shot at proving myself to you guys. You got any details for me?"

"I'll keep you posted as it's unfolding. The guy we're protecting arrives tomorrow. I'm gonna go scout out the hotel tonight. Take a tour of the place just to get a feel for it."

He put his hands down. "Oh, shit. Is this one of those 'undercover, you have to put on that suit' kind of deals?"

I licked my lips. "All you need to do is stick by your phone."

"Oh, fuck! You're gonna put on the suit! Damn, man. I haven't seen you in that penguin get-up in a while. You gonna take pictures?"

"I'll pull you from this shit in a heartbeat."

He rubbed his hands together. "I'm not trying to upset you. Just having a bit of fun. You're always so tense, Max. Need to loosen up a bit."

"Maybe when the job is done."

"How long is it supposed to run?"

I shrugged. "Ten days. A week. Somewhere around in there. You know how it is with Ashton and dates."

He nodded. "Well, you can count on me, no matter what you need."

"Well, when I need it, you better be ready to ride.

None of this 'I'll get back to you' bullshit you pulled last time."

"I was taking a shit when you called!"

"Well, shit faster next time. Or pick up the damn phone while you're pushing it out."

"Great. Yeah. I'll take the phone call in the middle of my grunts."

I shrugged. "You're the one who still has to prove yourself."

"Says the guy who refuses to give me a shot in the first place."

"You want work, or no?"

"No, no, no. I want the work. I just--"

I glared at him and he shut his fucking mouth.

"I'll pick up when called, boss."

"Good. I'll keep you updated."

I turned around and yanked the door open, startling a group of students just beyond the door. They looked up at me with wide eyes while a couple of the girls standing there licked their lips. I winked at the brunette before walking off, listening to her sigh as I brushed by. Making women weak in their knees came with the territory. And my fear was that Benji felt that was more important than the safety of the rest of the crew. Still, he was good at what he did. The boy could wield a serious gun and rode unlike anything I'd ever seen. You know, once he had a decent bike between his fucking legs.

He could prove to be useful if things got hairy with this guy.

Or if Rupert fucking insisted he come along.

I shoved my way out the front doors and hopped down the concrete steps. My bike glistened in the morning sunlight as I threw my leg over it. The cling of the kickstand coming up hung in my ears. My stomach was ready for food, and my veins were ready for some more coffee. But as I slid my helmet over my face, I gazed across the sidewalk.

And saw a very familiar set of eyes looking back at me.

Hello, Daddy's girl.

I cranked up my engine and revved the bike. I watched as she flinched, but she didn't take her eyes off me. The girl was something, that much was certain. She acted like she'd never see a bike before. Or a man wearing leather. It was cute. It added to her endearing nature. I decided to put on a show. One that would emblazon itself into her mind.

I spun out the wheels, filling the air with burnt rubber before I took off. I sped away from the curb, popping a wheelie before I took a sharp turn onto the main road. I cut cars off. They swerved and honked their horns at me. I chuckled to myself as I drew in a deep breath, resolving myself to a nice morning ride to my favorite breakfast place. I could get a decent cup of coffee there and a stack of pancakes all the way up to my eyebrows. Something my stomach needed immediately.

I listened to the sweet, soothing sounds of their cursing as I peered over to look at my rearview mirror.

Watching her as she watched me right back.

11

DANI

"Now, understanding human resources policy and administration might not sound as interesting as debate. But this class will provide a great deal of information that is going to be necessary for you to have at your disposal. Think of things like negotiation tactics as the icing on the cake, but classes like this are the cake itself. Which is why, in my class, you'll need at least a C+ in order for me to recommend a move-up on my behalf in this curriculum. Some of you are already forgetting that with the pop quizzes I gave you Wednesday."

The class groaned, but I didn't flinch. However, the groan did snap me out of my partial trance. The week had gone by incredibly slowly. But it was finally Friday, which meant the weekend was almost upon us. And with my last class of the day finally coming to a close, I listened to the professor repeat, over and over again, the mantra she thought was imperative to close every class with.

"I know, I know. It's usually a C- for the rest of the classes. But with something like this you need to do just a little better. Getting a degree in human resources is serious stuff. Might not sound like it, but it's important. HR is what stands between the employees and unlawful firings. HR is what keeps the peace in certain--"

My eyes panned over to the window and I gazed outside. From the building on campus, I saw the back of my dorm. A safe haven I had come to enjoy. And as I stared out the window, minding my own business, he popped up into my mind again.

Max.

I still smelled burnt rubber in my nostrils, even days later, after seeing Max speed off on his bike like that. I felt a smile slide across my face as his eyes popped to the forefront of my mind. Those brooding, dark green eyes. That softly crooked, stubbled jaw of his. The way he seemed unconcerned with the world around him. The expert way he popped that wheelie before blazing a trail into traffic.

I'd never seen anyone like him before.

"--and with that, I hope you all enjoy your weekends. And remember that your first pop essay is Monday morning!"

The groaning class pulled me from my trance yet again and I sighed. I couldn't live my entire semester this way. I'd never pass my classes. I took my time packing my things up and getting out of class. I needed to screw my head back on straight.

Why did Max distract me this badly?

I mean, he was a bad boy. The ultimate bad boy. He smoked cigarettes. He rode a bike. He was obviously into some trouble with that crew of his. Everyone was scared of him. He was big. A brute. Rude. Pompous. But here I was, remembering the smell of the rubber of his tires from four days ago.

You're infatuated with him.

I slung my backpack over my shoulder and headed outside. I needed to get rid of this infatuation. Because it wasn't like something would ever come of it. Max was way out of my league. No, he was in a completely different league of his own. I was in the 'good girl' league. I was the person that did as my parents told me to do, never questioned what was right for me, and never stepped out of the lines.

Max was the poster boy for 'opposite.'

"Doesn't matter anyway," I murmured to myself.

I mean, there were a plethora of reasons why Max and I couldn't work together. One, I was much too busy with my studies to go galavanting off on the back of his bike. Two? My father would never approve. Like, absolutely never in the history of ever. Three, I was a virgin. Therefore, I'd never be able to give a man like Max what he really wanted. And even if I could? That was probably the only thing Max was after with any given woman, and I deserved more than that.

So stop thinking about him. Go get lunch and focus on schoolwork.

I headed for the cafeteria, but the sound of a motorcycle in the distance caught my ear. I stopped in my tracks, almost getting run over by a crowd behind me, and my head started swiveling. Where was that revving coming from? Where was the bike? Was it Max? Was he on campus again?

You're in trouble, Dani.

The sound of the engine stopped and I shook my head. I needed to rip myself out of his trance. No. Max was scary. Intimidating. I had no business even thinking about a guy like that. My feet carried me as quickly as I could walk. And by the time I got to the cafeteria doors, I was in a full sprint. I panted for air as I ripped the door open, making my way to Hannah.

To engage in our daily lunch ritual.

"Hey there, girlie. How was class?"

Hannah's voice crooned next to me as I stepped into the lunch line.

"Ah, boring. As usual. But my classes are easy this semester."

She snickered. "Lucky you. I'm already dying in my math class. I hate math. Are you taking math this semester?"

I shook my head. "Got all my math courses knocked out last year for that reason. Math isn't something I want to drag out."

"Ugh, I should've done that. I did that with my history and science courses. Why do they make us take required courses like that? It only distracts from the classes I should be taking for my degree."

"Did you declare your degree this year?"

She scoffed. "Why, Dani, I'm thoroughly offended."

I grinned. "So, no on that degree declaration still."

She rolled her eyes. "I don't know what the big rush is."

I walked through the line and decided on breakfast for lunch. I mean, breakfast was acceptable at any time during the day. But especially at lunch. Hannah stood behind me at the panini bar, getting herself a hot sandwich to go with her soup. I took the liberty of getting our drinks and finding us a place to sit. Preferably by a window.

I enjoyed a nice view.

"Oh, thanks, girl. This diet?" Hannah asked.

I was still staring out the window when she sat down. Wondering if that bike I'd heard earlier would come cruising by.

"Hello? Earth to Dani?"

I blinked. "Yeah, sorry. Uh, yes. Yes. It's diet."

She furrowed her brow. "You okay?"

I picked up my fork. "Just drained from the week. You know, getting back into the groove and all."

"Well, you will be happy to know there's a party going on in the dorm beside us. Might be a nice way to wind down on a Friday night."

"That might be how *you* want to wind down. But what I want to do is order pizza, get into my comfy pajamas, and pass out after stuffing my face."

She pointed her spoon at me. "Now that's a plan I can get behind."

I gasped playfully. "What? You miss a party to be with little old me?"

Her face fell. "You're pushing it, Dani."

I smiled. "Which is why you love me."

"Wait, now? Seriously?"

My ear perked up at the sound of the voice behind me. It sounded an awful lot like Benji. That stupid jerk-off. But it was the voice that came after his that sent a shiver down my spine. And explained why I'd heard the motorcycle earlier.

"I told you to be ready once I called. This is me calling, since you don't want to pick up your damn phone."

I slowly peeked over my shoulder and saw Max hunched over a table with Benji. They sat a couple of tables down, in a corner that didn't have a window beside it. I quickly turned back around as my toes curled in my shoes. I heard Hannah talking at me, but I closed my eyes, trying to block out her voice so I could pay attention to them.

"Dude, I didn't do it intentionally. I was in class, remember? This morning? I got that class with--"

Max interrupted. "I call, you jump. That's how that works. You wanna be one of us? That's what it takes. This is the last time I'm tracking you down for a job. Got it?"

"Hey, Maxy-pad. You're the one who wanted me to--"

Max growled. "The fuck did you just call me?"

Hannah cleared her throat. "Dani? Are you listening to a word I'm saying?"

The growl that bubbled up Max's throat had me rooted to my seat. But Hannah's voice pulled me from my eavesdropping moment. I looked at her with wide eyes and she cocked her head, trying to figure out what in the world was wrong with me.

Join the club.

The scraping of chairs along the floor pulled my eyes over my shoulder. I saw Benji and Max get up from the table, heading straight for the exit. Max loomed over the lanky boy, his leather jacket pulled taut over his broad shoulders. And when his eyes roamed over the room as he stood by the exit, those dark green eyes I'd been daydreaming about all morning found mine.

I held my breath.

He stared at me as he held the door open for Benji. Even as Benji walked through it, he didn't move. I didn't dare move, either. I watched him lick his lips, causing my cheeks to flush. And when Hannah started laughing, Max slipped effortlessly through the door and into the exit stairwell.

"Wow, you've got it bad, Dani, dear."

I let out the breath I was holding. "I don't know what you're talking about."

Hannah's giggle told me she knew exactly what I was talking about.

And I didn't know how to feel about the predicament I found myself in.

12

MAX

With Rupert at my side and Benji directly behind me, the crew I had hired for this job rode up the driveway of my father's home. When my father jumped, everyone around him said 'How high?' So when he'd finally sent the text message this after-noon that we were to all assemble, I didn't bat an eye. I had been frustrated all week with this shit. What started out as a Tuesday afternoon job had turned into a Friday night job, per a last minute change on our client's part. That kind of shit didn't bode well for me and my boys. Especially since Mr. Dean struck me as the kind of man my father had become.

But the moment was upon us. We parked our bikes in front of the porch and made our way inside. The ritual was simple: Dad briefed us on the details of things now that everything was solidified, we would receive our tentative schedules, and if Dad wanted to make any changes to the crew members I had brought on board, he reserved the right to do that during the briefing.

Which he had done to me many times before.

We all walked up the steps and the heavy wooden door of my father's mansion magically opened. We marched into the foyer, taking up our stances while we waited for my father to appear. He enjoyed the theater of it all. The drama of us waiting for him while he entered a room by himself.

And when he appeared, I let out the breath I didn't realize I had been holding.

"Eight men?"

His booming voice made my ears twitch.

"Yes, sir."

He stood in front of me. "You only need eight men for this job?"

I looked him in his eyes. "You know too many bikers around these parts brings unwanted attention on the streets. If the client wants to be unseen, we have to be unseen with him."

He nodded. "Very well. Change of plans--"

"Go figure," Benji murmured.

My eyes slowly panned over to my cousin and I heard my father's anger already bubbling in his veins.

"What did you just say?" he asked.

Benji swallowed hard. "Nothing, sir."

Dad marched in front of him. "Don't you lie to me."

I butted in. "He's right, though."

Dad turned his anger toward me again. "Want to try that again?"

I shook my head. "No, I'm good."

He narrowed his eyes. "Yes, this week has been tense. Mr. Dean has pushed the date back on us a couple of times. That's what happens when delivering a premium service, however. People expect premium treatment."

I nodded. "Yep."

Dad stared at me for a long time. "Ready for the details? Or do you and the boys want to keep being smartasses?"

"Ready when you are, sir."

He nodded. "Good. Our client is already at his hotel. There's a business meeting he's conducting tonight. He wants the lot of you to meet him at the hotel, escort him to the meeting, and case the building while the meeting is being held."

"We can get it done."

"You are to stay with him during the meeting, then get him back to the hotel. I've already informed Mr. Dean that if he wants a change in the itinerary on your watch, you need to radio me first. Got it?"

I licked my lips. "Got it."

"Good. Now, get the hell out of here and get to the hotel. You're expected within the hour."

I whistled through my teeth and my men started for the front door. I stared my father down one last time, letting him know how absolutely disgusted I was with how this man was already yanking our chain. All week, we'd stood by our phones. All week, we'd waited for this inconsiderate asswipe to come into town. All I could hope for now was smooth transitions for the time we guarded this man.

Though I knew better than to expect something like that.

The guys fell in line behind me as we rode through town. The small mounted GPS on my bike handlebar guided me toward La Grenvan Rouge, and the closer we got the more expensive things became. The rundown brick buildings I was used to turned into fashion boutiques and overpriced coffee shops. The dollar stores became Targets and the seedy gas stations because 'refueling' stations. And when we pulled up to the front of the hotel, I gazed up at the reflective mirrored expanse of the hotel's black façade.

Yep. This place had some serious money sunk into it.

"Max?"

My eyes quickly found the tinny tenor voice that had dictated my name.

"Yes?" I asked.

A tall, spindly man came up to me and stuck out his hand.

"Mr. Dean."

I quirked an eyebrow. "You're Mr. Dean."

His hand fell to his side. "I might not look like much, but never underestimate a supposed underdog, Mr. Ryddle."

"Call me Max."

He nodded. "Very well. I'm due at my meeting in fifteen minutes. You and your men can ride behind me, but I want two of you at my side when I go in for this meeting. I assume you and your men are hot?"

I blinked. "Yeah."

"Good. See to it that it's always that way."

"Not a problem."

He walked off to the limo sitting down the block, and it made me wonder why the hell he wanted to walk to his limo. All of this smelled off. But I tried not to let it get to me too much. I twirled my finger in the air to round up the guys, and one by one we fell in behind the limo. We still hadn't been informed of this club destination. For all we knew, we'd be riding for the next fucking hour to this damn place.

But we surrounded the limo as best as we could to protect this man from any roadside onslaught.

Earpieces. We're going to need earpieces for this job.

The second we pulled up to the club, I gnawed on the inside of my cheek. This place wasn't a damn club. It was a seedy, sleazy, underground brothel-slash-casino ring. I knew all about it. Mostly because my father entertained a great deal of his personal guests beneath the crumbling walls of this dilapidated building. I shook my head as the guys all pulled up behind me. Our bikes surrounded the limo as Mr. Dean got out. He looked at me and crooked a finger, beckoning me to come with him. I looked toward Rupert and nodded my head, signaling that he needed to come with me.

After slinging my leg over my bike to get off, I held up the number 'two' in the air with my fingers. My men knew exactly what that meant after working together for so long. They got to work. All of our standard protocols had numbers assigned to them. Two was 'search and check.' My men were to case the outside of the building and cover all the exits with their guns ready to be drawn at a moment's notice.

"The hell's going on?" Rupert murmured.

I sighed. "No fucking clue."

Mr. Dean walked up to us. "Come with me, you two. We're going downstairs and into an office. You don't have to come inside the office, but I do want you standing on either side of the door until the meeting has concluded. Understood?"

I nodded. "Understood."

"Wonderful. Come with me."

The string bean with eyes turned on his heels and I looked over at Rupert. Even he had his eyebrows up as we walked behind this man. None of this was panning out the way we figured it would. And it had both of us on alert. We walked inside the club and cleared corners, making sure Mr. Dean was safe in this disgusting place. Then we followed him down a back staircase that led directly to a stark white door.

"You two wait here. I'll be out as soon as I can."

I nodded. "Understood."

Rupert and I took up our assigned places as Mr. Dean greeted, with great fervor, the person on the other side of the door. I didn't care to take a look. Or even try to eavesdrop. I didn't know what the hell this shit was about, and I didn't care to. It had nothing to do with me, so it wasn't my business.

"I hate this place," Rupert murmured.

"Shh."

"Seriously. It gives me the creeps."

I peeked at him. "Shut up."

He sighed. "It doesn't give you the--?"

The door swung open. "All right, gentlemen. With me."

I furrowed my brow as Mr. Dean came charging out of the room. The man hadn't been in there more than ten minutes.

Meeting must've gone bad.

I looked over at Rupert before we took off. I had my hand on my gun because my gut was screaming bloody murder. My eyes panned around the small corridors and the nasty building we walked through as we escorted our client back to his limo. But a voice behind us called out, stopping us in our tracks.

"Mr. Dean?"

Our client sighed. "Yes?"

We all turned around and found a very chaotic-looking man standing at the top of the steps we'd just come from.

"I forgot to mention something to you before you turned down my offer."

Our client rolled his eyes. "Yes?"

"I really can't allow you to leave."

Rupert reached for his gun, but I held my hand out. The man at the steps hadn't drawn a weapon, so there was no need for us to. Yet. Mr. Dean narrowed his eyes as he slowly walked toward the man. Rupert and I followed him, step for step, making sure we had his back while our hands hovered over our guns.

Yeah, we really need earpieces for this shit.

"And why is that?" our client asked calmly.

The club owner snickered. "I don't do business with lying bastards like you."

The second the man reached into his jacket pocket, I had my gun out and ready. Rupert made a run at the man, tackling him to the ground. Mr. Dean stood there with a grin on his face, completely immobile. As if he were a statue. And as I crouched down, silencing my footsteps, I watched my best friend wrestle this maniacal-looking man to the ground.

But not before he popped off a shot.

"Mr. Dean!"

I fisted the man's coat and tossed him into a darkened corner. Protected by the shadows, I leveled my gun at the club owner on the floor. Rupert jammed his elbow into the man's wrist, and I heard the 'snap!' as it dislocated. Another gunshot rang out, though, one that wasn't connected to the man on the ground. And as Rupert kicked the man's gun in my direction, I picked it up, dual-wielding weapons as I tried to find the source of the second shot.

13

DANI

"Hey, girl. You wanna go check out the party next door?"

I peered out the window with my cardigan wrapped around my body. I was already in my pajama pants and wondering about when I should order pizza. I gazed outside, my eyes gravitating across the street, watching that flickering lamplight illuminate the darkness, wondering if Max would magically appear before my very eyes.

"Hello, earth to Dani. I swear, you've been so--"

I sighed. "Distracted?"

I slowly turned away from the window and drew in a deep breath.

"I'm not okay right now, Hannah."

Her face fell. "Talk to me. What's going on?"

I leaned against the window. "I'm already struggling with my classes, and it's only been one week."

Hannah came over and placed her hands on my shoulders.

"That's a good thing, then."

I furrowed my brow. "What?"

She giggled. "The good thing is that it *is* only the first week. You've got plenty of time to focus and make things up. What happened?"

I shook my head. "No, no, no. It's not--it's not really grades, or anything like that."

"Well, then, what are you struggling with?"

I shrugged. "Just this whole…"

I looked over my shoulder to gaze out the window again and Hannah gasped.

"You're still thinking about that guy."

I paused. "Max."

"What?"

"He has a name. It's Max. I--figured that out Monday."

She swatted me. "You saw him this week and you didn't tell me?"

I rolled my eyes. "Trust me, it wasn't the best encounter there ever was."

"Why? The man's hot. Especially in that leather and black of his."

"He calls me 'Daddy's girl.' Even though he knows my name."

"Dani, you know boys pick on you when they like you, right?"

I grimaced. "That's a really stupid way to go about things. Why not just treat someone with respect?"

She giggled again. "Do those bike-riding guys

strike you as the kind of guys that give respect? No. What they give you is good times. And you're very overdue for a good time."

"Are we talking about my virginity again?"

"We're talking about your *everything* again."

I sighed. "Forget it. I shouldn't have said anything."

Hannah tugged me to my desk. "Oh, no you don't. You're going to sit right here and we're going to talk."

She pushed me down into my seat before pulling her chair up.

"So tell me everything. Exactly how often do you think about him?"

I shrugged. "Kind of hard not to. I mean, that Benji guy?"

"Who?"

"The one that was in the room that you had to kick out."

"Oh, that asshole? What about him?"

I snickered. "He's in my Monday and Wednesday morning conflict management class."

She paused. "Is he a human resources major, too?"

I shook my head. "I don't think so. That class also serves as a debate class requirement. Some people still knocking out their other required classes take it."

"So he's in that class with you."

"Yeah. And no matter where I sit in that stupid class, he always has to sit right beside me. Wednesday morning, I got there fifteen minutes early. And when he came waltzing into class twenty minutes late, he glared at the girl sitting beside me in the second row until she moved."

She laughed. "Oh, shit. That's some serious bull right there."

"Right!? It is. Not to mention, he's a jerk-off. Always picking on me. Calling me names. And every time he sits beside me, he makes me think of Max. Which starts me down this daydream spiral that I practically have every class. I don't know what to do. I can't even think clearly right now, Hannah."

She took my hands. "Look, Dani. All you have is a harmless crush. Every college girl gets them. Every girl, at least once in her life, has a major crush on some guy that doesn't suit her life. Or fit her parents. Or doesn't fall in line with what she wants in life. It's a rite of passage."

"How do I get it to go away, though? I can't do my entire semester this distracted. I'll fail."

"I know you, Dani. You won't fail. You might get some Cs, but you certainly won't fail."

"That's practically failing in my world."

She sighed. "Then you need to come out with me and make some real friends."

I rolled my eyes. "Please don't turn this into a way to get me to go to this party tonight."

She pulled me up from my chair. "You can either listen to me or not. But I'm telling you, once you surround yourself with good people it'll be harder for asshole bullies to get to you. That's what's happening right now. The two of them sound like bullies and they're getting under your skin."

"Then, aren't I supposed to hate them or something?"

"What you'll realize is that there's a very fine line between hate and love. Boys like those dickheads get off on getting reactions out of you. If you stop reacting, they'll stop teasing."

"In my experience, that just makes the teasing worse."

"For a while, sure. Until they get fed up. Take away the stimuli, and they'll eventually seek it elsewhere."

I paused. "Nice to see you're paying attention in your own classes."

She scoffed. "It's not like I failed any of my classes. I just know when to buckle down and when to have a good time."

"You're going to drag me to this party, aren't you?"

"You better believe it."

I groaned. "But crowds of people make me feel so-_"

She tugged me closer to her. "I know you're shy. I know you get anxious in crowds sometimes. But I'll be there. Being shy isn't going to serve you well anymore. Not here. Not in college. You need to be making connections. You need to be making friends. If you can't make connections here, then you won't be able to make professional connections out there. In the world. Once we graduate. Got it?"

I nodded. "You do make a decent point."

"I know I do. Now, I can introduce you to some nice people tonight. People who, if you give them the chance, will have your back after some time. How does that sound?"

"Sounds easier said than done."

"But does it sound like something you want?"

I sighed. "Yeah. It--it would be nice to have other people I could count on other than you."

She smiled. "Good. Wonderful. Okay. We're going to get you out of these pajamas and into something more party appropriate."

I rolled my eyes. "Nothing tight, okay? I really didn't like that white shirt."

"Then don't own any shirts like that. Throw it out. All of these things I'm dressing you up in are from your wardrobe. Take it or leave it."

"Fine, fine. Okay."

"Dani, I'll be by your side the entire night. Just trust me, okay?"

I sighed heavily before I pulled my hands out from the grip of hers.

"Okay. I'll trust you."

Hannah smiled. "Great. All right. Let's start by rummaging through your clothes and seeing what we can come up with."

The idea of my pizza night in quickly fell away as my best friend practically demolished my side of the room. She tossed clothes at me to try on before shaking her head and making me discard it. I had shirts and jeans and sweatpants crumpled on the floor and hanging off my bed. She started pulling things off hangers, tossing them to me and making me twirl for her. And after almost an hour of this nonsense, I finally had an outfit she approved of.

Where did I keep getting these tight clothes from, though?

Mom must've snuck them into my suitcases.

"You. Look. Amazing."

I tugged at the light blue tank top. "Can I wear something over this?"

She shook her head. "Nope. It's a warm summer night. Jeans and a tank top with those heels of yours is going to slay the competition tonight."

"Compet--what competition?"

"Hush. Quit panicking. It's a figure of speech. Girls always want to bring their best to parties like this. Especially parties in dorms that aren't theirs. Now it's my turn to get ready. Give me twenty minutes and we'll be on our way."

At least she's not putting makeup on you this time.

"Oh, and slather on some lip gloss. And use my blush, too. You don't want the lights at the party to wash you out."

I sighed. "I can do that."

While Hannah got ready, I gazed at myself in the full-length mirror on the back of our door. I swear, I'd never seen this tank top in my life. Nor had I seen these heels before. There was no question in my mind that Mom had snuck these into my wardrobe when I wasn't looking. But wouldn't I have seen them when I was unpacking?

Unless…

"Are you putting your clothes in my drawers, Hannah?"

She snickered. "Now, why the hell would I do that?"

I narrowed my eyes. "Hannah."

She clicked her tongue. "Hush, I'm putting on mascara."

"Are you sticking your clothes in my drawers so you can make me wear them for these parties of yours?"

She sighed. "I mean, you do look hot."

"Hannah!"

"What!? Dani, you have shit clothes. Baggy jeans, terribly scuffed tennis shoes, and baggy long-sleeve shirts. I don't think you even own a short-sleeved shirt! I'm not giving you good clothes. Just some basics. T-shirts, a tank top here and there. Heels I know I'm not going to wear."

"I like how I dress."

"Yeah, and so does the Catholic Church."

"Hannah, it's--"

She jammed her mascara closed. "Look, Dani. I know this makes you uncomfortable. But if you're going to complain about something? Be prepared to fix it. You want friends? They aren't coming to you. You have to go out and find them. And finding them means not blending in long enough so they can notice you. This isn't about vanity anymore, Dani. This is about you feeling comfortable enough in your own skin to show yourself to the world and say, 'Hey! I'm worth knowing.' And no one's going to know you how I know you if they can't even pick you out from a crowd."

She had a very good point.

"Okay. I'm sorry."

She packed up her makeup. "No need to be sorry. Just stop fighting me every step of the damn way and trust the process. I'm not trying to change you. I'm trying to elevate you a little bit. Plus, you're going to die of sweat in a long-sleeved shirt at something like this. Especially if you're drinking."

"I don't want a drink."

"Then take a drink and hold it so no one else gives you one."

The trick came back to memory. "Yes. I can do that."

Hannah slipped into her heels. "Good. Because I'm ready to go. You with me? Or are you going to keep complaining?"

She offered her arm to me and I slipped mine around hers.

"Ready when you are," I said.

The two of us marched out of our room and headed for the elevator. And I mentally prepared myself for finding a new friend tonight.

Even if I had to die of embarrassment in order to do it.

14

MAX

"Get him to the car. Now!" I roared.

I watched Rupert rip Mr. Dean off the floor as the shadows began to move. A bullet whizzed by my head and my vision started pulsing. Tunneling. Dripping with red as I aimed the sights of my pistols into the unseen corners. I popped off two shots while listening to my men scramble through the doors. Benji appeared, his gun drawn and his eyes wide. Panic settled in my veins.

He was much too good for this kind of life.

"Get down! Now!" I roared.

My men hit the floor, and relief flooded my veins when I saw Benji was out of harm's way.

"Fall back. Fall back now!"

I popped off a warning shot right beside the head of the club owner, letting him know exactly where my next bullet would go if he so much as got up from that fucking floor. I covered Rupert's escape as he dragged our client out through the front door, heading straight for that damn limo. I tucked my guns away and ripped the door open. Rupert practically threw the man into the backseat with his bare hands. And after closing the door, I banged on the top of the car, signaling the limo to drive away.

"Two! Six! Seven! Go with the limo, now!"

My voice boomed over the chorus of chaos before I heard bikes striking up. All of my men had numbers. Numbers that we were assigned at the start of every job. I never felt comfortable enough yelling their names, so numbers were the next best thing. And as I watched Benji ride off down the road with two other guys to follow that damn limo wherever it was headed, I drew in steady breaths.

Because we still had a job here to clean up.

The sound of glass shattering and tires screeching turned my head. I saw the club owner on the curb by the dark alleyway, his gun leveled at the limo. Rupert took off, ready to disarm the man as I pulled my guns back out. And as the limo careened around the corner with three of my men following it, I watched Benji turn around and pop off two shots that embedded themselves into the concrete.

Directly at the feet of the club owner from a fucking moving bike.

Boy's always been a damn good shot.

"One, look out!"

Rupert's voice grabbed my attention and my senses

went into overload. I felt the men behind me as I spun around, leveling my guns in front of me. The sound of gunshots rang out around us, filling the space with gunpowder, heat, and anger. I focused as I popped the men in their knees, refusing to kill anyone tonight. The guns lurched in my hands and explosive force emanated from my body as I focused my energy on getting my men the hell out of this shitstorm.

Then I saw a movement out of the corner of my eye.

A very broad man stood in the doorway of the club, but his gun was leveled in a different direction. I followed the barrel of his gun to find his target, and what I saw made my blood boil. I moved my guns toward him and fired without a second thought. He was staring right at Rupert. My best fucking friend.

The only sound that met my ears was a click.

I heard men chuckling around me. Gunfire sounded in the alleyway as Rupert pinned the club owner to the ground. And in a split-second decision, I dropped my guns, dug my feet into the concrete and took off at lightning speed, hunched over and ready to knock this asshole off his feet.

"Rupert, look out!" I roared.

My voice was distraction enough.

The man grunted as I ran straight into his stomach. I knocked him back into the club, onto the floor that kicked up dust around us. I straddled the man and threw the first punch, feeling his nose breaking against my knuckles. I watched him fiddling with his gun so I wrapped my hand around his wrist, smashing it against the ground, over and over, watching his grip weaken.

Finally I smashed his hand down against a rusty nail protruding from the floor.

"What the fuck!"

"Let go of the goddamn gun."

The growl of my voice sounded like someone else. I felt my nostrils flaring as the beast inside rattled against its cage. My eyes widened and I threw another punch. And then another. And then another still. I felt the man's faceplate shattering with every hit. He gurgled on his own damn blood as it poured from his nose and seeped from his ears.

I'd show this man no mercy for pointing a gun at Rupert.

I didn't even hear the gunshot before the bullet grazed my shoulder. The searing pain was enough to pull me from my trance. The man beneath me groaned as I hissed with shock. Then I felt someone grip my leather jacket.

"Get the hell off him."

I slipped out of my jacket and spun around, ready for another fight. The club owner stood there with wide eyes and disheveled hair. I mean, he looked like he was high on something.

"Bring it," I glowered.

"Guards! Get him!"

The trampling of feet behind me sprang me into action. I hooked around with my right fist, connecting with the club owner's jaw, knocking him out cold. I scooped up my leather jacket and tossed it around my shoulders as I ran out the door, my head swiveling to look for Rupert.

"Two! Where the fuck are you!?" I roared.

I heard a bike engine revving as footsteps grew louder behind me. Three short revs and a long one. Three short revs and a long one.

The club's universal signal for 'Get the fuck out of Dodge.'

With pain inching down my arm, I dashed for my bike. There were too many of those assholes around here for the five of us that were still left to take care of this place. I'd have words with Mr. Dean about it, but not tonight.

Right now, I had to get my men out of here.

"Two!" I bellowed.

I threw my leg over my bike as four brawny security men dressed in all black poured onto the sidewalk.

"Two!" I roared.

"Right here! I'm right here! Come on, One. We have to get out of here!"

I watched Rupert race down the road, leaving me in his dust. I counted my men as they filtered out of the alleyway, making sure I had everyone before I pushed away from the curb. Gunfire exploded behind us. Bullets whizzed and I heard the shattering of rear lights as we sped away. I pulled up beside Rupert and saw his bloodied nose. His eye was already swelling and turning black. And as I studied my men while making my way to the front of the pack, anger flared in my gut.

I hit the throttle on my bike, leaving that damn club in my dust with my men in tow.

We barely made it out of there alive.

As we cut our way through town, all of my thoughts fell back to my fucking father. He could've gotten us all killed with a job like this. I was under the impression that risks were minimized. That we weren't to expect firefights unless absolutely necessary. But a ten-minute meeting before the club owner opened fire on us?

It was almost like we should've expected war in the first fucking place.

It's a miracle no one's dead right now.

The pain in my arm blossomed like a damn flower all the way down to my fingertips. My men had gotten very roughed up tonight. And this was only the first night of guarding this asshole. I needed more information. I needed to know who the hell this character was, what the fuck had happened in that meeting, and I needed someone to foot the bill for the things we needed. Decent earpieces. Extra magazines to carry with us. Hell, some bulletproof gear, too. We weren't prepared for war. We weren't prepared to usher a slaughterer through these streets.

And if that was the expectation, then we needed gear.

I led the guys down Alleyway Cove, one of the main streets in our fair city where every single offshoot for three blocks was nothing but alleyways. Dark streets with no lamps that twisted and turned with one-way signs and yield signs for days. It was the perfect place to split up. To find our way back to our own home bases so we could recuperate and lay low.

So, with a flick of my wrist, I dismissed what was left of my crew.

Then I set my sights on that college campus to make sure Benji had gotten back all right.

15

DANI

The dimmed lights of the dorm building made it hard to navigate. But Hannah kept me close. With a cocktail of sweetness and rum in my hand, I followed her through the crowd, trying my best to put on a smile and not get grossed out at every person that shoved by me.

"Hey."

"Get out of the way."

"That's my man you're touching!"

Hannah whipped around. "She doesn't want your scrawny man. She's into men with muscles and substance."

I paused. "I am?"

"Yep. Now, come on. I want to introduce you to someone."

The more tense I grew, the more I watched people around me. All of them seemed to be relaxed.

Centered. Sure of themselves. And all of these people had one thing in common. They all had these red cups in their hands, filled with drinks they sucked down to keep them from sloshing over the edge.

Like the red cup I was holding.

"What's this drink, anyway?" I asked.

Hannah tugged me off to the side. "Dani, this is Rachel. She's in choir with me."

The girl waved. "Hi."

I paused. "I didn't know you sang."

Hannah snickered. "I don't. I just needed the elective."

Rachel sipped her drink. "What's your name again?"

Hannah laughed. "How many of those have you had?"

Rachel grinned. "Probably enough."

I watched her chug down the drink before I gazed into my own cup. The yellow liquid stared back at me with notes of coconut overwhelming my nostrils. It didn't smell terrible. And it didn't look unappetizing. I'd never had a drink like this before, though. A beer here and there with Hannah, sure. I hated beer, though. It wasn't hard to refuse a second one.

This drink made my mouth water.

"What's your major?" Rachel asked.

I took a sip of my drink and choked it down.

"Uh, human resources. You?"

The girl smiled. "English. I want to teach and write on the side."

I took another sip. "That's awesome. What year are you?"

"I'm a junior. And I know, I know. Still on campus and all. But I like the atmosphere and it saves me money on rent. Rent around here would be so much more expensive than just getting my own private dorm room."

I sipped again. "Wait, you can get your own dorm room?"

Hannah giggled. "Don't go getting any ideas, now. I want to be your roomie until we graduate."

Rachel gasped. "Oh, my gosh. You guys are room-mates. How cute! Sophomores, right? Did you guys room together last year?"

While the three of us talked, I continued sipping my drink. It didn't taste terrible, and it was helping me to relax. Maybe a bit too much, though. The second my drink was drained, the cup was plucked from my fingertips and replaced with another drink I started sipping on again.

"I feel all warm and fuzzy inside," I said.

Rachel smiled. "First time drinking?"

Hannah nodded. "Yep. That's why I'm cutting her off at three."

Rachel snickered. "Might want to cut her off after this one. I made this myself, and it's very strong."

I took a long pull from my drink. "And very good!"

"Move. Get out of my way. Get the fuck away from me."

The hardened voice turned my head and I staggered on my feet a bit. I squinted my eyes as I took another long pull from my drink, almost finishing it off. I felt someone hook a finger into the belt loops of my jeans. Was I teetering that much?

"Get the fuck out of my way."

Benji gnashed his teeth at people as he stomped down the hallway. I watched him shove others out of the way as he came straight for me. I stiffened. My knees went numb. My eyes followed him as he shot me a dark look before shoving himself into one of the dorm rooms. This wasn't his dorm. This wasn't our dorm, either.

So whose room had he just walked into?

"Benj!"

Max's voice boomed over the music and my lips parted in shock.

"Benj! Where the fuck are you?"

After finally focusing my vision on Max, I noticed how disheveled he looked. His shoulder looked slumped a bit, and he was limping. Or maybe that was the alcohol distorting my vision. I wasn't sure. I blinked in confusion as a hand darted out from the room Benji had just walked into. And the hand was covered in bruises. In blood.

At least, it looked like blood.

"Come on, we should get back to our room," Hannah said.

Rachel sighed. "Aww, you guys don't want to stay for another drink?"

I licked my lips. "What are they doing here?"

Hannah wrapped her arm around my waist. "Doesn't matter. Come on. Let's just get past the--"

"Is Bambi getting all liquored up?"

Benji's voice filled my ears as Hannah walked me past the open door.

"Hey! I asked you a fucking question!"

Hannah snarled at him. "Can it, you piece of shit."

"What did you just call me?"

I heard the stomping of footsteps and I leapt to the other side of the hallway. Everyone around us watched through their own liquored fog as Benji gnashed his teeth at me like some feral animal. Max loomed behind him in the shadows, his body still a bit hunched. But Benji's voice pierced through my thoughts.

"Bambi's getting liquored everyone! Open season for all the hunters."

Hannah pointed at him. "I don't know who the fuck you are or who you think you are, but if I ever hear you speak to my friend like that again--"

Benji turned to my best friend. "You'll what, dollface?"

That's it. I'd had enough of this asshole.

"Don't you dare," I glowered.

His eyes swept back over to me as I walked toward him.

"Don't you dare turn this on her. Don't you dare turn this on anyone," I said.

Benji snickered. "And what the hell are you gonna do about it, Bambi?"

I felt Max's eyes on me as I placed my hands against Benji's chest.

"What if I do this?" I asked.

I shoved him and he stumbled back into the dorm room.

"What the--?"

I grinned. "And what if I do a little of this?"

I balled up my hand and punched his arm. Not hard. But enough to startle him.

"Hey, get the fuck out of--"

"Or what if I do a little bit of this?"

I kicked his shin and he let out a yelp, causing Max to chuckle in the corner. Then I pointed at Benji as he stared at me with wide eyes.

"I don't know why you've sunken your claws into me. I don't know where you get off calling me names and talking to me the way you do. But it stops now. Do you hear me? It stops, or I report you. And I'll report you as much as I need to until you're thrown off campus and you can't terrorize anyone anymore. Understood, asshole?"

Hannah giggled. "Get him, girl."

Max's voice piped up. "Strong words for a Daddy's girl."

I whirled around on the brute of a man, ready to dig into him, too. Because if he thought he was innocent, then he had another thing coming. I pointed my finger at him in the corner. I stalked toward him, my eyes hooked with his. But when he stepped out of the corner and into the dim light of the moon filtering through the window, I saw it. The bruises along his jaw. His bloodied lip. His leather jacket, torn at the shoulder with what looked like dried blood around it.

The sight made me gasp.

"What happened to you, Max?"

His eye twitched before he leaned against the wall with his good shoulder.

"Best you don't know, Daddy's girl. Trust me."

Benji snickered. "I'm getting a fucking drink. Want one?"

Max didn't take his eyes off me. "No."

Hannah stepped up beside me. "Why are you here?"

Max shrugged, then groaned in pain. "Nice party."

I licked my lips. "This isn't your dorm room. This isn't your building. Why did you barge in?"

Max sighed. "Waiting for a friend."

I eyed him carefully. "To do what?"

But, when he didn't say anything, I looked around the room. I saw the textbooks strewn everywhere. Medical textbooks. I saw the half-open dresser drawer in the corner, with scrubs poking out.

"You came to see a med student," I said.

Max nodded, but didn't say anything.

"You need a doctor."

His eyes whipped to mine. "I need to get out of here. I only came here to make sure Benj was all right."

I nodded. "Then come with me."

I turned my back, but didn't hear him following me. So I turned around.

"You coming, or what?" I asked.

Hannah took my hand. "You know what you're doing?"

No. I had no clue what I was doing. But Max needed to be cleaned up. And, if possible, he needed to be convinced to get medical intervention. None of which would take place in the middle of a party.

"Yeah, I know what I'm doing," I said.

I cast one more look back at Max before I nodded my head. Part of me didn't think he'd follow me, so when he did, I felt relief. We left the party with him hovering over me, and I heard soft growls falling from his lips. As if he were staking a claim on his territory and warding off enemies of the night. The sound did something to me. The smell of his cologne and sweat mixed together made my fingertips tingle. And as we made our way into my dorm bedroom, I searched around for the first aid kit Dad had made me pack before sitting Max down in the chair at my desk.

"You really do need a doctor. This thing on your shoulder looks bad," I said.

"No hospitals for me."

"And why not?"

He shrugged, then groaned again. "Don't want attention from the police."

I ripped open an alcohol wipe. "Fair enough. Hope you're not averse to pain."

I slid the wipe over the gash on his shoulder and he grunted. Multiple times. I slipped his leather jacket off to clean more of the wound and rolled up the sleeve of his shirt. And there, emblazoned in red and black, were the words 'Red Thorns.' It wrapped around his bicep with a vine of thorns-sort of design dotted with small, red roses throughout. It was an intricate tattoo. One I let my fingers slide over. I lost track of cleaning up his wound as I studied the beautiful color and design against his skin.

"Is that the name of your crew?" I asked.

Max cleared his throat. "Yep."

"The Red Thorns."

"Uh huh."

"Interesting."

"Dangerous."

I nodded. "Figured as much by how beat up you look."

I went back to cleaning the indentation in his shoulder.

"How did you get this?"

Max snickered. "A bullet."

I felt my head spinning. "At least it didn't embed itself, I guess."

Wow, this guy really was a bad boy. Smelling of blood, and sweat, and cologne, and motor oil. Tattoos against his skin. Chiseled muscles that kept distracting my fingertips from their primary purpose. A stoic stare that could sink any person to their knees. Including myself.

I felt my blood pumping in my ears as Max's eyes panned over to look at me.

"Does that bother you?"

"Hmm?"

My eyes met his and I stopped cleaning again.

"Does that bother you?"

I blinked. "Does what bother me?"

He grinned. "The bullet. Does that bother you?"

And as my eyes danced between his, I figured the only thing I could do was tell him the truth.

D addy's girl licked her lips. "I... I don't think so. Never come into contact with someone who's been shot at before."

I nodded. "Fair enough."

I hissed as the alcohol wipe came down against my shoulder again. I looked down at my feet, trying to focus on something else other than the burn. I wanted to pull away. I wanted to growl at her to keep her hands to herself. But she was good at this. Her touch felt nice. Comforting, after an evening like this.

"All right. Where else?"

Her voice made me pause. "What?"

"Where else are you hurt?"

I shook my head. "Nowhere."

"I saw you limping. Did something happen to your foot, or your hip?"

I furrowed my brow. "What kind of question is that?"

"The kind a doctor might ask if you went there."

"You telling me you're a doctor?"

"I was going to go to med school, yes."

My gaze slid back up to hers. "Explains why you're good at this."

I watched her inspect my lip. She gripped my chin softly and tilted my head back. I knew what she was studying. I felt my jaw throbbing the entire way to this damn campus. I still didn't know when the hell I'd been clocked in my jaw. Or my face, for that matter. But things happened so fast tonight that I knew I'd never really be sure of anything.

Except the wrath I'd bring down on my father's head for this shit.

"Foot, or hip?" she asked.

I snickered. "Foot, most likely."

"Take off your boots."

"You really don't want me to do--"

She glared at me. "Take them off, or I will."

I sighed. "Suit yourself."

She sat down in front of me as I undid the laces of my boots. And when I kicked them off, a stench unlike any other filled the air. It wrinkled even my nose. My feet had always been a hazardous zone. But, for all the care I took trying to breathe, Daddy's little girl didn't flinch.

She simply took my bruised foot in her hand and started running her fingertips over my skin.

"Does this hurt?" she asked.

"Nope."

"What about this?"

"Uh-uh."

"And… this?"

She pressed down against the base of my middle toe and I wanted to blow through the fucking roof. But instead, I let out a soft grunt.

"Yep. Not fun."

She nodded. "Okay. Going to check your calf and your knee now."

I watched her closely as she rolled up my jean pant leg.

"Why didn't you go to med school?"

She sighed. "My parents pushed for it for a long time. My father is a pharmaceutical guy. Shocker, right? The Korean father wanting his daughter to follow in his footsteps, but take it farther. He wanted me to be a heart surgeon."

I nodded, but didn't say anything.

"But you didn't."

"Nope. The closest I ever got to wanting a medical profession was being a vet tech when I was a teenager."

"Lucky animals."

She blushed. "So I decided to study something that interests me more. And wasn't so intensive."

I flinched as she ran her fingers up the back of my calf.

"What are you studying now?" I asked.

She paused. "Did that hurt?"

"Answer my question."

"Answer mine first."

"Ladies first."

She snickered. "Like you're a proper gentleman."

I chuckled. "Maybe I pride myself on not being one. Ever think of that?"

Her eyes flickered up to mine and that gorgeous flush of hers deepened.

"Human resources."

I blinked. "What?"

"I'm studying human resources now."

I licked my lips. "That's a serious deviation from med school."

She nodded. "I know. It wasn't for me, anyway. I don't like blood."

"You seem to be handling it fine."

She shrugged. "I can if I have to."

I ripped my leg from her grasp. "You don't have to. I can take care of myself."

I stood up from the chair as my pant leg slid back down. I shoved my foot into my boot, trying my hardest not to wince. When the fuck did I break my toe in all this crazy bullshit?

Then Daddy's girl stood, too. "I know I don't have to."

I shoved my foot into my other boot. "Good."

She nodded. "Good."

"Time for me to go."

"Sure you're good to go?"

"Yep. Positive."

But she didn't move.

In fact, she stood so close to me that I smelled her perfume. Or was that her deodorant? She didn't strike me as the perfume kind of girl. But she also didn't strike me as a drinker. And the smell of rum wafted from her lips. The fruity scent of whatever she was wearing--or whatever she'd been drinking--filled my nostrils. And I knew this girl would forever be associated with pineapple and coconut in my mind.

Especially when my eyes fell to her lips.

They were perfect. That soft lower pout with an upper lip that disappeared whenever she spoke. That button nose, curved perfectly to offset the upward slant of her eyes. I wanted nothing more than to cup her cheek, feel the heat of that blush, and press my lips against hers. Even though she wasn't my type. Even though she wasn't the kind of girl I'd go for after a hard day's work.

What the hell.

My hand slid through the soft locks of her hair and I heard her gasp. My face dropped to hers, ready to capture those lips and make her mine. And when her warmth encompassed me, something inside me ignited.

I felt like I could take on the world after one simple kiss.

I gripped her hair tighter and wrapped my free arm around her. I picked her up off her feet and held her close to me, feeling her fist my shirt. Her legs dangled. Her tongue slid against my lips. And when I opened myself for her, she moaned so sweetly. So gently. So effortlessly down the back of my throat.

It took me no time to turn her around and pin her against her dorm door.

I felt her gasping for air. I pressed my hands against the flimsy wooden structure and pinned my knee between her legs. She sat there, her pussy warming and her tongue flicking over the roof of my mouth. She was a terrible kisser. Too much tongue. Our teeth were constantly clattering together because she didn't know which way to turn her head. And yet, it only added to her appeal. Her innocence. Her demeanor, that had somehow caught my eye.

I felt my cock stiffening against my jeans.

Benji.

My eyes flew open and I immediately pulled away. Her swollen, puckered lips searched for mine before those gorgeous eyes of her fell open. The flush had worked its way down her neck. What I wouldn't give to kiss it all the way down her breasts. Give her the time of her fucking life. But, Benji. She was just like Benji. Innocent and intelligent.

She had no business being wrapped up in the kind of life I led.

I mean, for crying out loud, I'd just been shot at! This beautiful girl, with her eyes holding my gaze and her soft hands cupping my cheeks, had a bright and bountiful future ahead of her. One that would be productive to society. One that would be filled with light and love and laughter and good feelings.

Getting tangled up in me would rob her of all that.

"Max?" she asked breathlessly.

I swallowed back a groan at the way she said my name. I watched her search my face, her beautiful eyes darting between my own. Searching for something I knew she wouldn't find. My hands slid from the door. I gripped her waist and removed my knee, easing her down to the ground. With all the pain in my body amounting to nothing but misery, I kept my grip on her. Tight. I moved her where I wanted her, over to the dorm bed in the corner, and hoisted her up. She squealed as I lifted her with my bare hands, settling her against the edge.

Then, I backed myself toward the door, making sure she didn't follow me.

"I still need to check--"

"Stay away from me, Danika. You know you need to."

And after watching confusion roll behind her twinkling eyes, I opened the door behind me and slipped out.

17

DANI

Three Weeks Later

I poked at the roasted chicken meal on my plate as I gazed around the dining room. I'd been looking forward to this long Labor Day Weekend for days now. I missed home whenever I came to college. Even though it was a nice escape. And being home for the long weekend felt, well, like home.

Something felt off, though.

I slid my eyes along the pastel walls topped with white crown molding and a median separator that glided along the wall. The white tiled floor of the dining room had a navy rug spread out underneath the kitchen table to unite the rest of the room. At least, that's what Mom said it did. The silverware on the table glistened, even after its use was complete. The crystal glasses that shone with ice water made me cock my head.

I never noticed before how much everything had its place in our house.

"Princess?" Dad's voice ripped me from my trance.

"Yes?"

"Something wrong with your food?"

I looked down at my plate and noticed how messy it had become. The peas were mixed in with the mashed potatoes. The skin of the chicken had been stripped and ripped into pieces by my own doing. The chicken had grown lukewarm and dry with the air being exposed to it. And the fruit salad I had in a bowl just above the plate sat untouched, marinating in its own juices.

"Yes, sorry. Just thinking about some things," I said.

Mom put her fork down. "Want to talk about it, sweetie? You've been very distracted since you got home Friday evening."

The torn meat of the chicken reminded me of the bullet wound. My gosh, Max had been grazed by a bullet. I looked up at the picture hanging on the wall. A beautiful picture of flowers in a meadow. But the red was all that jumped out at me. It reminded me of the red that had dotted Max's split lip. The dried blood against his skin I'd cleaned away with the alcohol wipe. I couldn't stop thinking about him. Even at home, where I felt most at ease, he invaded my dreams.

Leaving his motor oil scent in my nostrils to wake up to.

"Danika."

My father's voice grew stern and it made me jump.

"Your mother's speaking to you."

I nodded. "Yes, yes. I'm sorry. It's just…"

I placed my fork down and turned to my mother.

"Forgive me for being so distracted. School is just… taking a toll this year."

Mom grinned. "I don't know if its school that's got you all twisted up."

Dad paused. "What?"

I felt my heart stop. "What?"

Mom smiled. "Could it be a boy, possibly?"

Dad shook his head. "No, no boys. We had this conversation already. College is for studying. Dating is for after you get your feet set strongly on the ground with a career."

I felt myself turning bright pink as I shook my head.

"No, Mom. No boys. I made you and Dad that promise."

She winked. "You made your father that promise to help him feel better about you going to school ten hours away."

Dad shot her a look. "You're not helping."

Mom shrugged. "Fine. You're distracted because of classes, my little A-plus student. I'll accept that. For now."

Dad turned toward me. "So are you looking forward to Thanksgiving break?"

I took a small bite of my peas. "Actually, yes. It'll be nice to come home and spend some time actually resting instead of being locked in my room and studying."

Or daydreaming about Max while I neglect my studies.

"Well, your mother and I have invited some friends over for the holiday. Your mother's making a massive meal, so come a little hungrier than you have been tonight. And more talkative. They're going to want to know all about your studies and how your second year of college is going so far."

Mom asked. "Don't be so hard on her. College is hard. Remember when you were going through school? I had to force you to eat because all you did was sit at that desk and study."

"And I think my studies paid off, don't you?"

Mom giggled. "All I'm saying is I got out and made friends. Made memories. Did a bit of dating myself."

She winked at Dad and he grumbled.

"And I *still* opened my own business. Built my own career. And had the family I always wanted."

Dad cracked a smile. "Well, aren't you Superwoman."

Mom smiled. "Anytime, any day, anywhere."

I watched how quickly a disagreement between them dissolved into playful banter. My family wasn't perfect, by far. But the way they looked at one another was something I wanted for my life. Eventually, of course. I watched them kiss. Things like that never weirded me out as a child. I knew my parents loved one another. Fully and completely. No matter what they disagreed on or what they fought about, they always came back together. Time after time.

I wanted something like that in my future.

Maybe with Max.

"I'll clean the dishes," I said quickly.

I felt my thighs warming and needed to get out of the room.

After volunteering to wash the dishes and put everything away, I called it an early night. Instead of staying downstairs to watch a movie with my parents, I headed back up to my room. I needed time to myself. Time to think. Time to take a long, hot shower so I could scrub every last bit of Max off my skin.

Even though it felt as if I'd never get rid of him.

I flopped down onto my childhood bed and rolled onto my side. I gazed out the window, watching as my yellow sheer curtains fluttered softly as the air conditioning kicked on. Even my bed had been perfectly made. My pictures, straightened up on my bedside table. I rolled back over and looked at my dresser drawers. My mirror was perfectly straight on the wall. My knick-knacks were all in a pretty, unified row. My vision board for my life was hanging just beside the mirror, close to my bedroom door, and not a picture on the board was crooked. Or out of place.

I slowly sat up and ran my eyes along the pictures, thinking back to the life I wanted.

There was a picture of a headless man in a suit. A pristine suit. A clean-cut suit, with strong hands and broad shoulders. There was a picture of a Tudor-style home in the heart of Ann Arbor. Just a stone's throw away from downtown and all of the scenic and beautiful things it had to offer. Like the boutique stores and the holiday parades. The food specials and the friendly get-togethers. I had cut out pictures of beautiful cars. Rich green Jeeps and pearl white Mazda Miatas. Even a cherry red sports car I might surprise my husband with one day as a Christmas gift. Complete with a big bow on top.

One that still had side airbags, though. To keep our three children safe in case they wanted to take a ride with their daddy over to the lake.

I stood to my feet, walked over to the vision board and ran my fingertips over all the pictures. I fingered the headless man in a suit and couldn't stop thinking about how his hands were big, like Max's. I ran my fingertips over the cherry red sports car and couldn't stop thinking about how nice Max might look on a cherry red bike. I stared at the Tudor home, imagining living in it with its peaked rooftops, beautiful brown wooden exterior, cream-colored shutters and bright door to signal to everyone that they were welcome in our home.

And just beyond the door, I imagined Max and myself standing there. Dancing in the foyer underneath a chandelier while a pot of coffee percolated just for us in the kitchen.

How in the world could I possibly want a man that was so cruel to me?

18

MAX

I paced the floor of my father's study waiting for him to finally show up while John nagged me about how it was never good to barge in on him like this. I didn't give a shit, though. I'd been trying to contact my father for weeks about this job. About payment for services rendered. Ever since Mr. Dean finally left town, I hadn't heard a damn peep out of my father. Not a meeting. Not a payment in our accounts. Nothing.

Shit had finally hit the fan.

My temper boiled over. This entire ordeal had been a shitshow from start to finish. The job had been completed for weeks. Why the hell had we not been paid? My men and I had spent an entire week shadowing that fucker, making sure he got from place to place as safely as possible. Getting shot at. Almost losing men to this idiocy. Not to mention the other complicated scenarios in which we had bailed out Mr. Dean.

Though there hadn't been anything as bad as that first night.

My brother sighed. "Keep a level head, man. You've been busted up enough already over this. Your shoulder just closed up nice. Don't give him an excuse to rough you up even more."

I glared at my brother. "Three weeks. It's been three fucking weeks since this asshat left town. Three weeks, and not a word from him. We don't do a week's worth of anything without getting paid. Especially with the kind of shit we stared down!"

"Lower your voice. You know he hears you."

"Then let him hear!"

My voice echoed off the corners of the wall as I balled up my fists.

"Let them all hear. My father knew something about how dangerous this was. We weren't nearly prepared for the onslaught of that night. We needed devices we didn't have. Gear we didn't have the money for. All of us could've died. And you think I'm supposed to let that lie?"

"You nearly cost my client his life, you know."

Our father's voice rang out in the study as the door closed with a thud. I whipped around, glaring at my father as he stared daggers back at me. His lips were downturned in regret and his eyes narrowed to slits. With his hands clasped behind his back, he walked toward his desk. Easing himself down into the buttery leather chair as if he had a right to chastise me for the bullshit he put us in the middle of.

I felt myself bristle. "Yeah. And you nearly cost me and my club ours. Works both ways, Father."

I felt my brother stiffen as I challenged the man that single-handedly made our childhoods a living nightmare.

"And how do you figure?" Dad asked.

"How do I figure what?"

"How do you figure I put your club's lives at risk?"

I licked my teeth. "By withholding from us exactly how dangerous this was supposed to be."

"Did I not tell you to put your eight best men on this job?"

"I should've refused the job the second you didn't do a risk assessment!"

John butted in. "Wait, you didn't do what?"

Dad waved him away like a fly. "You can talk when I tell you to. For now, this is between myself and the incompetent president of your little club."

I pointed at him. "A club you founded. A club you started."

He slammed up from his desk. "And don't you ever forget it."

I walked up to my father's desk and placed my hands on the corner. Matching him movement for movement. He bent down, following my motions, trying to intimidate me like he did everyone else in his employ.

"You were reckless, Max."

"You withheld information, Ashton."

John tapped me with his can. "Max, cut it out."

I shook my head. "Not a fucking chance."

Dad's eye twitched. "You should have known something was off the second you got there. The second you saw where you were going."

"What? You're telling me you didn't know where your own client was going? Doesn't sound like you, Father dear."

"You mock me one more time, and you won't be alive to run that little haphazard crew of yours."

"The haphazard crew you started, Dad. Don't forget that."

His eye twitched again. "You should've been prepared for things to go south like that. That's your job."

I growled. "That's why we always do the fucking risk assessment."

"Fuck the risk assessment!"

Dad's voice boomed over our heads as he shot up, causing me to move with him so he couldn't gain the upper hand if he lunged at me.

"It's not my fault you don't have the gear you need! You get paid well over top dollar to do what you guys do. Buy your own fucking gear and stop assuming people will hand it all to you! That's your job, to have what your guys need to do their own jobs effectively. Welcome to being president, son. You're doing a shit job."

I pointed at him. "Own up to your part in this. You

didn't do the risk assessment with me because you knew what we were walking into. You knew we'd have to fight for the life of your client, and you knew that if I knew that, I would've never taken this damn job!"

"You're the president of the Red Thorns," Dad spit out. "Fucking act like it."

My head cocked. "And what does that mean, Ashton?"

John tapped me with his cane again, trying to get me to calm down. If he tapped me with it one more time, I'd shove the damn thing up his ass.

"What does it mean, Maxwell? Well, it means to stop walking around with your tail tucked between your damn legs. That's what it means. This life demands blood, Max. This life means sacrifice. John knew that when he became president, and I thought you did, too. If you're not willing to spill blood, then you're in the wrong business."

I rounded the desk and stood toe to toe with my father.

"Say that one more time, old man."

He grinned. "Maybe you'd be better suited to running errands and making my coffee."

I growled at him as my fingertips itched for the butt of my gun while Dad chuckled right in my fucking face.

"No matter. You'd find a way to fuck that up too. Like you fucked everything else up during your childhood. During the firefight that made your brother the cripple he is today."

I snarled. "You leave him out of this."

Dad kept going, as if I hadn't spoken. "Luckily, Mr. Dean got away with his life. I'm not sure how, and I can't say he's happy with how things were handled that week. But he's alive, and that's what matters."

"He's alive because of my boys. Mine. Do you hear me? So, why the fuck haven't we been paid for our time well spent?"

"You think that was time well spent? Well, your client didn't think so. You're in the pleasing business, son. And on that note, he's refused to pay you."

John scoffed. "Excuse me, what?"

Dad shrugged. "He's refused to pay you. Which I agree with."

I narrowed my eyes. "We saw the job through. That money belongs to my men. They earned it, and they will see you."

Dad hissed so hard he spat on my face. "You earned *nothing.* Now, get the fuck out of my house before I have the mind to balance out your bruises."

As I stared my father down, every single scenario of how to kill him ran through my mind. How quickly I could draw my gun since he wasn't packing anything but a knife in his pocket. How I could wrap my hands around his throat and close off his ability to breathe. Oh, the pleasure I'd get from watching the life drain from his eyes. Effort well spent, if I did say so myself. Then again, it would be poetic justice to turn my own father's knife on him and slit his throat. Covering his untouched manuscripts on the bookshelves with his own blood. My father had a hard-on for old books. His collection around the house of art and books and sculptures was worth at least forty million dollars.

What I wouldn't give to destroy it all in front of his eyes before watching him die at my feet.

"Come on, Max. Let's go."

I felt John tugging on me and I let him move me away from our father. Because out of all the times I had envisioned that man's death, I'd never quite craved his blood on my hands the way I did in that moment.

"Do your job better," Dad said.

John gripped me tighter. "He's not worth it."

"And teach your men how to protect better."

My brother groaned. "Shut up, Dad."

"What did you just say to me?"

Dad raced out from around his desk and I leapt into action. There was no way in hell I was letting him take on my brother. The man who almost gave his damn life to protect this club. A man that would never get on a fucking bike again because of what he did. Because of the situation my father put us in.

The second he charged John, I fisted his suit with one hand. I held him back, watching his anger boil over as spittle flew from his lips.

"Get off my property now. Both of you. And if either of you ever come in this house again, I'll have you both shot on sight. Both of you!"

I shoved Dad back and watched him stumble on his feet. Bodyguards popped seemingly out of nowhere and surrounded us, their guns drawn. I grinned as I held up my hands, backing toward my brother, who was already limping on his cane out the study door.

"Nice to know you'd kill your crippled son, Ashton."

And with a wink to my father, I turned my back on him.

Something no one but myself ever had the guts to do.

19

DANI

The ten-hour drive back to campus was excruciating. But I broke it up with naps on the side of the road and pit stops to pick up my favorite snacks. With my phone plugged into the auxiliary adapter of my SUV, I listened to the lectures of the past couple of weeks. I had sunken down to a point where I had to record them now. Because I was almost guaranteed to miss something. So, as I munched on sour patch kids and chugged down green tea, I listened to my professors talk at me through the speakers of my car.

For ten solid hours.

It was a great reinforcer of knowledge. Of the things I needed to know for fall midterms. I had to crawl through those before I could even think about Thanksgiving. And with how distracted I had been lately, I needed all the help I could get. Wanting to get back to campus as quickly as I could, I decided to get reckless and go eight miles an hour over the speed limit instead of only five. I wanted to get settled back into the groove of things.

And hopefully catch a glimpse of Max.

I didn't even try to fight it any longer. If the memory of him was going to haunt me, then I needed a way to embrace it. I mean, I hadn't seen him since that night anyway, the night he came stumbling in, all beat up and grazed with bullets. The night of that kiss, where he picked me up as if I weighed nothing and kissed me as if I were the only girl left on the planet.

My lips still sizzled at the memory.

I rolled through campus and parked my car. I heaved my bag out of the back and stowed my phone away in my back pocket. With my headphones in my ears, still listening to lectures, I made the trek across campus. Breaking a sweat in my jeans and my long-sleeved shirt just to get back to my dorm room before night fell.

And hopefully, before the bikes came out. So I could catch an unimpeded glimpse from my dorm room window.

You're hopeless, Dani.

I dragged my things into the elevator, huffing and puffing for air. I pressed the button for the top floor and closed my eyes, ready to be back in the safety of my dorm bed. The only other place I felt even remotely comfortable was in my dorm room. And as terrible as it sounded, I hoped and prayed Hannah wasn't in there.

Because I knew she'd try to drag me off to some party.

"Please don't be there. Please don't be there. Please don't be there."

I breathlessly chanted it down the hallway as I came to my room. I threw the door open, my heart sinking when I found it unlocked. I dragged my bag in and pulled the headphones out of my ears, preparing myself for the onslaught of convincing she'd need to get me to go anywhere tonight.

The room was empty.

"Hannah?"

I pulled my phone out and paused the lecture recordings as I gazed around the room.

"Hannah, you here?"

I closed the room door and locked it for safe measure. Then I made a mental note to talk to her about leaving the door unlocked when she was gone. I hoisted my bag onto my bed, preparing myself to unpack. To dig around for my books and settle in for a night of studying in my pajamas while listening to more lectures through my headphones.

My eyes kept gravitating toward my laptop, though.

"Dang it," I murmured.

I tossed my phone on top of my bag and dug out my laptop. I flopped down at my desk and quickly hooked it up to the charger I had forgotten to bring home with me. I knew if I didn't do anything about it now, it would simply eat away at me for the rest of the night. Being back on campus heightened the memory of Max. Thoughts were already spinning about him, including that steamy kiss.

I brought my fingertips to my lips as my laptop chimed to life.

"All right. Let's see what you've got for me," I murmured.

My fingers flew across the keyboard as I sat there, searching every keyword I knew that might come up with more information on Max.

Red Thorns.

Red Thorns motorcycle.

Motorcycle clubs in Ann Arbor

Max Red Thorns

Motorcycle gangs

The last search result was what yielded the most information to me. And even still, it wasn't what I wanted. After clicking through articles and blogs with red cursive writing and even Wikipedia articles for crews and gangs and tattoo symbols, I knew more about the culture than I ever wanted to know. I learned about gang tattoos. How different symbols and different pictures meant different things. I learned about the hierarchy of crews like that. A president, a vice president, a club arranger and a road guide. Or something like that. I read about meetings they held, called 'church' or sometimes a 'gathering.' I learned about prospects and initiation and how men like this usually made money.

And none of what I read sounded good.

After two hours of reading through all of this stuff,

my head spun with so many things. Initiation traditions and hazing. How to leave a motorcycle club and all the terrible things that happened to a person if they tried. Why gangs like this were stereotypically made of men and why they treated people the way they did. How crews like this came into being in the first place and how they funded themselves.

I didn't get what I was after, though.

Which was more information on Max.

I rolled my lips over my teeth. I could still taste him, even weeks later. How was that possible? How was it possible to feel this way and be so obsessed with a man who called me names? With a man who entertained company like this? With a man who clearly lived outside the law--or at least within the gray area of it?

Why did he treat me so cruelly if he didn't strike me as a cruel person?

I burned deep in my gut with desire for answers.

"Hey there, roomie! I was wondering when you'd get back."

Hannah's voice startled me and I slapped my laptop closed.

"Uh oh. What were we doing in here?"

I shook my head. "Nothing. Just some research."

I looked over at Hannah and found her smiling salaciously at me.

"What kind of research?"

I rolled my eyes. "Not the kind you're thinking of."

"Ah, don't worry. They don't allow my favorite porn sites to stream on campus anyway."

"That's goo--wait, what? You watch porn? Seriously?"

She threw her head back with laughter. "Dani, everyone watches porn."

"I don't watch it."

"You will eventually. You know, once you learn to create a bit of your own."

I wrinkled my nose. "I don't know what that means, and I don't care to know."

"So how was the time at your parents' place?"

She pulled up a chair in front of me and I shrugged.

"It was nice. Restful. Got a lot of studying done."

"And not looking at those porn sites at all. Right?"

I shot her a look. "Drop it."

She held up her hands. "Fine by me. I don't have much time anyway. I have to get myself a shower before I get ready for tonight."

"What's tonight?"

"I'm going out with some friends for drinks. Rachel's going to be there."

I nodded. "Have a good time."

"Yooooou… want to come with us?"

I shook my head. "I'm good. At least for tonight. The ten-hour drive was long, and I still have some reviewing to do before classes tomorrow."

"At least you have afternoon classes on Tuesdays and Thursdays."

"Right? Get to sleep in a bit after my wild night of studying."

She snickered. "You're a wild one, you know that?"

"I try my best."

"Well, if you change your mind, just shoot me a text. We're all going to be out pretty late, so no time isn't good for us. I'll let you know where we are if you want to hang out."

"Thanks. I appreciate it."

"Anytime!"

With a hum in her voice and a pep in her step, she gathered her things. Her towel. Her toiletries. Her robe. A few minutes later, she was headed straight for the co-ed bathrooms. I still hadn't gotten used to that. Showering with both boys and girls in the same massive space. I tried to slip into the shower during off times. Like early in the morning. Or really late at night, after I had finished studying.

"Yep. Shower late tonight," I whispered to myself.

I opened my laptop and forced myself to close the internet search. There wasn't anything on the Red Thorns at all, except for a couple of off-handed comments in a few local newspapers. Nothing that highlighted them or shed any light on them. Or Max. So my time was better spent listening to these lectures again and hoping I could pull my head out of my behind before midterms crept up on us.

I didn't even get the first one pulled up, though, before I heard that sound.

The revving of the motorcycle engine pulled me from my chair. I walked over to the window and peeked out, wondering who was down there. How many of them were down there this time? Three? Four? The whole entire gang of guys on their bikes? I glanced across the road and didn't see anything, which was odd. Because I heard the motorcycle engine, and I knew whoever owned it was close.

Then a shadow moved at the bottom of my eye.

Two figures emerged from beneath the awning of the first floor. And when they stepped out into the moonlight, I smiled. I saw Max down there, with his towering form and his broad shoulders, preparing another cigarette to be lit. And standing with him? Benji. That absolute jerk-off I never wanted to come into contact with again. Max struck a match and lit his cigarette, pulling on it hard. Then he passed the bundle of firesticks off to Benji, who struggled to light one.

I watched the way the cigarette lit up with every puff. How it dwindled toward Max's face before exploding from his lips in a cloud of smoke. I'd never been jealous of anything before. But as I stood there, watching his lips pucker, I realized I was jealous of that cigarette.

You're losing it, Dani.

I saw Max place his hand on his shoulder and roll it gingerly. And it ripped me back to that night. How deep that graze had been. How much blood I'd cleaned up. How badly he'd hissed with every swipe of that alcohol against his skin. He must still be struggling with it. At the very least, it was probably still bruised and sore.

"You should go check on him," I murmured to myself.

Yeah. Just to check on him. Just to make sure he was taking care of himself. Then I'd come right back up and continue on with my studies.

Right after I changed into something I hadn't been wearing for the past ten hours.

20

MAX

"So, that's what I was saying. Things could've been handled a lot differently, that's all. I think I should've stayed behind with you, too. I still don't know why you had me follow that stupid limo. You know the kind of shot I am. I could've helped you! I would've put a bullet in that club owner's--"

I shot Benji a look as I took the butt of my cigarette from between my lips. I squished it under the heel of my boot, watching as he shut up. He clamped his lips over his teeth and stared up at me with wide eyes. I made a decision as I pulled another cigarette from beyond the inside pocket of my leather jacket.

I'd start distancing Benji from this life.

It wouldn't be hard, either. The kid was already in college. Despite his attitude toward shit, he came out with all Bs last year. I was proud as shit the day he told me that. My cousin was destined for more than this life. Hell, I couldn't even pay him for the risks he had taken that night to keep Mr. Dean safe. It was a life I had to lead because of my father. My boys did it because they had no other choice.

But Benji? The boy was smart. The boy had choices.

Even if he *wanted* this kind of a life for himself.

"What aren't you telling me?" Benji asked.

I struck a match. "You talk too much."

"Do I dare ask why we haven't gotten paid?"

I lit my cigarette. "Depends. What kind of answer you looking for?"

"Dude, have you talked to your--"

"Don't. Ask."

"What? You think I don't have a right to know? You think none of us have a right to know? We've never waited this long to get paid for shit like this."

"You wouldn't know. This is only your second time doing something like this."

He snickered. "And after the shit I pulled on my bike to get that client back to his hotel room in one piece, I know it won't be the last."

I narrowed my eyes. "The hell does that mean?"

The sound of Rupert's bike pierced the air as I sucked hard on my cigarette. Benji put his out on the ground, stomping on it with his foot. Trying to look all tough, when really he thought this lifestyle was nothing but loose women and big bucks. I rolled my eyes and took another drag from my cigarette. The nicotine and smoke were the only things keeping my pain levels down right now. Because this healing shoulder was a fucking bitch. If the bruise it left behind wasn't throbbing, the wound itself itched. Not to mention how many times I had to slather that bitch in alcohol just to make sure it didn't get infected.

Sometimes, even *I* hated this fucking life.

"Boys," Rupert said.

He parked his bike on the curb and I walked toward him, leaving Benji and both of our bikes back near the dorm door.

"Hey, Rupert," I said.

He pulled out a cigarette and I handed him mine. I watched him light his as Benji trotted up behind us. Rupert stared at me with a flat expression, one he always gave me when Benji was around. And I knew what he was thinking. The same thing he was always thinking when he didn't want to say it.

Haven't broken the boy's heart yet?

Rupert handed my cigarette back to me and I took another drag. The anger I still had at how this job and shit with my father had gone down had me vibrating in my damn boots. I didn't know how to approach the subject with anyone. At my brother's insistence, I knew I had to tell them soon. I couldn't keep 'paying' the boys out of my own pocket whenever they needed a loan or some shit. We deserved the money we were owed. All of us had plans for that money.

Which meant I had to find a way to get it. And fast.

"So, Rupert. You think I should be on the team?" Benji asked.

I glared at him. "Shut up."

Rupert snickered. "What team? Ain't no sports team around here, as far as I'm concerned."

Benji rolled his eyes. "Dude, you know what I mean."

Rupert mocked him. "Dude, shut up."

I puffed out smoke. "Both of you shut up."

They each looked at me with quizzical expressions and a furrowed brow before I looked at my cousin.

"You. Go."

Benji blinked. "What?"

"Away. I need to talk to Rupert."

"And you can't say it in front of me?"

"No."

He scoffed. "Why the fuck not?"

I glared at him. "Because it's official crew business."

"Well, if you just made me an offi--"

"Now," I said hotly.

I took a step toward Benji and he held up his hands.

"Fine. Fine. I got better shit to do anyway."

Rupert chuckled. "Like study."

"Rupert," I said curtly.

My eyes slowly panned over to him and I watched his grin fall.

"Yeah, Rupert. Damn," Benji said, chuckling.

My eyes snapped back. "Don't make me even up those injuries you've got."

Benji snickered. "Whatever."

And as he walked back toward his dorm room, I let out a heavy sigh.

"I take it you talked with your father?"

I tossed my second cigarette to the ground and kicked it away with my boot.

"What makes you think that?"

Rupert snickered. "A line like that. And the anger in your voice."

I shook my head. "I really hate that man."

He clapped me on my good shoulder. "You and me both."

I felt sick with guilt as I watched Benji limp back to his bike. The boy was still in pain. We all were. All of us from that night. From that fucking week of work. I guess I could've paid the boy out of my own pocket to let it ride. But how did I explain that shit to the rest of the guys?

No, it was either all or nothing.

Because I had to protect my ass with them in all of this, too.

"What happened with Ashton?"

I sighed. "Nothing good."

Rupert squeezed my shoulder. "Then why don't you talk about it? I know you're shit at that. But this is a special circumstance."

I snickered. "Oh, really? And why's that?"

"Because even after talking with him, we still haven't gotten paid. Which means something really bad is happening right now."

I nodded slowly. "I went to go see him today. With John."

"John went?"

"He insisted he go with me."

"That long of a meeting or something?"

I faced him. "No. I was that angry leaving the house."

Rupert puckered his lips. "Oh, shit."

I sighed again. "Apparently, our client isn't happy with how things went down all week. He thought we could've tightened up the operation, and blames him almost getting killed on us."

He blinked. "Are you kidding me?"

"Nope. Mr. Dean has announced he isn't paying us for half-assed services, and my father agrees."

"We didn't half-ass shit."

"You think I don't know that? I told my father this is why we do the risk assessments for jobs. So I get the chance to decide what's better for the club. He didn't do the assessment, and I should've pushed harder."

"Max, you know how your father is. When he doesn't want to do something, he won't do it."

I growled. "Yeah, well."

"Seriously. This isn't your fault."

"Well, because he thinks it's our fault, we aren't getting paid. At least, until I find a reason I can shove down that man's throat to pay us."

"Like?"

I shrugged. "I'll let you know when I get there."

I wanted to tell Rupert more, but I was shaking with fury. I needed to calm down. I reached for yet another cigarette and put it between my lips, ready to strike it up. I needed all the nicotine I could get. Fucking hell, I needed the gum to chew at night in the middle of my sleep, too. If I was lucky enough, the damn thing would choke me and I'd be done with this bullshit life.

Rupert's focus shifted to something behind me.

"What the--?"

I turned around. "What?"

Rupert pointed, and I saw what he was looking at. I saw a pair of legs rushing for the curb as a mass of dark hair bounced around. I didn't even have to see the person's face to know it was Dani. My eyes whipped up to the dorm room and I saw the curtain of her window pulled wide open.

Fucking hell. I needed to find a better place to meet with Benji.

"What do you want?" I asked.

Dani came closer and the moonlight finally illuminated that beautiful face of hers.

"Hey there," she said breathlessly.

I blinked. "What. Do. You. Want?"

Rupert chuckled behind me as her eyes danced along my body.

"I, uh, just wanted to come out here and make sure you were okay."

He snorted. "Well, that's my cue. Have fun with your little pet, Max. I'll see you around."

I glared at him over my shoulder as his attention fell to Dani.

"And don't let him get under your skin, man. He'll drive you mad. And you know that's exactly what he wants."

My nose twitched at the way he winked at her. I didn't want anyone winking at her. Hell, I didn't want her anywhere near me. Or Benji. Or Rupert. Or anyone else, for that matter.

Rupert nodded. "Max? We'll talk soon."

I licked my lips. "Yep."

I watched him ride off down the road before my attention turned back to Dani, who was staring at me with her hands clasped in front of her.

"Change of clothes?"

She snickered. "No."

I grinned. "Cute."

Even in the dim moonlight, I saw her blushing. So I hardened my voice.

"I thought I told you to stay the fuck away from me."

Her face fell. "I want to make sure you're healing okay."

"I'm good."

"No, seriously. I want to check on your shoulder. I mean, your lip looks fine. Can't see the bruise on your jaw. But I do want to see your shoulder."

"No can do."

"Look, I feel a certain level of responsibility since I was the one who patched you up and all, okay? Just let me see it."

"You don't owe me anything."

She nodded. "I know that."

"So go away."

"Not until you show me your shoulder."

I took a step toward her and growled, but she didn't back up. She didn't cower away like normal.

Instead, she puffed out that chest of hers, raised her head high, and stared straight into my eyes.

"Now, Max."

I tried not to laugh at her. "I'm fine."

"Then you have nothing to worry about. I'm not leaving until you let me see."

"Hope you can sleep standing upright, then."

I stepped around her to walk past when I felt something tugging at my sleeve. I looked down and saw her small hand gripping my leather coat. Her small, delicate, dainty little hand. With her slender fingers and her soft skin and her effortless touch. It shot a shiver down my spine. A sensation that made me more alert than ever before. I wanted to pick her up, throw her over my shoulder, and drag her off into the shadows to do with her as I wished.

But instead, I made the decision to get her to go the fuck away.

"Fine," I said.

Her hand fell away. "I knew you'd see it my way."

I shrugged my coat off and pulled my T-shirt collar off to the side. I bent down while she stood on her tiptoes, examining it. Her fingers rested against my skin and my cock pulsed. She ran her hand over the bruising that was left and fingered the scab the graze had left behind. And all the while, it took everything in me not to kiss her breathless again.

Especially with her perfume filling my nostrils.

"Looks good. Thank you."

I stood up and put my coat back on. "Satisfied?"

She nodded. "Looks like you're healing well. I'm glad for it."

"I always do. Now, if you'll excuse me."

I walked past her and headed for my bike. But I felt her hot on my heels. I brushed it off as her heading back to her dorm. Which was where my bike was parked. I threw my leg over the leather saddle of my bike and reached for my helmet. I slipped it over my head and kicked up the stand. However, I felt a set of eyes on me that caused me to turn around. That caused me to flip up my visor.

And it didn't shock me when I saw Daddy's girl running her eyes over my bike.

She's curious.

"Ever been on one before?"

Her eyes snapped up to mine. "Oh, no. Nothing like that."

"Wanna go for a spin?"

She shook her head quickly. "No, no, no. My father would never let me around something like this."

I shrugged. "Don't see him anywhere."

"Yeah, but still."

"Sure you don't wanna go for a spin?"

She swallowed hard and I knew I had her on my hook.

"I really shouldn't."

I put my kickstand back down and slipped my helmet off. As I tucked it under my arm, I threw my leg over and walked toward her. Slowly. Deliberately. With my eyes holding hers as she backed her way into the shadows. Into a place where she felt shrouded and I felt at home. Her eyes twinkled in the darkness. Like diamonds amid dull gemstones. And when her back fell against the brick dorm building, she drew in a short breath.

"I really can't," she whispered.

I cocked my head. "Why, Bambi? You scared?"

Her nose wrinkled up. "No."

I pressed my helmet against her chest. "Then get on the fucking bike."

I felt her eyes on me as I turned around. I walked back to my bike, setting my sights on a different goal for the evening. One I hadn't planned on, but one I now craved. I slung my leg over the bike and sat there, watching the darkness. Waiting on her to emerge. And as the seconds ticked by, I counted the times my heart slammed against my chest. I counted the number of times my gut flared with delight. I counted the number of times my own mind wished and prayed and commanded her to emerge from that darkness with my damn helmet on.

Because I wanted to feel her cling to me as we roared down the road together.

21

DANI

I watched as his long, strong leg swung over the seat of his bike. He sat there, his eyes seemingly holding my own as he gazed at me through the darkness. I looked down at the helmet I held in my hands. It seemed so large. And yet it called to me. My eyes rose back to Max as a grin settled on his face. I wanted to know what he was thinking. How he was feeling. What he really wanted out of all this.

Could I really get on that bike with him?

My heart thundered in my chest. My stomach dropped to my toes. Adrenaline coursed through my veins and I felt myself fighting between what I wanted and what my parents wanted of me. I mean, seriously. If they knew I'd gotten on a bike with a man like this, they'd have my head. I'd be doing my college courses online from my room until I graduated. No. I had to give his helmet back to him. I couldn't get on this bike with him.

Could I?

If I go, where will he take me?

I started out of the shadows and made my way for his bike. He sat there with that cocky little grin on his face. The one that made me wonder if he already knew what decision I'd eventually make. Could he see the future? Was that a talent of his? Maybe this was another trick. Something else to tease me about if I told him no.

Maybe 'coward' is the next nickname he has planned for me.

No. I had to give the helmet back. I couldn't go anywhere with this man. I had classes tomorrow afternoon. I still had to study! Not to mention, he was a jerk. A real jerk-off, to me and to Hannah. He called me names. He leveled me with his stare. He kissed me, then told me to leave him alone like some brooding little… little jerk-off!

I need to find a better insult.

"So what's it gonna be, Bambi?"

I paused. "Why do you call me that?"

I held his helmet tighter as his eyes danced along my face.

"Why do you call me that name? Or any name, for that matter?"

He grinned. "Not a fan of a little flirting?"

"Not when it hurts, no."

He paused. "You getting on or not?"

"I--don't know."

He shrugged. "What are you waiting for, Daddy's girl?"

"See, there you go again with the names. I want to know why you call me those names."

"Will you get on my bike if I tell you?"

I didn't even bat an eye. "Yes."

He snickered. "Fine. I'll take that deal. Want to know why I call you these names?"

"Yes. I really do."

"Simple. They fit you."

His words stung more than I could've ever imagined. They should've pushed me away. But they only made me more determined to show him I wasn't the pushover he apparently thought I was. I glared at him before I picked up the helmet, lifted it over my head and made a show of slamming it down around my face. Grunting and groaning, I kept pushing it down to try and get it over the hump of my nose. I mean, I didn't think my nose was that big. So why wasn't the helmet going down any farther?

Max chuckled. "Try the other way."

"What?"

He turned me around and I heard something 'zzz-wp!' before I felt hot breath against my hair.

"Try the other way. You have it on backwards."

He continued chuckling as my cheeks flushed. I pulled the helmet off my head and quickly turned it around. I felt tears prickling my eyes from embarrassment, but I refused to cry. Not in front of him. I wouldn't give him the ammunition to make my life miserable so long as he came into contact with me. I was strong. I could do this. I was in college. I had a new lease on life. I was an adult, and I could make adult decisions.

Right after I got this stupid helmet on straight.

"Need help?"

I groaned. "No."

Max smiled. "You sure about that?"

When I finally got the helmet in place, I saw that full-blown smile across his face.

"Wow," I whispered.

"Quite a wrestle you had there."

I blinked. "What?"

His smile fell away quickly, much to my dismay. My gosh, he had a gorgeous smile. How his teeth were that white with all the smoking he did, I wasn't sure. But it lit up his face and made his green eyes sparkle. It centered his softly crooked jawline and somehow made him look even stronger than before. I wanted him to smile for me again. I wanted to catch a glimpse of that radiant light in his face one more time.

You have to be around him more to get something like that done.

And that was all the encouragement I needed.

After smoothing my hair away from my face, I lifted my leg. Max scooted up on his bike and I pushed my way into the back of it, grunting as I centered myself and gripped his jacket tightly. I felt myself sliding tighter against him before he leaned back. And when my chest sat against his strong back, warmth poured over me, wrapping me up in its tight grip and refusing to let go.

"Ready to live a little, Daddy's girl?"

I didn't even care that he called me that name again.

"Ready when you are, Max."

With a snicker on his lips, he cranked up the engine. It revved, vibrating beneath my thighs as I gripped the bike tight, an automatic reaction that I figured was probably right. I fisted his leather jacket tighter, wondering how in the world I was going to balance on a bike like this. I mean, the second he took a turn too tightly, wouldn't I go flying off? Wasn't that what seatbelts were for?

"Can you hear me?"

I nodded as his booming voice overpowered the roaring engine.

"All right. Squeeze with your thighs to keep a grip on the bike."

"Got that down. Thanks."

He tapped my knee. "Tighter. As tight as you can."

My eyes fell to where he tapped me and I wanted him to do it again.

"Like this?"

He peered down at my legs and nodded.

"That looks good for now."

I paused. "For now?"

He laughed. "Now wrap your arms around me and hold on."

"I am holding on to you."

He shook his head before steadying the bike underneath his legs. His hands pried my own from his jacket before he wrapped them around his waist. Like, completely around his waist. I felt myself blush from my cheeks to my chest. My hands splayed out across his abdomen, and even through his shirt I felt the rippling of his muscles. The rings of his abs. My mouth went dry as he shifted back against me. His butt moving tighter between my legs. Spreading my thighs and making me softly pant.

He smelled like leather and cigarette smoke.

And it was a smell I wanted to hold within my body for as long as I could.

"All right, hang on."

The bike took off with a roar and my head fell back. I had to clench all my muscles in order to get myself upright again. And when I did, I clung to Max as much as I could. My arms tightened around him. My thighs clenched the bike beneath me. I scooted closer to him, laying my covered cheek against his back. I felt his muscles rolling beneath his skin. With every movement he made and with every shift of the engine, he twitched against me. It felt like heaven, being so close to him. Holding him like this.

Knowing he wanted me there with him.

"All right, hold on tight, Bambi."

I looked up just in time to see a tight curve coming up. And when the bike leaned toward the ground, I let out a shriek. I looked behind me and saw campus quickly fading away into nothing, the darkness of the night swallowing it up as the horizon met the stars.

"You okay back there?"

Max took another turn and my yelps quickly devolved into laughter. Guttural guffaws of happiness as the adrenaline rushing through my veins excited me.

I felt free. Invigorated. Filled with an independence I'd never felt before. I tilted my head back and let out a howl. Like some idiotic wolf off in the distance who was just learning to howl for the first time. It was the only thing I could think of, though. You know, to put this nervous energy to good use.

And as I kept laughing and howling, even Max started laughing again.

Giving me a chance to catch his smile in the rearview mirrors mounted on his handlebars.

The engine roared with speed. The world raced on either side of me as I rested against Max's strength. The wind whipped around me with a velocity I couldn't process and I smiled as I drank it all in. The air was fresh and cool. The summer mugginess dissipated the farther we got away from campus. Worries of school and studies fell away from my mind, and all I thought about was how wonderful this felt. Or how lovely the bike felt vibrating beneath me. Or how perfect it felt clinging to Max on our ride to… wherever.

Or how close his butt is to my--

The wind suddenly died down and I realized I had my eyes closed. I opened them, peering through the visor of the helmet as the bike continued to roll at a slow pace. The wind no longer whipped around my body. The vibrations of the bike settled into nothing but a giant roar as we pulled into a small parking lot. The lamp posts around us had dead bulbs. No light, other than the stars and the moon, lit up our path. I furrowed my brow as Max rolled into a parking spot. Then he cut the engine and put down his kickstand.

I wasn't ready for the ride to be over.

"Where are we?"

Max slipped off his bike and pulled the helmet off my head. I gazed up at him, watching as his knuckles brushed away my tousled hair. That permanent grin was on his face, making me wonder what in the world he was thinking. And when my hair had been tamed by the brushing of his knuckles, he tucked the helmet underneath his arm.

"Hungry?"

I blinked. "What?"

"You asked what we were doing here. I'm asking you if you're hungry."

I paused. "Uh, I mean, I could eat. But I don't have my wallet or my purse or anything with me."

He shrugged. "Come on. I'm hungry. And this place has the best burgers."

"I will, once I can move my legs."

I watched him bury that beautiful smile and it made my heart ache. Why didn't he smile more? It looked so amazing on him. He hung his helmet on the handlebar of his bike, then wrapped his arms around me. I gasped softly as I wrapped my arms around his neck, trying to be careful of his shoulder as he locked himself around me. He inched me off the bike, giving me plenty of time to get my feet planted on the pavement. He held me close, much like when he'd kissed me.

And when he let me go to stand on my own, all I wanted was to pull him back into me.

"Ready, Bambi?"

I paused. "Seriously? I get on this bike with you and actually enjoy myself, and I don't get a new nickname?"

He chuckled. "All right, Daddy's Girl."

"Not that one, either."

He shrugged. "Sorry. The name picks the person. I don't have a say in it."

"Jerk."

"Tightwad."

I glared up at him. "I am not."

He winked. "Says you."

I shook my head as he walked in front of me, reaching for his helmet. And as he tucked it under his arm again, I felt a soft smile sliding onto my face. I forced my legs to do their job and I trotted up behind him, following him into the pub. The second the doors opened, the smell of sweaty men and fried cheese hit me. It certainly wasn't as enticing of a scent as Max. But I figured I could push through it if it meant more time with him.

"Hey there."

"Long time no see, Max."

"What's it been? A week?"

"Hey, man. Good to see you again."

"Max! Yo! Who's the girl!?"

He nodded and waved his hand at everyone that greeted him. Clearly, he was a regular in this place. A lot of the men were staring at me, though. With leather padding their bodies. Some of them had leather jackets. Some had leather vests. Some of them wore leather boots, or baggy leather pants. But, every man--no matter the size--had some sort of leather on him. Some wore bandanas. Some were tattooed from head to toe. And as I stared at everyone we walked by, I wondered if Max had any other tattoos.

"Here," he said.

I watched him slide into a booth before he pointed in front of him.

"Sit."

I slipped quickly into the sticky booth before someone came over and quickly wiped it up. I held my arms up as Max sat back against the cushions, his eyes dancing over the parts of me he could see. I was painfully aware of how hard he stared at me. And I prayed the flush of my cheeks didn't deepen.

But I spoke too soon.

Because I quickly felt the heat of his gaze dripping down the nape of my neck.

22

MAX

Her hair was still a mess. A wild, untamed mess. Her eyes were still widened from the ride. And the red tip of her nose from the wind battering her in the face held my stare. She looked positively delicious. Especially with the way she clung to me. No woman I'd ever had on the back of my bike held on to me as tightly as her. Mostly because they understood how to balance themselves. The women I found already knew how to conduct themselves on a bike. They were bike bunnies, girls and women that hopped from bike to bike, fucking around and having their fun while they could. And I entertained them. I mean, they were pretty in their own right. And no one wanted to be alone all the time.

But there was something thrilling about giving Danika her first ride.

I wanted to give her more firsts.

"So what'd you think?"

My grin widened as her blush trickled down the slopes of her neck.

"It was… exciting. Really, Max."

I leaned forward. "I get the feeling you don't do many exciting things in your life."

She leaned back into her seat. "I mean, I don't really know."

"Just tell me I'm right, Daddy's girl. Because I know I am."

She sighed. "Would it kill you to stop calling me that?"

I smiled. "Maybe."

Her eyes locked on to my face and I buried my smile. I hated my smile. It made me look goofy. Like some bumbling idiot. I didn't know why the hell this cute little girl made me smile so much, but I had to stop. Eventually, I'd have to leave her in my dust. I always did. And while I pissed many people off in my life because of that, it was never personal.

I just had to protect them from the shitstorm that constantly followed me around.

"The usual, big boy?"

My eyes turned up toward the waitress that had come over to take our orders.

"You know it. And get one for her, too," I said.

"What's your usual?"

The waitress smiled. "Double bacon cheeseburger with everything, a double order of crispy fries, and a beer."

Her eyes widened. "A beer when you have to ride your bike?"

The waitress slowly looked over at me. "She don't get out much, does she?"

I shook my head. "Nope. She doesn't."

Dani sighed. "I'm right here, guys. And I can order for myself."

I leaned back. "Go ahead, then."

She paused. "Well, is there a menu?"

Some of the guys sitting around us started roaring with laughter. I grinned at Dani, watching as she sank a little lower into her seat. Maybe if I showed her the kind of world I came from, she'd realize she didn't fit in and leave me the fuck alone for good. Because with the way she tugged at my groin, I knew I'd never leave her alone if she kept coming into my life. Walking up to me randomly. Enticing me with her perfume, and her hair, and those dazzling eyes of hers.

I meant it when I told her to stay away.

Mostly for her protection, but partially because I couldn't stay away from her. So her actions were her only hope for safety at this point.

"Take a risk for once, Bambi. It's not gonna kill you," I said.

She rolled her eyes. "Fine. Whatever. But no beer. Beer's gross, and I'm not caving to that."

I looked up at the waitress. "If you've got juice, I'm sure she'd be fine with that."

"Soda," Dani said curtly, "is just fine. Coke. Regular. Lots of ice."

I grinned. "Because tough girls need ice, right?"

She shot me a look that made me smile and I watched as her eyes danced around my face again.

The waitress nodded. "Soda and a beer coming right up. Anything else?"

I waved my hand in the air. "That's all. Thanks."

As the waitress went to get our drinks, Dani sighed. "If I answer your question, will you answer one of mine?"

I cocked my head. "What question did I ask?"

"Whether or not I take risks in my life."

"Ah."

"Question for a question?"

I leaned back. "Sure. Why not?"

She nodded. "All right. You're right, Max. I don't take a lot of risks in my life. I enjoy knowing what to expect. It keeps my anxiety down. I've never liked surprises. Or fast cars. Or taking rides from strangers. Or anything that might put me in danger or get me into trouble. An unknown outcome never sits well with me. It's just always been that way."

Wow. What a peaceful life to live.

Dani snickered. "You must think I'm incredibly boring right now."

I shook my head. "Don't ever assume what I'm thinking. Because people are always wrong."

"Well then, what were you thinking?"

I shrugged. "I was thinking that sounded kind of nice. To know what's coming all the time."

"What do you mean?"

"That the question you want to ask me?"

"What?"

"Question for a question. That the question you want to ask?"

She held my gaze for a long time before she nodded.

"Yeah. That's the question I'd like to ask."

It made me wonder what question she was casting off to the side.

"A regular Coke with extra ice for you, and an ice cold beer for you." The waitress broke our connection as she slammed the glasses down onto the table. "Your food'll be up in a few minutes. And if you want dessert, go across the street. We don't do that sweet shit here."

I chuckled. "Thanks for the update."

The waitress winked at me. "You know I have to do it for the newbies."

She walked away, leaving us alone again. And I saw Dani looking around. Oh, this would be rich. Because I knew exactly what the fuck she was searching for. I grabbed my beer and tipped it up to my lips. I chugged half of it down, quenching my thirst in the hopes that my greater thirst might dissipate. But as I sat my glass back down, I felt my need for this innocent girl grow.

Especially when she sighed.

"Something wrong?"

She blushed. "Nothing."

"Aww, come on. You know you can tell me."

She rolled her eyes. "All you'll do is mock me for it."

I gasped playfully. "Why, Bambi. I'm hurt by your accusation."

She snickered. "Jerk-off."

"Loosey-goose."

"Hey, I'm not loose."

"No, you're just cute. Searching for a straw to use like a big ol' grownup."

She sipped her drink. "Shut up."

"Oh, they grow up so fast."

She started giggling, and the sound held me hostage. It was glorious. A relaxing sound. One that soothed my beating heart and brushed away the pain I felt creeping up into my shoulder again. And as I sat there, watching her gaze around the dimly-lit pub, I got lost in my own thoughts.

Most men I ran with would've thought her life was boring. But I didn't. I wondered what it might be like to not have to worry about my crew all the time. I was always on edge. I never fully slept anymore. One eye was always open. One ear always listening. Waiting for the other shoe to drop. Waiting for an attack. Waiting for someone to come disrupt things and plunge us into another turf war that ended with one of us in the hospital for a damn month.

John…

We never even saw it coming. Dad sent us out after some bullshit gang that kept creeping up on our turf. Trying to peddle their drugs in our city. Trying to bring their dramatic assholery over the lines of Ann Arbor. We owned this town. We kept the people inside it safe from outside influences like laced drugs and faulty firearms that exploded in your face. We marked our territory everywhere we went. We opened fire whenever we saw something we didn't enjoy.

And it got us ambushed one night.

"Max? Can you hear me?"

Dani's voice ripped me from my thoughts. "What?"

"You're shaking. Are you okay?"

I looked down at my trembling hand before I slid it off the table.

"Yeah, I'm good. Blood sugar shit."

Worry filled her face. "Are you diabetic? Do I need to go up to the bar and--?"

I shook my head. "I'm fine, Bambi. Worry about yourself."

"Fine, sheesh."

The waitress came over with our food and I was thankful for the distraction. Because I needed one. I needed a distraction from the life I led. Sometimes, even the simplest of things gave me that same kind of anxiety Dani talked about. Even the ringing of my phone was bad. It could range from a group update to a group death. A group job to a group meltdown. There was no normalcy in my life. No pattern. Nothing to count on, except my father's sadistic, psychopathic tendencies.

I found myself envious of the life Dani lived.

"How's your burger?" she asked.

I picked it up and took a massive bite before I gave her a thumbs-up.

"Got a bit too much mayonnaise on it for me."

I shrugged, then took another bite of my burger. It gave me an excuse not to talk to her.

"Want some ketchup for your fries?"

I shook my head as I swallowed hard. Then drained the rest of my beer and slid the glass to the edge of the table, where the waitress scooped it up, ready to bring me another one. And a few seconds later, she slammed another brew in front of me.

"You sure you should be drinking so much even though you have to take me back to campus?"

I held her stare as I lifted the glass to my lips. I chugged, mouthful after mouthful, watching as her eyes widened like a deer in headlights. 'Bambi' suited her perfectly.

If only Benji hadn't used that shit as an insult.

After gulping down half my beer, I picked up a few fries. I shoved them into my mouth without ketchup and listened to Dani sigh. I was done with this question game. She had a way of getting under my skin that I didn't like. I didn't want to talk about my life anyway. I didn't want to tell her the number of times I'd gotten a phone call in the middle of the night, just to tell me a friend was dead. I didn't want to talk about my childhood, all the bullshit my father put me and my brother through. I didn't want to talk about the guys, or the gang, or anything that had to do with the shadows that followed me around. With the nightmares that clung to my mind at night.

Dani was a nice distraction from all that.

And I wanted to keep things that way for as long as I could.

"What's your favorite color?"

Dani's question caught me off-guard. "What?"

She smiled. "There's that voice of yours. I knew you had it in you, Buckaroo."

I furrowed my brow. "Buckaroo?"

"I'm Bambi, you're Buckaroo. Deal with it."

"You're not calling me that."

"You sure… Buckaroo?"

I heard a few guys snickering as they listened in on our conversation. I took another bite of my burger and chewed slowly, burrowing a hole with my eyes into Dani's face. She seemed undeterred. She sipped her Coke without moving her eyes away from me and ate a french fry from between the tips of her fingers as she held my stare.

"I'm waiting, Buckaroo," she said.

"Don't call me that."

She shrugged. "Then don't call me Bambi."

I licked my lips. "Red. Favorite color's red."

"Shocker. I guess you are a bit more predictable than you care to admit to."

One of the guys across the room roared with laughter as I took another pull from my beer.

"What's yours?" I asked.

"Yellow."

"That the color of your bedroom at home?"

"It is."

I grinned. "Makes two predictable people, then."

She shrugged. "I know I'm predictable. We just talked about that, remember?"

Now, even the waitress was giggling at us.

"You guys got nothing better to do?" I roared.

Dani's soft giggle filled my ears as everyone turned their attention back to their food. And their dates. And their fucking jobs.

"Getting irritated, Buckaroo?"

I sucked air through my teeth. "Okay, Bambi. My turn. Favorite ice cream flavor."

"Caramel. Yours?"

"Rocky road."

"Wow. Oddly normal."

I shrugged. "I aim to please."

"I'm sure you do."

Her words lit a fire under my ass. "Favorite vacation destination."

"The beach. Hands down. You?"

"The mountains. I enjoy the solitude and the aloneness."

"Throw in a hot tub and I'm down for it."

"Isn't that a given already? Who doesn't like a nice hot tub?"

"Weirdos."

I snickered. "Yeah. Weirdos."

She leaned forward. "Favorite movie."

I mocked her movements. "Top Gun. You?"

And when she smiled, my heart skipped a beat. "Any one of the Die Hard movies."

23

DANI

Max snickered. "You're a fan of the Die Hard movies? They're terrible."

I gasped playfully. "What did you just say?"

"They're shit movies. All of them. Bruce Willis is a lazy actor."

I put my hand over my heart. "You wound me with your words, Buckaroo!"

He laughed. "What? I'm just saying there's no plot substance."

"And you think Top Gun has plot substance?"

He pointed at me. "Hey. Hey, now. Don't you dare say anything about my Goose."

I shrugged. "I can't anyway. I've never seen Top Gun."

I watched as Max's jaw practically fell onto the table where we were eating.

"You've never what?"

I giggled. "I've never seen Top Gun."

"You've never see--Bambi. Your life is too plain."

"I watch the Fast and Furious movies!"

"Of course you do. More explosions with little to no plot."

"That's not fair. They have this massive overarching plot strung throughout all the movies."

"What? That some dude had a baby with some girl while he thought the love of his life was dead or some shit?"

"Shh! Spoilers, Buckaroo. Some guys in here might not have seen the movies."

And when he smiled at me again, I felt my heart stop in my chest.

"Favorite holiday, Bambi."

"Christmas. Yours?"

He sighed. "I don't know."

"Why not?"

He shrugged. "I guess I'd say Thanksgiving. I like all the food."

"Not really a holiday kind of person?"

"Holidays are for families. And I don't really come from a decent one."

I nodded slowly. "I'm sorry."

He waved his hand in the air. "It's fine. It is what it is."

"Want to talk about it?"

He paused. "No. Not at all."

"Fair enough."

As quickly as the conversation kicked up, it dissipated. And I found that Max was more normal than he appeared to be. We went back to eating our food, but there was no way on God's green earth I'd be able to finish all of it. I mean, I got halfway through my burger and was lucky to eat any of the fries. Which were outstanding, by the way. Max, however, wolfed down his entire meal. And then reached for a few of my fries. He drained another beer into his gut before he settled the tab, and the entire time I wondered what kind of family he came from. What made them so bad in the first place.

And how a family like that produced a beautiful man like the one that sat in front of me.

"All right, time to get you back to campus, Bambi."

I stood. "This place is great. I'll definitely have to come back sometime."

He snickered. "Not by yourself, though. These guys will eat you alive."

"Well, maybe you can bring me, then."

I looked up into his face and watched that wall come crashing back down, his eyes growing stern again. Stoic. Like they had been before we started talking. Started laughing. Started getting to know one another. He shoved the bike helmet into my hands and walked past me without another word. And as a heavy sigh left my lips, I saw the waitress was staring at me with an expression I couldn't read.

Without another word, I turned on my heels and followed Max out the front door. I slid the helmet onto my head the right way this time and we both got back onto his bike. The engine roared to life as I clamped my thighs. But he sped off before I could wrap my arms around him. And as they flailed around in the air, it took all the strength I had in my measly little body to pull myself upright.

"Could you be any less inconsiderate next time, Buckaroo?" I yelled the words at him as the wind howled around our bodies.

Despite the tension between us again, I held him tightly, squeezing my thighs around the bike and fisting his shirt in my hands. I leaned my covered cheek against his back, closed my eyes, and drank it all in. The speed. The wind. The way his muscles twitched with every movement, whether it was to stabilize himself around a tight corner or scoot a bit further into me.

Nestling his butt right between my thighs.

I didn't want the night to end. But all too soon, we pulled up to campus. He rode me straight to the door of my dorm, parking us just underneath the shadows of the awning. I opened my eyes and sighed with disappointment before slipping off the back of the bike and tugging the helmet off my head. I brushed the hair out of my face, hoping I'd get to feel Max's knuckles against my skin one last time.

He didn't move to help me, though.

Just kept staring at me until I handed his helmet back to him.

"Thanks for tonight. I needed a distraction from studying."

He nodded. "So did I."

"From what?"

He grinned. "Nice try, Daddy's girl."

"No more Bambi?"

"When I'm feeling up for it."

"So now we're back to Daddy's girl? Where I don't get to tease you because you're trying to play the tough guy routine to push me away?"

His eyes narrowed. "Good night."

I gripped the handlebars of his bike. "Can I ask you something?"

He licked his lips. "Sure. I'll bite."

I stood up. "Why did you take me out tonight?"

"Why do you care?"

"I mean, the last time we saw each other, you told me to stay away from you. Now... now you're taking me out on your bike. And I'm pretty sure that's about as close as we can get. You know, our bodies and such."

"You think that's as close as two people can get?"

"Well, yeah. With clothes on, at least."

He grinned. "What about with clothes off?"

It felt like someone had caught my tongue in a vise grip. Because every time I went to talk, I couldn't. My mouth didn't move. My voice didn't come up my throat. I watched him put his kickstand down and pull a cigarette from inside his leather jacket. He popped it between his kissable lips, struck a match and I listened to the end of it sizzle. He drew in a long pull and blew out the smoke, battering my face with it.

I refused to move, though.

I wanted an answer to my question.

"Did you like it?"

I blinked. "Yeah. I mean, I told you the bike ride was fun. But--"

He slipped off his bike. "Not the bike, Daddy's girl."

He stepped toward me, closing the distance between us. His warmth wrapped around me as our legs touched. Smoke trailed in wisps from the end of his cigarette as he gazed down at me with a playful stare and a crooked grin. I held my breath as the shadows swallowed us whole. The puttering of his bike engine backdropped the moment, covering up just how loudly my heart thundered in my ears.

Max took the cigarette between his fingers and flicked the ash off. But he didn't return it to his lips.

"Did you like being close to me, Bambi?"

His hand came up to cup my cheek and my eyes fluttered closed at the heat. I nuzzled against his palm, answering his question with my movements. But he still waited for an answer to fall from my lips. I drew in a broken breath. My eyes slid open and I found him grinning wolfishly down at me. His hand held my face and I felt his thumb stroking along my lower lip. It sent shivers of electricity jolting throughout my body, puckering places on me that would surely anger my father. I knew if I let this go any further, I'd have more problems than I could manage. I knew if I didn't step back, I'd have more than just daydreams about this sexy biker on my mind. Impure thoughts rattled around in my brain as my eyes fell to his lips.

Those lips I couldn't stop thinking about kissing.

"Answer me, Daddy's girl."

I swallowed hard. "Y--yes. Yes, I--I did."

He leaned in closer. "Prove it."

I felt his breath against my lips. I felt his body press into mine. His hand slid into the tendrils of my loose hair, gripping it softly, commanding my stare to stay with his. My half-hooded eyes danced around his face, watching his eyes turn to black as wisps of cigarette smoke wrapped around us. Like imaginary ropes pulling us together. Forcing us into one another's orbit.

"Like this?" I whispered.

I pressed my lips against his and squeezed my eyes shut. I held my position, wondering if I was doing it right. I heard something flick. I felt Max pull back. And when I heard the soft sizzle of his cigarette, I peeked an eye open.

"Was that…?"

He blew smoke into the oncoming fall breeze. "You're stiff, you know that?"

Disappointment filled my gut. "I guess I don't really have--"

"If you're going to kiss someone, kiss them like this."

His hand fisted my hair and he pulled my head back. His lips crashed against mine, swallowing the gasp that bubbled up the back of my throat. I slid my arms around his neck, feeling his tongue slide across the roof of my mouth. He invaded me, backing me up until I felt myself being pressed against the outer brick wall of my dorm room. Then I felt his knee press between my legs.

"Yes," I moaned.

He chuckled as his tongue slid against my own. The taste of beer and burger and cigarettes overwhelmed me. I slid my hands through his hair, clinging to the perimeter of his leather jacket. I stood on my tiptoes, pressing myself tighter into him as he sucked on my lower lip, drawing from me an involuntary sound that I didn't know how to describe. Finally he pulled away from my lips.

But I wanted to make that sound again.

"Come back," I breathed.

I fisted his shirt and captured his lips again. Only this time, I mimicked his movements. I raked my teeth along his lower lip. I let my tongue slide over the roof of his mouth. I tamed his tongue with my own, tasting him as my hands danced around his chest. Up and down his torso. Heck, I even slid my arms underneath his leather jacket just to pull him closer to me. I heard that telltale flick again. His hand gripped my hair and he pulled my lips away from his. I whimpered for more as he took one last drag from his cigarette.

Then he put it out against the brick right by my head.

"You're a quick teach, Bambi."

His cigarette smoke wafted against my face, but it didn't stop me from smiling. I felt alive. I felt as if I had stumbled into heaven without even realizing it. I felt my nipples pucker hard against my bra, my thighs aching with a need for rest, even though I didn't want the moment to end. I settled myself softly against his knee—his thigh, really, since it still sat between my legs. His thumb slid along my lower lip one last time. He dragged it down slowly, watching as my lip bounced back into place once he released it.

"Oh, Bambi," he growled.

And the sound made me moan again.

It was the most intense moment I'd ever shared with a man. I wanted to do it again. I tried to catch my breath, steadying myself against the wall as he backed away. I wanted to reach out for him, to draw him back to me so we could recreate the moment. But my arms felt like jello. My legs felt like mud. It was as if every single bone in my body had evaporated with the heat of his kiss. And when he turned to head back to his bike, I pushed myself off the wall.

"Wait!"

He slung his leg over his bike and grinned at me with that cocky pride of his.

"I'll see you soon, Daddy's girl."

I snickered. "Really? Back to that one?"

He winked. "Do me a favor, though, will you?"

"Anything."

He chuckled at the breathlessness of my voice and I felt myself turn bright pink.

"Don't go around kissing any other guys. I'm bad at sharing."

I smiled. "Oh, you don't have to worr--"

Before I could reassure him I wasn't that kind of girl, his engine revved. He slipped the helmet onto his head and peeled away from the curb, leaving a soft cloud of burnt rubber in his wake. I walked to the edge of the curb and stood there, watching his tail light fade into nothingness as he turned the sharp corner at the end of the road and sped off into the night.

I didn't even realize I had been holding my breath until the sound of his bike faded away completely. When I finally let it out, I placed my hand over my heart.

Dani? What in the world are you doing?

24

MAX

Her lips tasted like cotton candy and sunshine. My hands fell to her hips, pulling her closer against me. Her hands rumbled over my chest, peeking underneath my shirt as if she didn't know where to go next.

"Come on, Daddy's girl. What are you waiting for?"

I growled as I hoisted her against the wall. With every second that passed by, my cock grew more for her. I felt myself leaking against my boxers. Every moan she pushed down my throat made me spiral into an endless abyss I never wanted to return from.

"Dani," I growled.

I wrapped my arms around her and pulled her away from the wall. We fell onto the bed behind me, her lips trailing kisses down my neck. I fisted her hair. My cock swelled with need for her. I kicked my boots off, digging them into the floor and praying to God she'd know what came next.

But her fingertips stopped just underneath my shirt.

I lifted my head and saw her eyes dancing along my abs. I

grinned as I watched her study me as if she'd never seen a man's body before. How cute she looked, with her eyes wide and her lips parted in shock.

"Go on. Do it."

Her eyes slid back up my body until she gazed into my own. I sat up on my elbows, bucking softly against her warmth. My, my, how her pussy had warmed for me. How her thighs clamped around me as she straddled my hips. She gripped me like my bike, holding on to me with a strength I wouldn't have ever noticed in her. And as her hands fell to the button of my pants, I chuckled.

But it didn't deter her from her goal.

Off came my pants and my boxers. And when she gasped, I felt her hot breath falling softly against it. My head fell back to the bed, my hand fisting her hair. Her hand wrapped around the base, stroking me but unsure of her movements.

And yet, they were somehow perfect.

"Dani," I grunted.

"I don't know what to do," she whispered.

"I'll guide you. Just follow my hand."

I guided her lips down to my cock and she kissed its tip. Her soft, pillowy lips made me leak and I heard her gasp again with shock. Her innocence did something to me. I wanted to rid her of all of it. I wanted to show her things her family wanted to keep her locked away from forever.

Starting with the pleasure a real man could give a girl like her.

"Lick it," I growled.

"What?"

I peeked my head up and found her wide eyes staring back to me.

"With your tongue. Lick it up. See if you like it."

I watched her with a heated stare as she looked back down at my dick. Precum dribbled over the side, quickly making its way to her fingers. She dipped down and lapped at my cock, causing me to grunt as her warm, wet tongue connected with the ridge of my girth that pulsed for her. She giggled as my precum became wetness against her skin.

"It's…"

She clicked her tongue inside her mouth before a smile spread across her cheeks.

"I don't hate it."

I grinned. "Then I've got plenty more for you."

I shoved her face back down to my cock and she opened her mouth. I felt her gag around me as my head fell back to the bed. I cupped her cheek and massaged her neck, helping her to relax as she took all of me she could. The tightness of her throat called to me. The spit from her mouth dripped down my balls, coating me in her own mark. What I wouldn't give to feel the tightness of her pussy around my dick, to make her orgasm over and over until she begged me to stop because she couldn't take it any longer.

"Max," *she moaned.*

The vibrations made my dick jump as I sucked in a shallow breath.

"Hold it there. Just--like that."

My eyes twitched as the memory faded. Wait. No. It wasn't a memory. It was…

A dream?

"Fuck," I groaned.

Every move I made had me wincing. My cock was stiff as a board, and I felt something damp against my skin. I forced my eyes open and I found myself gazing at the ceiling. My chest was still panting for air, my hand still warm from the phantom tendrils of her hair.

I peeked underneath the comforter before I grumbled to myself.

"Great. Gotta change the damn sheets."

I was a grown fucking man. Why the hell was I having wet dreams? I rolled over onto my side and drew in deep breaths. I had to get this behemoth erection to go away before I could even think about sitting up. I closed my eyes and shook the last of the haze from my mind. I rubbed my eyes, trying to bring myself back down to the land of the living. Sure, I'd had a good time with the girl last night.

But now I was already dreaming about her?

"She did a number on you," I murmured.

I drew in a deep breath before I forced myself upright. My balls hurt. Physically hurt. And my thighs felt as if I'd just run a damn marathon. How long had I been dreaming about her? I had no clue. All I knew was that my boxers were sticky, my comforter was damp, and my sheets were crusted over.

Telling me this had happened more than once last night.

"The fuck?" I growled.

I shuffled into my bathroom. I needed a long, hot-ass shower. I had no idea what drew me to this girl so much. Her innocence? I mean, sure. I guess. Those doe eyes. The fact that she didn't know shit about the world was kind of entertaining. Was it the way she looked at me with those beautiful eyes of hers? Like I was a good man or something?

The way her nose wrinkled when she laughed?

The way her giggle made me smile?

The way she called me Buckaroo?

You're an idiot, Max.

I peeled my boxers off and tossed them to the floor. After fiddling with the water for a hot shower, I stepped into the stream. I hissed as it battered against my back and shoulders. But damn, it felt good. I leaned my forehead against the tile wall and sighed. I still heard her voice whispering my name in the recesses of my mind. Calling out to me. Asking me to go back to sleep. Telling me she'd meet me there if I simply lay back down.

"You're losing it," I grumbled.

Yep. I had finally cracked.

I washed myself down while I pissed in the shower. It hurt like hell, but it needed to be done. I groaned as the bubbles popped against my skin. The smell of coffee trickled into the bathroom. That meant my brother was already up. But, when I heard another voice in my house, I bristled.

Benji.

I quickly got out of the shower and dried myself off. I slipped into my slippers and pulled on some pajama pants, ready to figure out why the hell this boy had come by so damn early in the morning. I checked my phone to see if I had missed a phone call. Was there something I needed to know? But the only thing I'd missed was a text from John an hour ago. Stating that Benji had stopped by to talk.

"Knock knock."

His voice emanated from my doorway, making me toss my phone to the bed.

"Don't you have classes or some shit?"

Benji snickered. "That how you greet someone who brings you coffee?"

I turned around. "Yeah, when the person bringing me coffee is probably doing it for information. What do you want?"

He handed me the mug. "Damn. Can't family get together just because?"

"We never get together just because."

"Fine, whatever."

"What do you want, Benj?"

He grinned. "Saw you riding off with that uptight chick from my dorm last night."

"And?"

He crossed his arms. "What did you two get into?"

I sipped my coffee. "None of your business."

He barked with laughter. "She's a brat, you know. And a goody-good. Sits in the front rows in all her lectures and shit. It's annoying."

"I said it's none of your business, Benji."

John chuckled. "Oh shit. Better back off, Benji. This sounds personal."

My brother limped from around the corner and took up residence in my doorway, too, so that the two of them were preventing me from going anywhere.

"You know, it's not every day you have a girl on your bike, but wake up alone the next morning."

Benji smiled. "No, it isn't."

John smirked. "She turn you down or something?"

I quirked an eyebrow. "Ever heard of a girl saying 'no' to me?"

Benji paused. "Well, no."

I nodded. "Then what makes you think I didn't turn her down?"

John barked with laughter. "Max, you don't turn anyone down."

Benji thumbed over his shoulder. "He's right. I mean, no offense or anything, but you don't have the highest standards when it comes to women."

"Remember the girl that kept coming back over? You know, the one with the armpit hair?"

I shrugged. "Body hair doesn't bother me."

"Or the one who interrupted a club meeting just to see if you were feeling better because you kept dodging her by saying you were sick?"

"Oh, oh, oh! What about the one who flattened his tires at her place?"

"Yeah, that girl was a fucking psychopath. She would've been better off with your father."

"Come to think of it, I don't think she shaved her legs."

John laughed. "I hope this new girl shaves her everything. You need some sanity in your life right now."

I glowered. "That's enough."

Benji rolled his eyes. "You're welcome for the coffee."

"Get your ass to class before you're late and flunk out."

He grinned. "I never flunk. I'm too smart for that

shit."

Just like you're too smart for this club. "Out."

John patted his shoulder. "Come on. I'll walk you out and let Groucho here catch up on his caffeine intake."

Benji shot me a glare, but he followed John out of the house. I chugged back the hot liquid, trying to erase the taste of Dani's tongue from the back of my throat. She haunted me like a nightmare. And yet she was quickly becoming the most gorgeous girl I'd ever had anywhere near me. The guys were right. I didn't have standards when it came to women. Mostly because it was about getting my dick wet. Nothing else. I didn't lead the kind of life that did relationships. Or love. Or marriage. Or romance. Or any of that other shit.

Dani was in a completely different league, though.

And I wasn't sure I was the man to step up to the plate for it.

"Still daydreaming about her?"

John's voice snapped me out of it. "Benj gone?"

My brother grinned. "So you're really not going to talk about this girl?"

"Nothing to talk about."

"I'd beg to differ."

"Well, you've been wrong before."

I nodded to the cane he now held in his hands and he scoffed.

"Always with the cheap shot, huh?"

I shrugged. "It puts you in your place when I need it to."

He sighed. "Fine. Want to talk about why you're being a dick to Benji?"

"He complaining to you now?"

"He says you aren't giving him a fair shot at the crew. And bitching about how he hasn't gotten paid yet."

"Join the club."

He chuckled. "That's what Benji's wanting to do."

"And I won't let him."

I shot John a look before I set my mug onto the bedside table.

"I take it you won't talk about that, either?"

I shook my head. "Nope."

John sighed. "Fine. Then let's talk about Dad."

"Are you fucking kidding me with this shit right now?"

"He called me last night."

"Yeah? Well, what did the asshole want? Because I don't have any missed calls from him."

He smiled playfully. "Because I'm the favorite."

I snickered. "And you can have that title, as far as I'm concerned."

"He wants me to keep an eye on you."

My eyes found his. "What?"

He limped into my bedroom. "Max, this is getting serious. You need to watch yourself. If he thinks, for any reason, you're straying from the crew, he's going to test your loyalty in ways you can't even imagine."

"I'm not straying. He's got no fucking business having you spy on me. For fuck's sake, he's the one not paying us for a job we took from him without a risk assessment!"

"You know how Dad is. You know his reasoning is always screwed up."

"Do you think I'm straying from the family? From the crew?"

He furrowed his brow. "Of course not. I know you're not that stupid. But Dad is a paranoid bastard. It's how he got to where he is. It's how he keeps his millions and his status in the underworld. Keep your head down, Max. Finish the next job *right*. No mess ups. No fuss. And no Benji, if you don't want him around this shit. Show Dad he doesn't have to worry about you."

I didn't like John's tone of voice. It hadn't been full of this much worry since he woke up in the hospital after the turf war.

The one that almost killed him when he was president of this club.

"You know you can count on that."

He nodded. "Good. Because I am counting on it."

Then he turned around and limped out of my room.

But not before peering at me from over his shoulder first.

25

DANI

My last class of the afternoon dragged on and on… and on. It seemed as if the professor had nothing better to do except tell us personal stories of the stuff he'd been through as a child. At this point, his stories didn't even have anything to do with the lecture material. He was just talking to hear himself talk.

I couldn't wait for this class to be over.

I already had my swimsuit on. I had a towel and my goggles stuffed down into my backpack. I wanted to race to the pool and swim laps until my head was clear again. All night, I'd dreamt of Max. Of his touch. His kiss. The way he pinned his body against mine. The way the smoke of his cigarettes played against my tongue. It was a smell and a taste I never thought I'd enjoy. And yet, I adored it on him. It suited him, with the leather and the motor oil and the cologne.

I knew it was cologne now.

I'd been close enough to him for long enough to pinpoint it.

The more my professor droned on, the more I thought of Max. I had questions. So many questions I wanted to ask him. But one question kept popping up into the forefront of my mind, haunting me all throughout my morning while I tried to study. To focus. To get prepared for my afternoon classes.

What is our relationship to him?

His comment about not kissing other guys really threw me off. Were we a thing? Had we gone on a date last night? Was this the beginning of a thing? Is that how this kind of thing worked?

I cursed myself for not having any experience in the area. Because not having the answers to these questions was maddening.

I mean, sure, I could talk to Hannah about it. If I wanted to endure relentless teasing and jokes about my virginity before she gave me any advice. I swear, she and Benji would be perfect for one another. They enjoyed teasing people more than anything else. I leaned back in my front-row chair and sighed, tuning back in to the professor long enough to hear him wrapping up some story about how he met his wife.

What that had to do with talent sourcing and acquisition, I'd never know.

"All right, class. Make sure to read the fifth chapter in your textbooks and come prepared for a round-table discussion!"

I couldn't gather my things up quickly enough.

I raced out of the room and barreled down the

hallway. I could almost smell the chlorine of that pool, ready to wash me clean of my sins. With all eyes on me, I barged through the glass double doors and hopped down the concrete steps. The pool was clear on the other side of campus, but I knew a shortcut. And hopefully, the safety of the pool locker rooms would shake away the feeling of being analyzed by everyone around me.

I ran past the parking deck and cut through the grove of transplanted trees. I rushed up the brick pathway and ran between a couple of the dorm buildings on campus. Through the main campus square, past the cafeteria, until I saw the onyx black steps of the indoor pool on campus.

A figure came out of nowhere and I ran straight into them.

"I'm sorry. I'm so sorry. Are you okay? I didn't hurt you, did I? I wasn't looking where I was--"

"Where ya goin' in such a hurry, Bambi?"

Benji's voice prickled the nape of my neck as I paused. With my stuff sprawled out at my feet, I traced my eyes up his skinny legs, past his baggy shirt, all the way up to his menacing eyes. I looked around me, wondering if Max was with him, if they were walking campus for some reason. Maybe looking for me?

"Aww, don't look so disappointed. Max has better things to do some days."

I reached for my things. "I have to go. I'm sorry for running into you."

Benji knocked my backpack to the ground again. "Stay for a while. Let's chat."

"I'm late."

"For what? Isn't this your last class of the day?"

I paused. "How do you know that?"

A wild smile spread across his face. "I know a lot about you, Bambi."

"Don't call me that."

"Bambi."

"I said stop calling me that."

He snickered. "Okay, Daddy's girl."

"Not that either."

He narrowed his eyes. "Why? Because they're only for Max to call you?"

My brow furrowed. "Why in the world would you care anyway?"

He shrugged. "He's family. I'm his cousin. And you distract him."

"So?"

"So that's not good for business, *Bambi*."

I pointed at him. "I said stop it."

"Or you'll what?"

I bent down to pick up my things again. But Benji stepped on the strap of my backpack. I'd had enough of this asshole. Enough of this--this needless scrap of human flesh. Without thinking, I pressed my hands into his chest, shoving him with all my might, causing him to stumble back. And as my eyes widened in shock, his filled with fury.

"Looks like Bambi's got a bit of fight in her."

I quickly gathered my things. "I have to go."

He gripped my arm. "Not so fast."

I ripped away from his grasp. "Touch me again, and Max will know about it."

I hustled away from the boy, holding my backpack close to my chest. I felt his eyes burrowing into me from behind, but I didn't stop to look back. I tried my best to ignore him. Ignore his words. Ignore his stare. However, when I got to the top of the onyx steps, I caved.

I turned around and searched for him. Wondering where he was and what he was doing.

He was nowhere to be found.

"Okay. This isn't terrible. You're good. Everything's good. Let's go swim."

I pep-talked myself all the way inside the building. I scurried to the locker room and picked one toward the door. Not back in the back, where I usually resided. Because if Benji came to look for me again, I wanted the greatest chance at getting away. What in the world was it with him? Why did he hate me so much? I didn't even know the guy. I hadn't done anything to him!

What business was I distracting Max from?

More questions to haunt me with no answers in sight.

I stripped my clothes off and shoved them into the locker. I pulled out my goggles and my towel before shoving everything else in, too. And after closing the metal door, I made my way to the pool. I was ready to swim until I couldn't move any longer.

The water felt wonderful against my skin. From the second I dove in, I felt it washing me clean. My slick body glided down the lane like a mermaid in the depths of the ocean. My arms pumped, pulling me forward. My legs kicked, propelling me toward the wall. And as I circled around before pushing off, everything finally fell away.

Lap after lap after lap.

Blood pumped through my veins. My heart surged to life. I moved faster. Swam harder. Until my sweat mingled with the chlorinated water, bleaching my skin of its dirtiness. Around and around I went. Butterfly. Freestyle. Backstroke. I'd loved being on the swim team in high school. The competition of it all. Spending time with friends and kicking everyone's butt in the metered races.

I slammed both of my hands against the concrete wall before I looked up, sloshing water over the edge. I drew in a deep breath, flipping my hair back. As I panted for oxygen, I heard footsteps walking along the edge, squishing into the puddles of water I had left behind.

Then he bent down and showed me his face.

"Didn't know you looked so good in a bathing suit, Bambi."

The foolish grin Benji had on his cheeks made my blood run cold. There was something in his eyes I didn't like. Had he been watching me this entire time? I quickly pushed off the wall and swam away from the pool's edge. Anything to get away from this man. The sight of him made everything in my body run cold, despite the fact that I knew I was sweating from head to toe. I forced myself to tread water, even though my muscles screamed for rest.

I decided to swim to the other side of the pool.

"Oh, no you don't."

I heard him get up and race around the pool. As my hands touched down onto the concrete, I saw his shadow rounding the corner. I drew in a deep breath and pushed off again. Maybe I could wear him out and find an opening. I swam back across, but he kept up with me. Back and forth. Back and forth.

How in the world could I possibly feel cornered in a pool?

"I just want to talk!"

His voice echoed off the walls of the pool, rattling my ears.

"Get away from me, you freak!"

He chuckled. "That's rich, you calling me the freak, Bambi."

"Ah!"

I let out a frustrated cry and dove underneath the water. I used my feet to splash him, hopefully distracting him long enough to get to the shallow end of the pool. If I could get my legs underneath me, I knew I was faster than him. So even though my lungs screamed for mercy, I moved as fast as I could. I opened my eyes under water, feeling them burn as my goggles slipped off my face. I pushed the water behind me with my cupped hands, hoping and praying I had beat him.

But when I came out of the water, I felt a tight grip around my wrist.

"Let me go!"

Benji laughed. "No wonder you've piqued Max's curiosity."

He tugged me over to the steps as I tried to pull away from him.

"I said let me go. Now."

He snickered. "You're a feisty little thing. Sexy in a swimsuit. Those toned little legs of yours. Your tits are bigger than your shirts show, too. Lucky man, my cousin."

"Help! Someone help me!"

"Aww, does Bambi need her father?"

I finally wrenched away. "Get the hell away from me. Now."

"Oh, and she curses! Does that make you feel bad, Bambi? Did Max teach you one of those words, Daddy's girl?"

I turned around to dive back into the pool, but I felt an arm wrap around me and hot breath on the nape of my neck. Benji. He had me. Panic rushed through my veins. I dug my nails into his forearm as I tried to jam backward with my elbow. But he was protected by the leather of his jacket. And the punch I delivered with my elbow didn't seem to do anything but tickle him.

"Benji, put me down!" I shrieked.

He lifted me out of the pool. "And easy to toss around! Oh, Max is really going to like that."

My legs flailed. "Stop it! Please! Someone help me!"

"Oh, quit your shouting. I just want to talk to the girl who's got my cousin's dick all twisted up in knots."

"We aren't sleeping together."

His lips pressed against my ear. "Oh, but you will, Bambi. You will spread those legs for him. All girls do eventually. And do you know who swoops in for another round once he's done?"

I grimaced. "I would rather die."

He chuckled. "Until I show you what heaven really feels like, huh?"

26

MAX

I rode by Dani's dorm room and frowned. All the parking spaces next to the damn place were taken up. So I throttled it around campus and found something much too far away. I had to get away from the house. After my talk with John, sitting around was doing nothing but making me feel fucking paranoid. I wanted something to distract me, lift my spirits. Because every time I crunched numbers to see if I could get the guys paid out of our own club fund, it pissed me off that I couldn't.

Not without some serious outside help.

As I parked my bike and walked across campus, that little voice in my mind nagged at me. It told me to stay away. To do what was good for me. To stay at the house and keep my head down, just like John told me to. It burned my blood that Dad called him. That Dad wanted my own damn brother to keep tabs on me like that. It took me damn near twenty minutes to just get out of the house without telling John where I was headed. And even then, we still fought over it.

In the end, though, I won.

I always fucking did.

Girls giggled and pointed. I felt them running their curious eyes up and down my body. I didn't care, though. For once, I didn't give a shit. I had a final destination in mind. I had someone I needed to see. A girl I had become weak against. My own version of kryptonite.

The saving grace I didn't deserve.

Something about this girl made me crazy in all the right ways. She captivated me in a way I'd never been before. I had to find out why. Uncovering the secret to her mesmerizing presence would help me wash her away forever. Maybe I had to sleep with her. Maybe I had to fuck her out of my mind. Maybe once I dove between those legs and visited that sweet place for myself, this would all go away.

She could go back to the light, and I could retreat back into the dark.

"You're an idiot, Max," I murmured to myself.

That had been my mantra all fucking morning. What an idiot I was being. How stupid this was becoming. She was just some girl. Some college girl who didn't know shit about the world. To many people, I lived an exciting life. What did I want with some girl who didn't even know how to kiss?

That was the beauty of her, though. That was the meat of it all. She didn't know about these things. She still saw the world through rose-colored lenses. If she was lucky, she would forever. She'd see this place as good. She'd see people as good.

She wouldn't become like me, if she was lucky.

As I crossed through a random grove of trees, I came to the back of Dani's dorm building. Well, I still had a ways to walk. But it was there. I grinned as I started up the hill. Every step I took brought me closer to her. I felt myself picking up the pace, moving faster and faster until the only thing I focused on was that damn back entrance.

Into the stairwell that took me all the way to the top.

"Hey! I just want to talk!"

"Leave me alone!"

My head whipped to the left as Benji's voice sailed along the wind that had kicked up. But it wasn't Benji's voice that kept my eyes searching the grounds. It was the voice that came after. The high-pitched, panicked voice of the person that answered.

Dani.

I diverted my path and headed toward the voices. People knocked into me and fell to the grass, cursing my existence and shooting profanities my way. And while I usually stopped to pay them a bit of attention with my snarl, I didn't dare stop.

Dani sounded scared.

And I wanted to know what the fuck Benji had to do with that.

"Wait up, Bambi! Can't we just have a chat?"

"Keep your hands off me, you jerk!"

My eyes widened. My back bristled. Hands. He put

his hands on her? I broke into a dead sprint as I crested the hill. I turned around, trying to figure out where the two of them were. I panted for air. My nostrils flared with anger. My blood bubbled in my veins as my vision dripped red.

No one touched Dani.

No one touched what was mine.

After searching the space around me, I gazed down the hill. I saw a girl rushing steadily up it with a back-pack slung over her shoulder. I took a step forward and studied her. The way she hunched over, wiping at her face. The way she tried to make herself as small as possible while her towel hung out of her backpack. The hair gave her away, though. That soaking wet, almost-black hair that swung with every step she took.

Is she crying?

"I swear to fuck, if you don't stop--!"

"Leave me alone," she said breathlessly.

My skull pounded with anger. The second I heard her sniffle, my world exploded with fury. I watched Dani come up the hill, knowing that if I intervened before I could get my anger in check, I'd kill him. I'd kill my own damn cousin for this girl.

You're in deep shit, Max.

Benji burst into a full-blown run, racing to catch up with her. He had his eyes locked on her, coming for her as quickly as his feet would let him. When I saw the glistening of her tears from the corner in which I stood, I came out and reached for her, cradling her elbow in the palm of my hand.

"Dani, it's me."

"Just stop touching me, Benji!"

The way she jerked away from me made me sick. But what she said confirmed my suspicions.

"Max?" she asked breathlessly.

"Bambi, when I ask you to do something, you--"

I saw Benji's hand come out of nowhere, ready to touch down against her shoulder. Oh, hell no. Did he not realize I was standing right here? Was he that thick-headed? My hand moved at the speed of light, slapping around his wrist and yanking him away from her. I pulled him to my face, standing him on his fucking tiptoes as my free hand fisted his leather jacket.

"Hey! Max! Uh… you mind putting me down?"

Dani sniffled, and I had to draw in a few deep breaths to keep from strangling the kid.

"Want to tell me why she's crying and trying to get away from you?"

He snickered. "You serious right now?"

She drew in a shuddered breath. "He cornered me in the pool."

Benji scoffed. "I'm not even wet."

She interjected. "He wrapped his arm around my waist and physically pulled me out of the pool. I tried to get away from him at the shallow end--"

"Wow, you've really got a mouth on you, Bambi."

I narrowed my eyes. "Don't you call her that."

I tossed him to the ground, sending him sprawled out on his back. Right on his fucking ass. I took a step and straddled him, looming over him as my body blocked out the afternoon sun.

"He's not worth it, Max. Really. I'm okay."

Her sweet voice was the only thing keeping me on my fucking leash.

"What the fuck, Max? Are you serious?"

Benji's growl infuriated me. "Is he bothering you, Dani?"

He chuckled. "Oh, so she's 'Dani' now? When the hell did that happen?"

I pointed at him. "Stay there, or you're done. You hear me?"

I peered over my shoulder at Dani and saw her still wiping at her face.

"Is he bothering you, Dani?"

She swallowed hard before she nodded. The damn girl couldn't even catch her breath enough to speak to me again. Her chest jumped with soft sobs, and I had no clue what to do. I knew what I wanted to do. I wanted to strangle Benji until his eyes popped out. I wanted to hang him up under a bridge for all the world to see as a warning.

This is what happens when someone messes with what is mine.

"Fucking hell, my goddamn back. Dude, have you lost your shit or something?"

Benji went to get up, but I pressed my boot against his chest, pushing him back down to the concrete.

"Let me the fuck up. Right now."

I licked my lips. "You're going to stay the hell away from her from here on out. You hear me?"

He shoved my foot away. "Fuck you."

I reached down and fisted his shirt as people gasped around me.

"Max, please," Dani pleaded.

Benji wrapped his hands around my forearm. "Your brother's going to hear about his."

I glared at him. "She's off limits. Understand?"

He glared right back. "We have classes together. The fuck do you want me to do about that?"

I seethed. "Sit in the back row."

I dropped him to his feet before backing up and standing next to Dani. Shading her from the prying eyes that were wondering what the hell was going on.

"Fuck you, Max."

I cocked my head. "Want to try that again?"

Benji snickered. "No, actually. I don't. She's just some college chick. Some slice of pussy you'll get before dumping her, like you do every other girl. But, me, I'm fucking family. I'm your crew. I'm your flesh and blood. You're going to choose a bitch over me?"

"Max!"

I didn't even register the movement until it was too late. Dani yelling my name was the last thing I heard before I felt something warm against my knuckles. It seemed like I blinked, and then Benji was down. In the blink of an eye, my fist had connected with his nose and put him on his fucking back again. Blood dripped down the sides of his face. I looked at my hand and registered the blood splattered against my knuckles. People around us gasped. I looked back at Dani and watched her eyes widen with shock and fear, her hands covering her mouth.

"So that how it's gonna be?"

I panned my head back around and watched my cousin peel himself off the concrete.

"You and this girl, against everyone else?"

I lowered my fist. "You leave her alone for good. Got it?"

He spat blood at my feet. "Fuck you and your morals. Dumbass piece of shit."

I lunged at him, but I felt a pair of hands grip my leather jacket. I heard her shuddering breaths as I turned around, knowing damn good and well who was holding me back. Her hands fell away from my jacket. I heard Benji cursing to himself and storming off as the crowd quickly dissipated. And as I gazed into Dani's frightened eyes, I sighed.

"I'm sorry."

The shock was evident on her face as her hands slipped to her sides.

"It's--it's okay. I--Thank you."

I nodded. "Anytime."

She furrowed her brow. "What are you doing here? It's, like, four in the afternoon."

I chuckled. "Think I only dwell at night, Bambi?"

She smiled softly for me. "Maybe."

My eyes slid down her body. "Did he hurt you?"

"What do you mean?"

My eyes snapped back to hers. "If you have to quantify the statement, you might as well tell me what he did."

She grinned. "Quantify. Big word for Fistman."

I paused. "Fistman?"

"It's either that or Buckaroo."

"I've grown partial to Buckaroo."

She smiled. "Then that's a big word for you, Buckaroo."

"Just because I don't use them doesn't mean I don't know them."

"Seems I still have a lot to learn about you."

I nodded. "Right after you tell me whether or not Benji hurt you."

And when her face fell, I braced for the worst.

Because if he had hurt her, my morals were clear. An eye for an eye. That's how I lived my life. If someone hurt me, I hurt them. If someone stole from me, I stole from them. If someone killed someone I loved, I gave them that fate right back. That's how the Red Thorns operated. 'Rogues in Arms.' Taking up swords and guns and war for those who couldn't fight themselves. Exacting revenge as we saw fit, making money as we could, and making sure this world always stayed at an even keel around us.

If Benji had hurt her, he'd suffer the same fate. Something I needed to prepare myself for.

I held my breath as her lips parted to speak.

27

DANI

"No, he didn't hurt me. He just scared me."

I watched relief flood Max's face as he sighed so heavily I thought he might've been holding his breath.

"I'm sorry," Max said again.

I shook my head. "It's not your fault."

"He's my responsibility."

"He's not a child. He's his own responsibility."

He snickered. "You don't understand."

I cleared my throat as my heart winced. Was it possible for hearts to wince? I wasn't sure, but that's what it felt like. The struggled beat that finally rang through my body caused me to grow dizzy. His words stung because, well, he was right. I didn't understand. Max and I came from two very different worlds. Two very different walks of life. I couldn't even begin to understand what reality looked like through his eyes.

What kinds of pressures he had on his shoulders. For all I knew, nothing was the same between us.

"Well, uh, thank you. Again."

Max drew in a short breath. "What happened?"

I shook my head. "I really don't--"

He took my hand in his. "What happened, Dani?"

My entire body stopped. Dani? I was 'Dani' now? Why did that feel like such an accomplishment? Why did it have to be an accomplishment with him? His eyes held mine as I drew in a heavy breath. The weight of the world seemed so much sometimes. And yet the stroke of his finger against the top of my hand somehow made it better. Made it easier to carry.

I wondered if I made him feel that way, too.

"I uh, headed to the pool after my last class. Just needed a nice swim. To clear my head."

Max nodded. "I get that."

"You do?"

He grinned. "Sounds like me and a good ride."

I smiled up at him. "Yeah. About like that."

"So, what? Benji found you in the pool?"

"Well, I ran into him on my way to the pool. I was practically running there."

"Why?"

To get away from my mind. "To try and just... wash myself."

I figured he'd question me. Implore for more of an answer. But his eyes filled with understanding. As if we were standing on the same plane.

And I felt like his equal again.

"Anyway, he kind of tried to stop me from going to the pool."

He furrowed his brow. "How so?"

"Max..."

His voice grew curt. "How so, Dani?"

I shook my head. "You aren't going to like this."

"I already don't like it. But I want to know what my cousin did to you."

"So you're cousins."

"Don't change the subject."

"Just learning more about you, that's all."

He licked his lips. "What did he do to try and stop you?"

"He was so insistent on talking to me. He said--"

I wasn't sure if this was something Max needed to know. But I knew I'd already said too much.

"Dani."

I shook my head. "Sorry. He just--he thinks I distract you, and he doesn't know why. I guess because I'm not like most girls you're usually with? I don't know. I tried to step around him and he grabbed my arm to prevent me from leaving and--ouch!"

Max dropped my hand. "I'm sorry. Shit."

I shook my hand. "No, no. It's okay. It's--it's fine."

"It's not fine. Not if you get hurt. I hurt you."

He ran his hands through my hair and turned his back to me.

"Max, look at me."

He shook his head.

"Max, come on."

He shook his head again.

"Don't make me bust out the big guns, Buckaroo."

He snickered. "Now I'm curious to know your big guns."

I balled up my fist and punched him in the butt cheek. Before I could even think, my knuckles connected with his butt. And holy crap, it was rock solid. He whipped around with surprise in his face and I shook out my hand, murmuring 'ouch' underneath my breath. He took my hand back in his and massaged it softly, trying his hardest to swallow down his laughter.

"That uh... those the big guns?"

I snorted. "I hate you."

He smiled. "I really don't think you do."

I sighed at the beauty of his smile before I stepped closer.

"Why don't you smile often?"

It fell from his face. "Don't have much to smile about, I guess."

"What makes you smile?"

"You do."

I blushed. "What really makes you smile?"

"You punching my ass does."

I giggled. "You're a jerk."

"And you're the cutest thing I've ever laid eyes on."

I felt my blush work down my neck. "After I was done swimming laps, he was there. Benji. I tried to get out, but he--"

"He won't bother you again. You have my word."

I paused. "Don't you want to know what--"

"Not at the expense of hurting you, no. All I ask is

that if he does mess with you ever again, you need to tell me. All right?"

I nodded. "All right."

The wind kicked up and something cold on the edge of my eyelash made my eyes water again. Max's hand came up to me, wiping away the tears still clinging to them. I sniffled again as his hand cupped my cheek. Another tear worked its way down. Then another. And another still. Only, they weren't tears of sorrow.

Nevertheless, it didn't stop Max from brushing them away, erasing their existence as his warmth kept me company.

"Let me make it up to you."

I paused. "What?"

"Today. The pool. My cousin's assholery. Let me make it up to you."

"I--you--how?"

He grinned. "Got any more classes today?"

I shook my head. "Not until the morning."

"Great. Let's drop your things off and take a ride."

"Max, you don't have to--"

"Come on, Bambi. We're burning daylight."

He tugged me softly toward my dorm entrance and the two of us walked up. We took the back stairwell, keeping in step with one another until we got to the top. It didn't shock me one bit that Hannah wasn't in the room. Part of me was relieved. The last thing I needed was her questioning why I was randomly with Max. Nor did I want her flirting with him.

That idea made my lips turn down.

"Can I get out of my bathing suit first?" I asked.

"You didn't change out of it?"

I paused. "I didn't really get a chance to."

His nostrils flared. "You do whatever you need to. I'll be right outside the door."

I nodded. "I won't take long."

The second he closed the door, I jumped around. Taking off my wet clothes was the hardest thing I'd ever done. Especially when I went to wiggle out of my suit. I tossed everything into my hamper. I knew it would grow musty overnight, but I didn't care. All I cared about was piling my hair on top of my head, putting on some fresh clothes, and going anywhere and everywhere with Max. I pulled a pair of my comfy jeans up my legs, opting for a long-sleeved shirt since my hair was still wet. After sliding on a bit of lip gloss and dusting on some blush like Hannah had shown me, I smiled at myself in the mirror.

Then I opened the door.

"Ready?"

Max's eyes fell to my jeans, but the look he gave me wasn't one I'd ever seen in the movies. I mean, I didn't expect to sweep the man off his feet or anything. But did he really have to look so put-off by them?

"How long have you had those?" he asked.

I paused. "Uh, since high school?"

"What year in high school?"

"Do they look bad or something?"

He slowly shook his head. "They're just… loose."

I smiled. "That's what makes them comfortable."

"They have holes in the knees."

"Does that bother you, Mr. Leather Jacket?"

His eyes found mine. "My jeans don't have holes in the knees."

"Well, all right, Mr. Perfect."

"Come on. I know exactly where I'm taking you."

He took my hand and started down the hallway, with me falling in step behind him. We made our way to the elevator, taking the easy way down to his bike. Being able to wrap my arms around him again felt wonderful. It was something I hadn't been sure I'd ever experience again. But as campus fell away behind us, I felt freer than I had in a long time.

And the ride was substantially longer this time around.

With every bend in the road, I leaned into him. Grounded myself with my arms wrapped around his waist. I clenched the bike with my thighs, even though they were tired. My abs screamed for mercy and my arms wanted to hang limply in the air. But I didn't give in. I wanted to know where he was taking me. I wanted to know what was in store for us this evening. As the sun began to sink in the sky, colors splashed across the horizon. Pinks and blues and purples that backdropped shadowed trees and rolling green hills.

We finally pulled into a parking lot.

"Where are we?"

Max cut the engine and put the kickstand down.

"Come inside and find out. That's how most adventures start."

I slid the helmet off my head. "Mike's Bikes and Boots?"

He held out his hand. "You coming or not?"

I slapped the helmet into his hand before wiggling my way down from the bike. I followed him inside, and I instantly regretted my decision. Everywhere I looked, there was biker apparel. Leather jackets on hangers in the corners. Boots lining the back wall. Gloves, jeans, and T-shirts, all lining the aisles in the middle of the store. The cashier was blowing bubbles with her chewing gum, her voluptuous curves barely stuffed into the tight leather pieces she wore.

"Need anything?" she asked flatly.

I shook my head. "No, ma'am."

She scoffed. "Fine, then."

Max took my hand. "Follow me."

I don't know what in the world would possibly possess him to bring me here or how this was making anything up to me. But I went with it. As much as I could, anyway. He tugged me all the way to the back corner of the store, where there was a door with a crooked sign that said 'dressing room.'

"What are we doing here, Max?"

He reached for a pair of jeans. "You need new pants."

"Wait, what?"

He turned around and let his eyes fall down my legs.

"Preferably, a pair that fits."

I scoffed. "Oh. Oh, I see. You're wanting me to get into some tiny little leather gear just so you can see what's underneath these baggy clothes. Well, I'm telling you right now, Buckaroo, that ain't happenin'."

He grinned at me. "That your 'tough gun' voice?"

"I'm not living that down, am I?"

"Oh, never, as long as I'm alive."

I rolled my eyes. "Give me those."

I snatched the jeans out of his hands as he laughed. I smiled to myself as I walked through the door, only to find myself face to face with a full-length mirror. Oh, this was the dressing room. I figured this was a backroom with multiple dressing rooms.

No matter. These jeans looked so small I probably wouldn't fit into them anyway.

"When you're done with those, toss them over and tell me how they fit."

I slid my jeans over my hips. "What? You don't want me to come out and model them for you?"

"We're here to find you some clothes that fit. Not tease me. My treat."

My cheeks were on fire with his words. "I'll throw them over once I'm done."

"Already found another pair you can try. Incoming!"

I looked up and saw a pair of jeans being tossed over the top of the door. Well, they were supposed to be jeans. I held them up to myself and my eyes bulged when I saw how skinny the legs were. I mean, the roundness of my thighs didn't even fit behind the outline of the fabric!

"Max?"

"Yep?"

"Are you sure this is you making things up to me?"

Another pair of jeans came over the door. "Why do you ask?"

I sighed. "Oh, you know. Because these jeans are really tight. And I'm thinking this might secretly be about you, because you want to see me in a…"

I tried to stretch the jeans out a bit, but they didn't budge.

"… much tighter pair of jeans," I grunted.

He chuckled. "Why can't it be both?"

The fabric I was pulling at fell from my hands as my body froze up.

"No."

"Nope."

"I can't even zip these up. How small do you think I am?"

"The legs are too long."

"This makes my butt look big."

I snickered. "At least you have a butt in these."

She poked her head around the dressing room door. "What was that?"

I grinned. "Nothing. I'll go get you another pair. But I'm also going to get you some other things to try on in the process."

She sighed. "What exactly are you getting me? Because you aren't throwing over very good jeans."

"Like my leather jacket?"

I watched her head disappear before I heard the sound of a zipper.

"I'll try on one jacket," she said.

I smiled. "Perfect."

Even though she kept vetoing the jeans I sent her way, I refused to stop. The clothes she wore on a regular basis practically swallowed her whole. And they did nothing for the beautiful body I knew was underneath. Yes, clothes needed to breathe. But they didn't need to be two sizes too big in order to do that. I shoved the jeans into the arms of the woman following me around the store. I felt her staring at my ass, but I didn't care. I put on a nice show for her to be entertained with while I picked out clothes for the only girl I had my sights set on right now.

Dani.

I plucked two different kinds of black shirts off the rack, although I already knew which one she'd feel more comfortable in. Then I walked over to the leather jackets. I had to grab a couple of different sizes because I wasn't sure which one would fit her. But she definitely wasn't bigger than a medium. After gathering the last of the clothes, I walked over to the dressing room. Dani had already pushed two other pairs of jeans underneath the door.

I pushed all the clothes over the top of the door and listened to her yelp.

"Max!"

I chuckled. "Yep?"

I heard the pouting in her voice. "The hanger hit my head."

"Might want to start choosing some clothes, then. Because there's a lot more where that came from."

"Jerk off."

I grinned. "Gorgeous."

She snickered. "You really need to stop calling me things like that. You might not be able to get--"

She bit off the last of that sentence, but I knew what she was about to say.

You might not be able to get rid of me.

I think I could stand something like that happening. With her, at least.

After hearing her muttering and sighing behind the door for another twenty minutes, the doorknob finally twisted open. My heart leapt into my throat as I pushed away from the wall, waiting to see what she had chosen for herself. Her eyes were the first thing I saw. Apprehensive. Worried. Unsure of herself. But as my eyes traveled down her body, I prayed to God on high she didn't see my cock growing against my pants.

Because the skin-tight dark-wash jeans looked fantastic on her.

"Wow," I breathed.

Dani paused. "Not too much?"

"Turn around."

She held out her arms and did a slow turn for me, giving me a second to salivate over her. Holy shit, the ass she had underneath those clothes would fit perfectly in the palms of my hands. The scooped-neck black shirt showcased the soft slope of her waist and the blossom of her tits. Breasts I wanted to taste, like the perfect mouthfuls they were. And the leather jacket? Fucking hell, that was the best part. She faced me and zipped it up, stopping just below those tits of hers.

And damn it, I wanted to rip those clothes right back off.

"I feel silly," she said.

I blinked. "You look hot as sin, Dani. I'm serious."

She shook her head. "It's not me."

"Says who?"

She paused, and my eyes found hers. I forced myself to pull my bulging eyes away from the perfection of her body and made myself study her face. And what I saw was a storm raging behind her eyes. I saw her fighting herself. While she wanted to retreat back to those old clothes of hers, I saw a confidence flourishing in the way she stood in front of me. Her shoulders weren't slumped. Her head held itself a little higher. She didn't look so confused as she stared up into my face.

She looked more grounded than I had ever seen her.

I walked over to her and looped my fingers into the belt loops. I pulled her close to me, feeling her breasts gracing my torso. Her hands held my arms while my eyes held hers. And as my hands settled onto her hips, I gripped her softly, holding her in front of me so I knew she was listening.

"Listen, Daddy's girl. The girls I ride with dress like this. The girls I ride with aren't afraid to look good. They aren't afraid of themselves. That's what makes a girl a woman. Confidence. Knowing herself. Being unafraid to take what she knows is hers and make it her own. So if you don't like it, I won't force it on you. That's not my style. But if you *do* like it? There isn't a damn thing in this world to feel embarrassed about."

She swallowed hard. "Yeah?"

I nodded. "Yeah. You're sexy, Dani. Really sexy."

A smile curled her lips. "Am I really hearing you call me 'Dani' now and again?"

"So what if I do?"

The smile that took over her lips made my chest swell with pride. This was the girl I saw behind those eyes. She was more powerful and much stronger than she recognized. And I had a feeling that had to do with how she was raised. Raised as a girl to keep her head down and her nose in books. To speak when spoken to, and nothing else. To follow the commands of others instead of the beat of her own drum. And while I was guilty of playing on that with her in the past, I made a promise to myself as my smile slowly grew to match hers.

I'll help you find yourself, Bambi.

"I like the jeans." Her voice broke my trance.

"I figured you might."

Dani swatted my chest. "Yeah, after tossing me seventeen different pairs."

I paused. "You counted?"

"There are a lot of things I do that you don't realize."

My hands slid to her lower back. "Well then, I can't wait to figure out what the rest of them are."

"I really do like these jeans, though. How much are they?"

I shrugged. "Why does that matter?"

"Well, I was hoping to get myself another pair. Maybe in… black?"

I growled softly. "What makes you think I'm letting you pay for anything?"

"You don't have to pay for everything. I do have some money to throw around."

"And I promised you I'd make things up to you. Let me do this. Just go with it."

She sighed. "Fine. But I buy food next time."

"Oh, no. Not a fucking chance."

"Hey, I'm serious now."

"So am I. When you're with me, I pay."

"When do I get to pay, then?"

I shrugged. "When we're ordering takeout. But I'm still the one tipping the driver."

She giggled. "Oh. Oh, yeah. Right. Of course. *Totally*."

I narrowed my eyes. "Are you mocking me?"

She smiled. "If you have to ask…"

I swatted her ass cheek. "Bad."

Her cheeks flushed that beautiful color I never could ignore. "Max."

"Too far?"

"No. I mean, I don't know. Just--well…?"

I waited for her to gather her thoughts as my hands slowly slipped down to her ass cheeks. I cupped them softly, massaging them for the first time. I liked how they felt. Malleable, but strong. Her body leaned against mine, her hands sliding along my torso. She threaded them underneath my leather jacket. I felt her hands splayed out over my back. And as I held her close to me, I placed a soft kiss on the top of her head.

And not once did she smack my hands away.

"Not too far," she whispered.

I grinned. "Come on. Let's go find that black pair of jeans."

With a soft pat to her ass, I released her from my grip. What I wanted to do was pull her into that fucking dressing room and have my way with her. Not the time, though. There was a time and a place for that. And now wasn't it. I wanted her to walk out of here with some clothes. Some decent clothes. Ones that made her feel as confident as she did right now.

"Here. These," she said.

I draped them over my arm. "Want a light-wash pair, too?"

She furrowed her brow. "How do you know so much about jeans?"

I shrugged. "Comes with the territory."

"Uh huh."

"So what do you think?"

She slid the light blue faded jeans off the rack before smiling.

"I think I could wear these."

I took them from her. "All right. Three pairs of pants. You'll need at least six shirts with these."

"Six!? What's wrong with the one I've got on?"

I shrugged. "That's fine. Let's get five more of them."

"I don't want them in all black, though."

"Then let's find them in other colors."

As we walked around the store, I reached for a bike helmet hanging on the wall. She needed her own so both of us could be safe while riding around. I tucked it underneath my arm while she kept holding shirts up to herself. Watching her settle into the niceties of clothes shopping made my grin grow from ear to ear. She tossed me shirts, then another pair of jeans. She even found a leather belt she wanted to wear, so I told her to hand it to me. I didn't care how much money we spent today. That wasn't an object right now.

The whole point of this was confidence. Helping her bloom into the woman I knew existed underneath those baggy-ass clothes of hers.

And it seemed to be working.

"Okay, that's definitely enough," she said.

I nodded. "Sure about that?"

"Yep. And I'm helping you pay for this."

I thrust everything onto the register counter. "Not a chance."

"Max."

"Daddy's girl."

"Hey. What happened to my name?"

I grinned. "When you earn it back, you'll hear it."

"By doing everything you ask me?"

"By knowing when to step up and when to back off. I'm treating you, Bambi. Let me do that."

My hand covered the total as it mounted and mounted. I knew these clothes would cost me damn near eight hundred bucks. Especially with the helmet I was buying for her. I didn't care, though. I more than had the money. For now, at least. And she needed some nice things in her life. I wanted to give her those nice things.

So I paid without her knowing the price and we headed outside.

"Max?"

I tucked the bags into the storage compartment of my bike. "Yep?"

I felt something warm press against my cheek and it gave me pause. My eyes fell closed and a sigh left my lips as her own lingered against my skin. I leaned into her. I didn't even notice I was doing it until she puckered her lips and kissed me again. And again. Shooting electricity through my body and sparking a fire in my gut.

"Thank you. For everything."

I nodded. "Of course."

She kissed me one more time on my cheek. The softest, most innocent of kisses I'd ever experienced in my life. And I felt my cock rising to the occasion again. I straightened up and handed her the helmet I purchased for her. All black, with red trim that matched the colors of my bike. She snickered as she took it from me. She slid it over her head with ease. And when she popped open the visor like a pro, I knew I had made the right decision.

"Hold your thoughts. Because we have one more stop to make, Daddy's girl."

She rolled her eyes. "Whisk me away, Buckaroo."

And with a chuckle, I threw my leg over my bike, giving her my hand to help her on behind me.

29

DANI

I closed my eyes and tried to get comfortable with the way my clothes hugged me. And the more we traveled away from the clothing store, the more alive I felt. I didn't hear my clothes whipping around in the wind. All I heard was the sound of the bike's engine and the muffled world as it rushed by me. I didn't feel so off-kilter on the back of the bike, either. Like my clothes were dragging me in all sorts of directions. I felt more stabilized, more grounded.

It didn't keep me from clinging to Max, though.

The way he swatted at my butt made me feel things I'd never felt before. It didn't even hurt, either. It just… shocked me. And that shock turned into a desire that clenched my heart. When his hands slipped over the globes of my butt, I felt held by him. I know it sounds stupid and weird. But I'd never felt safer than when he held me like that. As if he were cupping the entirety of my body and protecting it, all at once.

I almost groaned with disappointment when his hands moved.

My arms wrapped around him as we sped down the street on his bike. And while I wanted to close my eyes, I made myself look at the world around us zooming by at lightning speed. Or, at least it felt like we were going that fast. I giggled and clung to Max as we took tight corners. My hands splayed along his abs as I rubbernecked to look around. Shops passed by in a blur and groves of trees melded into blobs of dark green and brown.

I wondered what the changing of the leaves might look like going this fast down the road.

When we pulled into what looked like a subdivision, though, I perked up. Where were we going? We had been riding for a while. At least, it felt like a while. How long had we been riding around?

Pay more attention, Dani.

We rode through the subdivision and out a back exit. The road we turned onto was lined with trees and ditches on either side, and riddled with potholes. I felt my gut growing nervous. Where in the world was this man taking me?

My question got answered, though, when we pulled into a driveway.

The leaning trees shadowing the concrete expanse gave way as we pulled up to the house. My eyebrows rose as I studied it, trying to come to terms with it. I don't know, it felt... out of place. The white exterior. The pristine porch. The uncracked driveway that looked as if it had been recently poured. The red shutters made sense, though. Blood red, like the roses on Max's arm tattoo. Blood red, like the colors of his bike. Of my helmet.

Of the Red Thorns.

"Where are we?" I asked.

Max didn't answer me. He simply turned off his bike and put the kickstand down.

"Coming inside?" he asked.

I pulled my helmet off. "Is this your place?"

He shrugged. "Mine and my brother's place, but yeah."

"You have a brother?"

He pulled his helmet off. "You coming or what, Bambi?"

I grinned. "Oh, I'm coming all right. Just let me get... off... ugh."

His hands fell to my waist and he practically picked me up off the bike. He set me down onto my feet before taking my helmet from me. Then I watched him hang both of the helmets on either side of his handlebars. Mine was slightly smaller than his. I liked the way they looked side by side on his bike. His hand fell to my lower back and he guided me to the front door. The blood red door that matched the shutters.

Once I got inside, I couldn't keep my shocked gasp inside any longer.

"What? Did you think I'd live in a dump?"

My eyes took in the vaulted foyer ceiling. "I don't know what I expected. But it wasn't this."

"Nicer than you expected?"

I didn't want to answer his question because I didn't want to seem mean.

"Eh, it's fine. This is the house I grew up in, actually. Sits on seven acres, got a lake on it if you ride far back enough into the backyard."

I turned to face him. "Maybe we could go see it?"

He grinned. "Sure, sometime."

I nodded. "So is your brother around? I'd like to meet him, if that's okay."

"John's not here right now. Just the two of us."

Butterflies erupted in my stomach. They flew around, fluttering so hard I thought I'd take off toward the vaulted ceiling. I swallowed hard as nervousness crept up my back. Did he bring me here to--?

"Breathe, Bambi. Don't forget to breathe."

I drew in a broken breath. "Sorry. Yeah. I--yeah. Yes. Okay."

His smiled at me like a hungry beast. "You didn't think you'd be able to get away with looking that hot today without me needing you, did you?"

I blinked. "I… I--it--"

He walked toward me. "And those kisses. So soft against my cheek. Did you know what you were doing? Or did that simply come natural to you?"

My back fell against the front door. "I--well, it--"

His hand fell beside my head. "Use your words, Daddy's girl."

I licked my lips. "Please, call me Dani."

His other hand came down against the other side of my head. His eyes held mine. And as his hot breath pulsed against my lips, I wanted to lean forward and kiss him.

"Okay, Dani."

I should've been scared. But I wasn't. Not of Max, anyway. The look in his eye seemed carnal. I'd never had a man look at me like that before. It was intoxicating. The feral growl falling from his lips. The way his breath tasted good. How was that possible? For breath to taste like something? My eyes danced between his. My elbows tingled and my knees grew weak. His nose nuzzled softly against mine, and I knew he was waiting for me to speak. Or move. Or do something.

I knew he didn't want to move until I did.

"Max?"

"Dani."

I smiled softly. "Kiss me?"

His eyes ignited with fire. "Don't mind if I do."

His lips fell against mine and I fisted his leather jacket in my hands. I pulled him closer to me, standing on my tiptoes. He rose in front of me, like a bear finally being let out of its cage. His arms wrapped around me and he picked me up, pulling me flush against his body.

"Max," I whispered.

"You're coming with me."

I kissed across his cheek. I tried to recall every romantic movie I had ever watched to try and figure out what came next. I cursed myself for being weird about porn. I bet if I watched it, I'd know what to do next. I wrapped my legs around Max's body as his hands cupped my butt cheeks. I kissed along his jawline, listening to him grunt and growl as he walked us down a hallway. I licked at his neck. I kissed it. Sucked his skin. Ran my teeth softly over it. I didn't want to hurt him. But all of this felt so right.

"Dani," he growled.

I felt my body dropping away from his.

My back bounced against something soft. I looked around me while Max shed his leather jacket. I was in a bedroom. On a bed. Was this his room? I wanted to have a chance to take it in. To see his style. How he laid out his own space. My mother always said you could tell a lot about a person by the way they kept the rooms in their home. Where their safe places were. What their mindset was on any given occasion.

However, I felt something strong wrap around both of my ankles and then I was being pulled.

I yelped.

Max's chuckle graced my ears as my shoes went falling to the floor. He pulled off my socks and kissed my toes. I giggled and jerked around, rolling onto my stomach.

"I'm ticklish. Max!"

He grunted with delight. "I'm coming for you."

"Max!"

He grabbed my ankles and pulled me back again, causing me to burst out in laughter. He gripped my leather jacket and hoisted me up, settling me down onto my knees. My jacket came off. His lips came down against my neck. And as my head fell off to the side, his hands roamed my clothed body.

Massaging my breasts.

Gripping my waist.

Sliding up and down my thighs as I moaned for him.

I felt my defenses coming down, the fight draining from my veins. His fingertips slid underneath the hem of my shirt, and his touch made my skin prickle. The hairs on my arms stood on end. My toes curled as he hooked his fingers into my belt loops again. He pulled me back, grinding his pelvis against my butt cheeks. Something large pulsed against me. I felt his chest rising and falling with his breath. But when his hand gravitated to the button of my jeans, I froze.

And he stopped with me.

"What is it?"

My eyes slowly fell to his fingers, watching them as they settled over the button of my new jeans. What was I doing? Could I really do this with him?

He needs to know.

"Dani, talk to me."

I sighed. "I don't want you to go away once I do."

He kissed my neck. "That could never happen. What did I do wrong?"

I shook my head. "You did nothing wrong. It's me."

His kisses made me moan as my head fell to the side again.

"You could never do anything wrong."

I paused. "Maybe take off my shirt first?"

He chuckled. "Don't mind if I do."

I shivered as I knelt there on the bed, with his chest pressed into my back. I lifted my hands as he gripped my shirt, and for the first time in my life, I felt a man take off my clothes. It was invigorating. I felt alive as my bare skin came into contact with the air of his room. His lips fell against my shoulder as I heard my shirt bunch up onto the floor. Then, Max stepped back.

"Where are you go--"

I peeked over my shoulder and watched him slip his own shirt off. And when I saw his torso for the first time, my jaw fell open. Because he did have more tattoos.

He grinned. "Like what you see?"

I reached out for him and his shirt fell from his hands. He came closer to me, and I let my fingertips run along the ink embedded into his skin. Over his heart, there sat a circle of interwoven vines, like the ones wrapped around his bicep. There were thorns on the vine, with little roses. It was almost identical to the one around his arm. And in the middle of the circle was a red rose. A large one. And behind the entire thing was a sun rising over the hill of his chest. I traced the colors with my fingertips. The sunrise itself spanned almost the entire width of his chest.

It was mesmerizing.

"Rogues in Arms?" I asked. I hadn't noticed the words underneath the circle of thorns until my eyes followed the colors down in that direction. "What does that mean?"

My eyes rose back up to Max's and I found him staring at me. Hard.

"It's the Red Thorn mantra."

I paused. "What does it mean?"

He cupped my cheek. "Maybe someday, I'll tell you."

"Why can't you tell me now?"

He grinned. "Because that might ruin the mood."

He went to capture my lips again, but I pulled back.

"Dani?"

I swallowed hard. "There's really something you should know before this goes any further."

He furrowed his brow. "I don't think there's anything you could tell me that I don't already know."

"Wait, what?"

30

MAX

Fucking hell, this girl was the cutest thing I'd ever come across on the face of this planet. Her lips were swollen from my kisses, her cheeks pink from how turned on she was. My cock was rock hard, ready to go and be played with however she wished. I felt myself already leaking against my boxers. My hands were ready to explore her folds, tease her until she was wetter than she'd ever been in her wildest dreams.

I knew what she was about to say.

"You know?" she asked.

I smoothed my fingers along her cheek. "Why don't you act like I don't?"

The second she pulled away from me, I knew I had fucked up. I wasn't sure how, but I had. She fell to the bed and curled her knees to her chest, trying to cover herself as much as possible. The pink of her cheeks turned to red. Arousal to embarrassment. I didn't like seeing her that way. I didn't like her caving back in on herself like that. But I understood it.

This kind of thing was different for girls.

"Here," I said.

I scooped my leather jacket off the floor and handed it to her. She eyed it carefully before taking it and quickly wrapping it around her body. I turned my back to her and jammed my hand down my pants. As much as I wanted to make this girl orgasm until she begged for mercy, I couldn't do that without her permission. And I sure as hell couldn't do that when she was so uncomfortable with the situation.

Fucking idiot. I'm a fucking idiot.

With a heavy sigh, I turned around and crawled onto the bed. Dani had scooted herself up until her back sat against the wall. Her feet were tucked under the covers and her knees were still up to her chest. And with my leather jacket draped over her body, I couldn't see a damn part of the beauty I had successfully uncovered.

A shame, really.

"Whenever you're ready," I said.

I slipped underneath the covers and folded my arms over my chest. I peered over at her, waiting for her to say whatever it was she had to say.

"If you know, why say anything anyway?"

I shrugged. "Because it looks like you need to say it."

She snickered. "Why bring me here if you know?"

Her eyes slowly panned up to mine and I grinned.

"Simple. You're hot. I'm drawn to you. Your kisses

turned me on. Figured this was a nice setup, especially with my brother not being around."

She nodded. "So that's all this was? Just… to have sex?"

"Would it bother you if I said yes?"

She paused. "I'm not sure."

"Would it make you uncomfortable to lay down with me?"

"Might not be comfortable in this leather jacket."

"Then take it off."

She swallowed hard. "Then I'll be--"

"--covered by your bra, Dani. Which I won't touch unless you want me to."

"Promise?"

I nodded. "You have my word."

She quickly tossed my leather jacket off the side of the bed and hunkered down beneath the comforter. Watching her dark hair splay across my pillow made my heart skip a beat. The confident woman I'd brought to my house had given way to the self-conscious girl I always found on campus. And I wasn't sure how to draw that confidence back out again. My cock still wanted to bury itself inside her. My gut churned with a need to taste what was between her legs. And my head? Well, it wasn't thinking straight.

Because the only thing it told me to do was pin her down and take what was mine.

"Max, I'm sorry. It's just--"

I shook my head. "Don't apologize."

She paused. "What?"

"I said don't apologize. If you do something, mean it."

"But I know you're--"

"Fuck me, Dani."

She grinned. "That's what you were hoping for, at least."

I chuckled. "There she is."

"There who is?"

"That playful, confident woman stuffed into the body of a self-conscious college girl."

She sighed as I slid down underneath the comforter with her.

"You have to learn to own your actions, no matter how they make others feel. You can't be so scared to walk around in this world. It'll eat you alive if you are."

She nodded. "I know."

"You got uncomfortable. I saw that and stopped. Don't apologize for that. Talk to me about why. Don't apologize. Just explain so I can better understand."

"I'm a virgin, Max."

She blurted out the words so quickly it made my eyes widen.

"Well, that's one way to do it, I guess."

She sighed. "I'm sorry. I just--I've never been in this situation before and I've never felt these things for anyone before and I've never had my clothes taken off or anything before and it just--just got--"

I let her ramble until the words finally came to her.

"I got overwhelmed and wasn't sure what came next," she said.

I nodded. "I wasn't sure, but I had a feeling."

"When did you have that feeling?"

"The first time I kissed you."

She sighed. "That bad?"

I snickered. "Trust me, I've known plenty of experienced girls who were terrible kissers."

She winced. "How many girls have you been with?"

"Bad question to ask."

"I mean, you know I'm a virgin. Wouldn't hurt to know what number I am."

"Dani…"

"Max."

I snickered. "There's that confident voice again."

She looked me straight in my eyes. "Am I just another number in your life?"

Her question caught me off-guard, and now I was the one struggling with what to say. So many things were swirling around in my head. Like how much of an oaf I was for letting my cock dictate what came next. I had asked her for too much too soon. This girl was nowhere near ready for the shit that came with me. Then again, I always got what I wanted.

And what I wanted was her.

"Dani, I don't know what you are to me right now."

Her voice fell flat. "How romantic."

"If you're looking for romance, you're barking up the wrong tree. I'm not a romantic guy. When I want something, I get it. Always. That's how I've lived my life, and it's gotten me this far."

"Are you happy, though?"

I took a chance and reached out for her. I let my hand settle into the natural crook of her waist and felt her skin jump underneath my touch. But she didn't pull away, so I scooted closer to her. Just to be nearer to her warmth.

"I don't think 'happy' is the word," I said.

She sighed. "Then what are you when you're with me? Why put all of this energy into a girl who you had a feeling couldn't give you what you usually want from women?"

I shrugged. "You... make me feel something."

"What do I make you feel?"

"I don't know, Dani. Usually, I don't feel anything. The other girls I'm with? They're a way to pass the time. I feel time passing with them. That's what I feel. But with you, it stops."

"What stops?"

"Time stops."

She blushed. "Oh."

I slid my hand over the swell of her hip and down the side of her thigh. She moved her leg toward me and I opened my own, capturing her against my body. With her leg pressed between my own, I rested against her. I scooted closer, letting my hand slide back over her waist and around to her back. She kept jumping. Flinching. But her skin puckered and her eyes fluttered closed. I kept shifting closer until her chest fell against my own. Until our bodies rested without a space between us.

Her eyes opened and found me again.

"Hey there."

She smiled. "Hi."

"Feeling better?"

She drew in a deep breath. "Much."

"Dani, I don't have answers for you. The only thing I know is that I want you. I've wanted you since the first moment I saw you. I don't know what it is, and I don't know what is different with you. I just know it is different."

"I feel the same way. I think that's part of why I'm so confused. I don't know why I'm drawn to you. I just am."

My hand slid up to her cheek. "So with all of that said, I'll wait as long as it takes. You're not ready for sex? Fine by me. There are plenty of other things I can do to your body that would make you scream, beautiful."

She blushed deeply. "Those might be fun."

I chuckled. "Trust me, they are fun. But if you really want this, if you really want to stick around, you need to listen to me. Are you listening?"

"Yes. I'm listening."

I quickly rolled her over onto her back and she yelped. I pinned her down with my pelvis, feeling her legs automatically spread for me. Her chest rose and fell with her short breaths. Her eyes widened as she stared back at me. I planted my hands firmly on either side of her body as I scooted closer. Tighter, between her legs. Until I sat on my knees and her ankles locked around me naturally.

As if her body were made for mine.

"Mark my words, Dani. You'll be mine. All of you.

Every inch of you. Until you're covered in me. And when I finally get what I want, I promise you one thing."

She cleared her throat. "What's that?"

I leaned my lips down to her ear. "You'll scream my name at the ceiling when I make you come."

I kissed the shell of her ear and heard her gasp. Her neck turned the cutest shade of pink as I dragged my lips softly along her skin. She turned her head and captured my lips. My tongue found hers as her hands landed on my back. I felt them roaming, her fingertips rumbling over my muscles. I sucked on her lower lip and dragged my stubble along her neck before I placed a kiss within the valley of her breasts. And when her nails dug into my skin, I laid my teeth into her. Sucking and licking. Softly chewing and biting.

Marking her left tit as mine already.

"Max," she moaned.

I nuzzled the teeth marks I left behind. "Dani?"

She fisted my hair. "Come back."

"As you wish."

I kissed up her chest. Up her neck. I kissed along her jawline again before coming across her cheek. I planted a kiss against the tip of her nose. The middle of her forehead. Then I pressed my hands back against the bed and lifted myself off her. I hovered over her, watching as her eyes grew wide with want, though I still saw confusion behind them.

"If you need me to wait, I'll wait. You have my word."

She nodded. "Okay."

"Just know that when the time comes, all of you is mine."

The smile that crossed her face made my cock leak heavily against my boxers. It made me wonder about all the things to come. How I'd take her virginity, make her come for the first time on my cock. It sent my head spiraling into a dark abyss I wasn't sure I'd ever return from until I finally felt her shaking around my girth.

"Deal," she said.

I'll hold you to it, too, Dani.

31

DANI

*T**alent acquisition is a little known fact in the human resources world. When the company first opens a job, it is up to Human Resources to utilize the resources around them to find who might be a nice fit for the job. For example…"*

I blinked as I drummed my pencil against my open textbook. The sound of an engine outside distracted me. Not a bike engine, of course. The backfiring of a car engine. So I got back to work.

For example, online websites where resumes are posted. It is not only HR's job to scout those who have public resumes and email them, but it is also up to HR and those working within the department to…

I heard the revving of an engine in the distance and perked my head up. The sound faded away before it crept closer. Which meant, back to reading.

…and those working within the department to…

"Wait, what?" I murmured.

It is not only HR's job to scout...

I sighed. "For example. Online websites where resumes are poste--why don't I remember any of this?"

I slammed my pencil against my textbook. I leaned back as my highlighter fell to the floor. With my fingers drumming against my desk, I looked up at the ceiling and tried to manage my frustrations enough to focus on schoolwork. I couldn't retain anything, though. Over half of my book was highlighted to try and make sure I understood what in the world I had to know for these upcoming tests of mine. Precursors to our midterm exams that were creeping up faster rather than slower.

But all I could focus on was Max.

I closed my eyes, letting my body prickle at the thought of him. Yesterday had been outstanding. The shopping. The bike ride. Feeling those clothes tight against my body.

Feeling Max take them off.

"Mmm," I hummed.

My mind drifted to Max's bed. How comfortable it felt. How quickly he pinned me underneath his body. How close I had come to giving him everything. His lips against my skin made me shiver. I felt my thighs warming as the memory of his teeth against my breast made me gasp. I sat up and pulled out my shirt, peeking underneath at the soft purple mark against my left breast.

It made me smile as I gazed upon it.

I had almost given myself over to him. I had

almost given him everything. And I would have, had I not stopped myself.

I still wanted to.

I didn't know how this happened to me. For years, I hadn't even looked in a boy's direction. I kept my nose in my novels and my mind in my education and paved a path for myself. I had a ten-year plan. A plan that required me to graduate. For heaven's sake, I had a vision board of my life, where I wanted to be and what I wanted out of my existence.

Nothing else mattered, though.

Not when Max took over my mind.

Have I lost my mind?

"I feel like I'm going crazy," I whispered to myself.

I stood up from my desk, walked over to my bed, and jumped up onto it. I snuggled down beneath the covers, ready to take a nap. Maybe I was tired. Maybe sleep was what I needed. Maybe that was the secret to all of this, getting more than five hours of sleep before waking up with Max on my brain. I closed my eyes and curled up into a ball. I felt the tight jeans against my skin stretching and screaming for mercy. I felt my shirt buckling and tightening around my waist. I even felt the leather belt around my waist pinching me at my sides.

All of it reminded me of him.

"Damn it," I murmured.

I slipped out of bed and ripped the clothes off. I tossed them to the floor and dug around in my dresser for my pajama pants. What was so wrong with my clothes, anyway? Why did he feel he had to change me? I kicked the outfit underneath my bed and pulled on my pajama pants and the baggiest sweatshirt I could find. I sighed with relief before I climbed back into bed, ready to relegate myself to a three-hour nap.

My mind still didn't stop.

How had I fallen for a guy so quickly? Especially a guy like Max. I knew he had skeletons in his closet. I knew he was bad news. I didn't know anything about him, or this gang he ran with. I didn't know what they did, or what kind of trouble they got into, or what kind of life they afforded themselves. I didn't know what Max had done in his past to warrant that stoic stare or that gruff voice. Or the scars I sometimes saw on his knuckles.

I don't care.

The truth froze me in my tracks. I curled up into a ball and stayed like that as I squeezed my eyes shut. If I could just fall asleep, it would all go away. The thoughts. The feelings. The warmth. The truth.

The fact that I wanted to be with him still.

I mean, he made me feel alive. Cherished. Protected. Beautiful. Every time he kissed me, I felt like the only girl in the world. Being spoiled like that yesterday? I'd never had that happen before. Mom always bought my clothes and brought them home for Dad to either nod yes to or toss out the door. Max was everything my life hadn't been. Max was everything I hadn't yet experienced.

And I wanted all of him.

You want to have sex with him.

I growled to myself as I turned over onto my back.

My eyes fell open effortlessly and I sighed with frustration. I wasn't tired. I was distracted. And I realized that all I really wanted was to have sex with the man. I wanted to know what that felt like—with him. I wanted to feel all of those things. With him.

Max was my person.

And I wanted to give him my virginity.

Dad would have a fit.

I didn't care, though. What used to be a threat was nothing more than an empty thought. As much as my parents talked to me about saving myself for marriage, that wasn't what I wanted for my life. I just wanted the right person to come along so I could have a positive experience. I'd heard so many horror stories about someone's first time going wrong. Being ripped away from them or being given up just to make a boy shut up about it. I didn't want things to be like that with me.

"It wouldn't be like that with Max," I whispered.

Sure, the man wasn't the definition of the 'right person.' At least not by society's standards. But I'd never wanted this with anyone else. I'd never even wanted to look at a boy like that before, until he came along. Until I laid eyes on him my first day back to campus and couldn't stop wondering about him.

He might not be Mr. Right. But he was my Mr. Right Now.

And just thinking about him turned me on so much.

I rolled over and faced the wall. My hands trembled as I thought about how I'd felt that bulge against my back yesterday. I felt how big he had grown. The man was a behemoth compared to me. Strong. Muscular. He could pick me up without hesitation with his bare hands. And I wondered if my first time with him would hurt. My toes curled at the thought. I didn't want it to hurt. Would he go slow if I asked?

Stop being so scared all the time, Dani.

I wasn't scared. I really wasn't! Well, maybe a little bit. But I wasn't scared about the sex as much as I was scared about what would come after. He stopped when he saw how uncomfortable I was. If I told him to go slow, I knew he would. I trusted that.

I didn't trust him to not discard me later, though.

He'd said it himself! All the other girls that had come before me were just ways to pass the time. What if we got to the end of things, and he decided I was just another way to pass the time? The thought hurt. It hurt so much it brought tears to my eyes. I sniffled and wiped them against my pillow, feeling more stupid than ever before.

"Why are you already crying, you weak little idiot?" I murmured to myself.

I didn't want him to cast me off to the side. I didn't want to be just another number to him. I wanted to be part of his life. I wanted to be at his side after it was all said and done. That meant I'd have to be part of his life somehow.

And that meant understanding more about this crew of his.

I rolled onto my back again and blinked. As my tears dried up, I drew in a deep breath. That settled it. The next time I saw him, I'd get to know more about

him. About his life. About his past. About his childhood, and the guys he rode with. Even if that meant
talking about his cousin, Benji. I grimaced at the
thought. I didn't want to talk about that jerk. But if it
got me closer to Max, I'd talk about anything.

Especially if it got me closer to him.

I wanted to be his. I wanted to be Max's woman.
The girl at his side and on the back of his bike. The
idea made me smile. My head rushed as the room
tilted over onto itself. Yes. That was it. I'd talk with him
about becoming his, just like he'd said I would be. I
wanted a definition around that. I wanted to know
what that meant to him. Because if it meant what I
wanted it to?

Then I was all his.

"Hey there, roomie!"

Hannah waltzed into the dorm room and I drew in
a short breath. "Heya."

Hannah stood beside me. "Nice to see you resting
for once. Wanna go for coffee? My treat."

I turned toward her. "Can you give me ten minutes
to change?"

"You mean you aren't going dressed as you are?"

I thought about the clothes under the bed. "Nope.
I want to show you something new I bought."

"Wait, you went shopping without me? Ah! Dani!
I'm so hurt. Why would you do such a thing?"

I threw the covers off me. "Trust me, you're going
to like this outfit. A lot."

"Then thrill me with it, sunshine."

As I pulled the outfit from underneath my bed, I

already heard Hannah gasping, clapping her hands, and cheering me on as I jumped into the skin-tight jeans. I knew I'd be asked a lot of questions, but I didn't care. I wanted to talk to Hannah about this. I wanted to tell her what was going on.

I just didn't want to dump it all on her at once.

32

MAX

I sat on the rolling seat and cranked the wrench against my bike. It was making a funny sound, and I had been trying to chase that shit down all fucking morning. Every time the engine revved, it sounded like a fucking tin can was rattling around somewhere. It pissed me off.

"Come on," I grunted.

I finally got the nut off and tossed it into a rusted tin can. Taking a motorcycle apart was always fun. If it was for restoration purposes. Doing it to actually chase down an issue was bullshit. It felt more like work than anything else. Still, I busted a damn sweat sitting there, pulling off metal side panels and setting them down on towels so the concrete slab of the double garage I'd laid last year wouldn't scuff up the newest paint job.

"Having troubles?"

I paused as my father's voice rang in my ears. I slowly slid my eyes over toward the door of the garage and pivoted my entire chair to face him. I saw him standing by a completely blacked-out car. Very much his style. He leaned against the door in a suit that matched the car: all black except for the blood red pocket square against his chest.

When two burly men got out of the back seat, I stood up.

"Father."

He nodded. "Max."

I pointed to the two guys. "Something wrong?"

Dad snickered. "Oh, these guys? They're my associates. You know how it goes."

You mean bodyguards. "Yeah. I do."

They were two new guys this time. Not the regular men I usually saw with him. They both loomed in the sunlight, casting a hazy shadow over my father as he closed the car door. He walked to the entrance of the garage, just barely crossing the threshold before stopping again. As I dropped my wrench, Dad nodded.

"So I hear you've been spending some time apart from the boys."

I blinked. "Have I missed any meetings I didn't know about?"

He clasped his hands together. "I don't know. Have you?"

I shrugged. "Nope."

"So this is all hearsay?"

"Far as I'm concerned."

He nodded. "All right. That sounds acceptable."

"Anything else?"

"Let's say, for scenario's sake, you have been spending time apart from the boys."

"For scenario's sake."

He took a step toward me. "Yes."

"You don't have to come any closer."

"I can do as I please."

"Not on this property you can't."

He snickered. "Pretty sure I own it."

I grinned. "Pretty sure you've forgotten that John and I refinanced it."

His face fell. "Why have you been spending time away from the crew?"

My defenses instantly went up. "What makes you think I've been doing that?"

"Let's call it a little birdie in the tree."

"I'm assuming you mean Benji."

"We don't have to name names."

"If you don't think I see the game you're playing, you've clearly underestimated me. I'm not spending as much time at the house, so John is no longer a player in your schemes to keep an eye on me. So you enlist the help of my cousin. Benji. Who you find out has been seeing more of me since I've been around campus. He comes whining to you about something, probably because I won't initiate him--"

He took another step toward me. "Yes, let's talk about that for a second. Why not make Benji a member?"

"Other than the fact that you can manipulate him easier than you can John? He's better than us."

"Enlighten me on what that means."

I took a step toward him. "He's got a real future ahead of him that has nothing to do with your influence."

I held my father's gaze as a smile broke out on his face. I hated seeing him smile. Every time he did, I saw myself in him. It's why I didn't look in mirrors. It's why I had mine in my bathroom covered up with a fucking sheet. I hated looking in the mirror and seeing that man smiling back at me.

But there he was. With that sadistic smile I had inherited.

"My, my. She must really have you knotted up inside."

I quirked an eyebrow. "She?"

"Hmm? Oh, yes. Um... Dani. That's the name. Dani Young."

I tensed. Holy shit, I didn't even know her last name. This was bad. Very, very bad. Benji had gone and flapped his fucking jowls like the asshole he was, and now Dani was in my father's crosshairs. That was never a safe place to be. More people than not died once my father set their sights on them. A chill worked its way down my spine as my father closed the distance between us. I stood my ground, keeping my face as stoic as I could. But I knew my silence had already given so much away.

"You've fallen for a girl who's messed up your priorities, son."

I licked my lips. "I've fallen for no one."

"I told you this gallivanting around with strange

women would catch up with you soon enough. How do you think you and your brother came along?"

I grinned. "When a psychopath and a drug addict love one another *very* much--"

"Even the strongest of men can be deterred by beauty!"

His roaring voice bounced off the walls of the garage as his spittle hit me in the face. In any other moment, with any other person, I would've strangled the asshole. But killing my father came with consequences that would get everyone else around me killed. Hell, even hurting my father would get people killed.

Dani included, now.

"I don't like this. I don't like her, and I don't like you. Keep your head in the game, Maxwell. There are big jobs coming down the pipeline. Massive ones that will pay you more than Mr. Dean ever could have. Work through your pitiful anger and screw your head on straight."

I grinned. "How is our duck-and-run client anyway?"

Dad raised his finger into my face. "Clients are counting on me to provide quality men. As in you and those Red Thorns. I established that crew from nothing. I endured torture after torture to establish this gang. To run it as I saw fit. With morals and an ethical code that got shit done. And ever since it got handed to you, the only thing that's happened is that the moral fiber of this crew has dropped."

I shrugged. "Or changed."

He licked his teeth. "I will not have the president

of this club throwing his future away because he wants to screw around with some college cunt on my dime. Women are a distraction. Nothing else. Fuck her, get rid of her, and get back to being president."

My body hummed with fury. I felt my nostrils flaring as my father's eyes raked down me. He took a step back and adjusted his suit coat. As if I had somehow knocked it off-kilter with my voracious stare. I didn't want to make a scene. Not with two massive brutes packing all sorts of heat just outside my fucking garage. Because I knew my father. And complicating Dani's life to keep her away from me wasn't something beyond the realm of his abilities. The last thing I wanted was for my girl to get dragged into this shit sto-

-

My girl?

Since when the hell had Dani become my girl?

"Do we have a deal?"

Dad's voice ripped me from my confused mind. "I can take care of my own affairs."

He chuckled. "Or maybe you just need something else to occupy your time."

"What does that mean?"

Dad snapped his fingers. "Go ahead."

"Wait. Wait a second. What--hey!"

The two goons standing by the car waltzed their way into the garage. My garage. With my personal things hanging on the walls. I watched them grab everything from pictures to tools and throw them onto the floor.

"Hey! Cut it the fuck out!"

I watched them tip over my tool chest, and the contents came spilling out. Nails and bolts. Hammers and wrenches of all shapes and sizes. My anger grew out of control. I didn't even see red. I simply saw black. My anger blacked me out as my fists started swinging. I felt bones beneath my hands. I heard men growling. Grunting. I felt something around my neck before I bit down into the skin just beyond my chin. I stomped on bones that crunched as growls poured forth. And it was all I could do to keep myself from drawing the weapon that sat right there on my hip.

Until I felt a hand at the back of my neck.

The pain that ricocheted through my forehead snapped me out of it. I groaned as my vision slowly came back to the light. And when I saw the wall coming at me again, I held my hands out. I stopped the bashing from happening again as the world tilted around me. Then a pair of hands gripped my shoulders.

Before my father's face came into view.

"You listen to me and you listen good, son. John would've never pulled this kind of shit with me. He knew what loyalty looked like. He knew when to buckle down and work, and when to fuck off in his spare time. He knew what family looked like before--"

"--before you sent him out to get shot," I hissed.

Dad's eyes widened and I braced myself for another fight. His goonies were pulling themselves off the floor, blood dripping down their faces. Good. They needed to know what the hell came with my father if they were going to keep riding around in cars with that maniac. However, it shocked me when my father released me.

Especially since he stayed quiet.

I narrowed my eyes and dabbed at my forehead. I had blood on my palm, but I didn't feel dizzy. That was good. No concussion, possibly. I did feel blood trickling down my face, though. It would definitely need stitches.

I kept my eyes locked on my father. He stared down his nose at me, as if he were somehow better than all of us. When really, he was the worst of us all. He kept his mouth shut as he backtracked to his car, refusing to turn his back on me. Smart. Because if I had to, I'd kill the man in a heartbeat.

Maybe.

Possibly.

Once I can get Dani's name out of his mouth.

"We'll talk soon, son," he said.

"Not if I can help it," I murmured.

He and his bodyguards got into the blacked-out car and left, leaving me with new bruises, a fucking mess to clean up, and an anger that made me quake with every step I took.

33

DANI

I smoothed my hands over the black T-shirt and sighed. I don't know. It just didn't look right on me. T-shirts were for looser jeans. The tight shirt with the tight pants didn't fit me well. I felt too cramped up. Too stifled in all the tightness.

I ripped the T-shirt over my head.

"All right. Time to find something else," I murmured.

I walked over to the few things I had hanging up on hangers and tried to make a decision. I wanted to make the right decision, because when I woke up this morning, I found a note slid under my door. It had nothing but a phone number on it and the letter 'M.' And that started my day off better than any cup of coffee could have.

Max left me a note.

I was lucky that I had gotten up before Hannah this morning for classes. If she had found that note, there would've been so many questions I still wasn't prepared to answer. I ended up chickening out at the coffee shop the other day. I had planned on telling her about Max and everything that had transpired. If anything, just to get her take on things. But I'd gotten too paranoid to tell her. Why?

Because even in my head, it sounded insane.

What in the world was I supposed to do? Tell my roommate that the jerk-off biker guy wasn't terrible and now, after a few weeks, I suddenly wanted to sleep with him? I mean, even Hannah would've thrown a fit at that. I decided not to tell her anything. I decided I didn't want anyone talking any sort of sense into me. I wanted to ride this rollercoaster as long as it would last. Because it was the most excitement I'd ever felt in my life.

And wherever it led--whatever consequences became of it--I'd take it like a woman.

"There we go," I said with a smile.

I reached into the back of my closet and pulled out a white blouse. It was the only kind of blouse like this I owned. Yet another secret purchase my mother had stuffed into my things before sending me back to campus. But for this particular occasion, it fit what I wanted to do. I slipped the blouse off the hanger and over my head. The flowing fabric caressed my skin instead of adhering to it, and I felt much more comfortable. The tight, black skinny jeans looked great with the fluttering blouse made of soft, silky materials that moved and swayed every time I did. I slipped the leather belt out from my belt loops, since I really didn't need it. And after sliding the leather coat Max had purchased for me over my shoulders, I smiled at myself in the mirror.

Perfect.

Max and I were going out on a date. A true, bonafide date. Not my first date, but it might as well have been. I was nervous, but in a good way. Adrenaline coursed through my veins as I tried to figure out what kind of shoes to wear with this outfit.

I didn't seem to have any that looked right, though.

I reached for my phone and turned on the screen. Crap. Max would be here in less than ten minutes. I had no idea where we were going, so I hoped I had nailed the look for the night. If I could just find some shoes that weren't my darn tennis shoes. Eight o'clock was looming. I knew I'd hear the sound of his bike outside any minute.

"What are you wearing?"

Hannah's voice stilled me as I whipped around, seeing her standing in the doorway.

"Hey! How were classes today?" I asked.

She quirked an eyebrow. "I've never seen that outfit before."

I looked down. "Uh, yeah. It's new. Just trying out some different things."

"I like it. It suits you."

I snickered. "Yeah. Much better than the black T-shirt I had on earlier. It feels more… me."

She furrowed her brow. "Uh huh."

I paused. "What?"

My roommate walked into our room and I took a

step back. Uh oh. She had that look on her face. She knew something was up. She knew I wasn't telling her the whole truth. I felt myself panicking. What in the world was I supposed to do to get out of this situation?

"You have new jeans," she said.

I nodded. "Yep."

"And a new jacket."

"Mm-hmm."

"Is that a new top, too?"

I snickered. "Something Mom snuck into my clothing bag after Labor Day. I found it after unpacking all my stuff."

She licked her lips. "You look great, Dani."

My eyebrows rose. "Really?"

She nodded. "Yeah. You look hot. I mean, I've never--I didn't know you could pull off edgy."

"Edgy?"

"Yeah. I mean, look at you! Rockin' the leather coat. The tight jeans. Wait--is that eyeliner you have on?"

I paused. "I might have borrowed it from you. But don't worry, I didn't use much at all. And I washed the brush before--"

Her gasp cut me off as she pointed at me.

"You're going on a date!"

My jaw fell open. "I--you--what?"

She pointed at me. "Danika Young, you're going on a date and you didn't tell me about it!"

I held my hands up in mock surrender. "I swear, I'm innocent!"

She charged me until my back fell against the wall.

"You tell me right now who it is. You're a terrible liar. Who is he? What's he like? And why in the world did you go shopping without me?"

"You really think this outfit looks good?"

Hannah quickly stepped back and pulled me with her. With her hands holding mine, she turned me around, watching how my blouse fluttered. She released my hands and twirled her finger around, signaling for me to spin for her. With my arms out while I held my breath, I did as she asked.

My eyes found hers. "I feel like it might be a little too much. Like maybe I'm trying too hard?"

Hannah bit her lower lip. "You doing anything with your hair?"

"I… was just going to leave it down."

"That doesn't really work with a coat like that. It's going to get trapped underneath the collar and it's going to be a mess. Rule of thumb for a date: if the top or your coat has a collar, your hair is better off up. Come here, I've got a great style that would--"

"It's not the collar or anything. It's the helmet."

I blurted out the words before I could stop myself. And that caught my roommate's attention.

"I'm sorry, did you just say 'helmet'?"

Dang it. "I… uh…"

She narrowed her eyes. "Dani?"

"Yes?"

"Who are you going on a date with tonight?"

I shrugged. "Just a guy."

She wagged her finger at me. "Nuh-uh. That's not gonna fly. You just said 'helmet.'"

"I just meant--"

"And you're wearing a leather jacket."

"Fall is coming quickly. It's getting cold."

Hannah gasped again and I knew I was sunk.

"Are you going out with *him*?" she squealed.

I winced at the high-pitched sound. "Who?"

"Oh, don't you dare, Danika. Don't you even try. You know exactly who I'm talking about."

"Hannah, don't freak out."

"Oh, my God! You are! Mr. Sexy Leather Biker Baddie! You're going out on a date with him! I didn't even know you two were talking. How in the world have you been keeping this from me? I feel so hurt. I thought we were friends. When is he supposed to be here?"

I blinked. "Don't call him that, please."

"So is that who you're going on a date with?"

"Hannah."

"You have to say it."

"He's going to be here any minute."

"Is the leather-clad sculpted mound of muscle on the bike who you're going out with tonight?"

I paused. "What did you just say?"

She sighed. "Okay, I'm assuming it is. Now, for my next question. Is this the best idea?"

I rolled my eyes. "I have to leave."

She gripped my wrist. "Hey, cut me some slack. I'm just now figuring out about this and I'm trying to make sure my best friend's okay."

"I'm going to be fine. Thanks for your help."

She spun me around. "He's not a raging criminal or shit like that, is he?"

I sighed. "He's not what you think he is, Hannah. And I have to go. We can talk about this later. But right now, I need some shoes and I need to get downstairs."

"Oh! I have the perfect pair. Here. You can borrow mine."

She rushed over to her closet and I spun around, reached for the floral-printed scarf my father got me for my birthday last year, and tied it around my neck. A pop of pattern to the muted tones of the white and the black. Hannah turned around with heeled boots in her hands and sighed. She smiled at the scarf before she tossed the boots to me, and my eyes widened at the heels.

"Are you crazy? On the back of a bike?"

She giggled. "Put them on and get out of here. They're only three inches high. You'll be fine. And as payment, I expect details when you get back."

I leaned against my bed and pulled the boots up my legs. I zipped them up, figuring they'd fit me oddly, or be uncomfortable. But the heeled black boots actually made me feel more powerful. I nodded at Hannah as she held the door open for me, leaning against it with a crooked grin on her face.

"Be safe, beautiful," she said with a wink.

I shook my head as I headed out into the hallway. I took the stairs to try and get used to the heels on my feet. The last thing I wanted to do was trip and fall in these suckers right in front of Max. Hannah was right, though.

They weren't hard to navigate. They weren't much taller than the one pair of heels I owned, so it didn't take long for me to feel stable in them. I really hoped Hannah didn't stay up worrying about me. The last thing I needed was someone blowing up my phone just to figure out what I was doing. Because I knew Max would never hurt me. I knew he'd never put me in danger.

I trusted that more than anything.

I trust him more than anything.

"Rein it in a bit, Dani," I murmured to myself.

The sound of the bike engine in the distance made me shake. A smile broke out across my face as I pushed out the main glass door and walked across the lawn to stand underneath the broken, flickering lamp light. The engine grew closer, roaring and revving off in the distance. I checked to make sure my phone was in my jacket pocket, along with my wallet and dorm keys. Then I zipped the pockets and fluffed my hair one last time, hoping and praying I looked all right.

My ribcage rumbled as Max grew closer. I smiled when he turned the corner, making his way to me. He puttered to a stop right in front of me, his hands poised to pull his helmet off. When he did, I wasted no time in leaning in to give him a kiss before squeezing him in the biggest hug I could.

I felt him wince.

"You okay?"

Max chuckled. "Never better. Ready to go?"

I pulled back and furrowed my brow at him. "You sure you're okay?"

His gaze slipped down my body. "I'm great, and you're beautiful."

I blushed. "Not too much?"

He wrapped his arm around me and pulled me close.

"Never too much."

His lips captured mine again as my hand landed on his cheek. Our tongues came together as his bike vibrated between his legs, calling for me to get on and forecasting the fun tonight would bring us both. I moaned softly down the back of his throat. Our tongues did battle while his cologne filled my nostrils. I felt his arm tighten around me, making me groan against his lips. As if he couldn't get me close enough. A sensation I adored more than anything else.

Then, once he finally pulled back, he flashed me that charming smile of his.

"Your helmet's in the storage compartment. Get it and get on."

And he sure as hell didn't have to tell me twice.

34

MAX

The feeling of her arms wrapped around me. The way she leaned her helmeted head between my shoulder blades. The way her legs clenched on to me. It felt right, having her on the back of my bike. And the way she squealed and laughed as we banked tight corners made me smile.

I never smiled like that with anyone, except her.

I came up to the last light, the one I had to take a left at in order to get to our final destination. But I found myself staying straight instead. I wanted a few more minutes of her to myself, on the back of my bike. Clinging to me, her laughter filling the space around us as I revved the engine and blew through stop signs.

"Woo hoo! Yeah!"

I chuckled at her bombastic sounds.

You're going soft, Max.

I pushed the thought from my head as I drove farther away from our destination. More time to get back there meant more time to spend with her all to myself, instead of allowing the general public to invade our personal time together. I had half a mind to take her back to my place, to shut her up in my room and tease her with my tongue until she begged me to take what was rightfully mine. I knew I could do it. I knew I could coax it from her. I knew I could give her the time of her life. A moment she'd never regret.

Your father's on to something.

I growled as I whipped a U-turn in the middle of the road. I heard Dani gasp as she held me tighter, her hands fisting my shirt. I could've sworn I felt her fingernails rake against my abs, and it caused me to growl. Heat rushed through my body. A need for her against me rose up the back of my spine. No, I wasn't going soft. My father wasn't right.

Dani was exactly what I needed in my life.

This college girl was beauty incarnate for me. Untouched by the darkness of my life. Untouched by any darkness, really. She was safe. Cute. A breath of fresh air. Pleasantly ignorant to the crime that crept up into the corners of poor old Ann Arbor. A blind citizen that still enjoyed something as simple as getting coffee without having to look over her shoulder.

I liked that about her.

You love that about her.

I gnashed my teeth as I pressed onward.

Dani was everything I didn't deserve. She was everything I longed for, and everything I dreamt about at night. All wrapped up in one innocent, clumsy package. She didn't understand darkness. She didn't understand the underworld. She didn't understand abuse and mental illness and all of the things that crept up into the lives of the people around me on a regular basis. To her, the worst thing imaginable was a stormy night with no power. Or the possibility of being broken down on the side of the road.

I enjoyed her youthful ignorance and her bountiful laughter. I enjoyed everything about her, because she was mine.

Even if only for a little while.

I grinned at the thought. I'd make her mine. Even if she didn't stick around for the long haul. Hell, even if she didn't stick around into next week. I'd find a way to get what I wanted. To show her exactly how a man treated a woman like her. She deserved that much. She deserved to have that kind of a bar set in her life. How a man should spoil her. Kiss her. Whisk her away, and make her feel alive. She deserved a man who knew how to rile her up in bed. Who knew how to throw her over the edge until she begged for mercy. And then did it again.

Dani deserved every kind of beauty this world had to offer.

And I was determined to give as much of it to her as possible.

We rode back up to the light and I took the turn I needed to. I was still disappointed at the ride not taking longer than it had. But I tried my best not to show it. I pulled up to the curb and parked in an open space right in front of the pub. With its flickering neon sign hanging crookedly on the brick façade, I put down my kickstand and cut the engine to my bike. Even slid my helmet off to draw in the all-too-familiar scent of stale cigarette smoke and frying grease.

"Brick's?"

I slipped off my bike and watched Dani take her helmet off.

"Yep."

She loosened the scarf around her neck. "Well. Uh. This is… not what I expected."

I heard the nerves in her voice, and it made me chuckle.

"This is my clubhouse."

She blinked. "Your what?"

"My clubhouse. This is where my crew and I socialize. And I want you to see what it's like being me."

The sweetest smile tugged at her lips. "Really?"

I shrugged. "We're here, aren't we?"

She slid off my bike. "Well, okay then. I'm honored. But you're sure I'm not going to stick out like a sore thumb in a place like this?"

I chuckled. "Oh, you're *definitely* going to stick out, Daddy's girl. But that's all right. I don't date women who blend in anyway."

She tucked her helmet under her arm. "Date, huh? And here I thought you were scared of the word."

I smiled. "Guess even I can surprise."

I held my arm out for her to get in front of me, and together, we started into the place. The club had bought this ratty, rundown pub years ago. Closed it to the public, mostly. Except for a few occasions where the squirrliest of individuals came out and filled our registers with their blood money. But for the most part, this place was privately owned by the Red Thorns. Specifically, by whoever the president was at the time.

My father had owned it when he ran this crew. It was then passed to my brother when he took over. And once I stepped up to the plate, it was transferred to me.

I owned this cigarette-smoke filled dump now.

With my hand on Dani's lower back, I escorted her through the fully-tinted glass door. When I walked through the entrance, a chorus of voices rang out my name.

"Max!"

"Maxy-boy! The hell have you been!?"

"Max! What's shakin'? The fuck you got going on lately?"

"Long time no see, asshole. How ya doin', Max?"

And when I looked down at Dani, I saw her lips curled up into a full-blown smile.

"Looks like you're popular," she yelled up at me.

I winked. "Comes with the territory."

Dani tucked herself close to my side, so I took the liberty of wrapping my arm around her shoulders. Signaling to all the men staring at her that she was already spoken for. I didn't mind, either. She fit nicely at my side. The perfect height for me to rest my arm around as we fell in step with one another. Left foot. Right foot. Left, then right. All the way up to the bar, with all eyes on us.

"Whatcha havin'?" the bartender asked.

I looked down at Dani. "Well?"

316 | REBEL HART

She licked her lips. "Um, do you have something that isn't beer?"

The bartender quirked an eyebrow. "Seriously?"

I glared at him. "Answer her question."

The man sighed. "We got cider and Coke. Some vodka, too."

Dani nodded. "Got any rum?"

The bartender looked at me and I nodded my head.

"Got a personal stash in the back, yeah."

Dani smiled. "I'll have a rum and Coke, then."

I nodded. "And I'll have myself a couple of beers."

The bartender shooed us away and I led Dani over to a table to sit with me. She seemed nervous. Her eyes kept darting around everywhere, as if she were on her guard, wondering who might walk in and cause trouble at any second. It was a very unnatural look on her. And it was a look I wanted to wash away. She was safe with me, wherever we went. No matter where we were, or who surrounded us.

I put her back to the door and sat across from her, just in case someone decided to come through those front doors and kick up a stink.

"Am I doing okay?"

Her hushed voice was almost swallowed up by the massive men behind her roaring with laughter. But it didn't stop me from registering her question. Nor did it stop me from taking her hand to try and soothe away her fears.

"There's nothing to worry about in a place like

this. You're safe. None of these men will hurt you. You have my word on that."

She chewed on her lower lip. "I'm sorry. It's just-- my father's told me about places *exactly* like this. And he always says there are many things to worry about."

"Like what?"

She sighed. "Promise you won't get upset?"

I shook my head. "Not if you're honest with me."

She nodded. "He says these are the kinds of places where drugs are dealt. Where unsavory people come to dump money they shouldn't have on them, or hook up with others to commit crimes. He always told me to stay away from places like these, for my safety."

Smart man. "Anything else?"

She paused. "Is he right?"

"About?"

"About there being drugs and all kinds of criminals that come in and out of these places?"

"Do you want a logical answer? Or an honest one?"

"There's a difference?"

I nodded. "There is."

She licked her lips. "An honest one. Seriously, Max. Do I have something like that to worry about?"

A devilish smile crossed my cheeks. "Not when you're on my arm, you don't."

35

DANI

"Welcome back, Max. We've missed you. Who's your friend?"

I looked up at the woman who had approached our table and I couldn't take my eyes off her. The painted-on leather pants. The biker boots she wore, laced all the way up her shins. The red tank top she spilled out of and the matching red lipstick she had on her over-sized lips. She looked like a punk Barbie doll. Her hair was curled and teased, and there was a choker around her neck. Multiple rings sparkled on her fingers as she poised the pen she held over her pad, ready to take our orders.

I'd never seen anyone like her before.

"Now, you know you don't miss a crotchety man like me," Max said.

The woman giggled. "You're the head of this place, you know."

I furrowed my brow. "The head?"

Max winked at me. "Hungry?"

"What does she mean?"

"Do you want food, Dani?"

He said my name, but it was a bit sharp. Curt. And the look behind his eyes told me to stop what I was doing. I wasn't sure why he wouldn't answer my question, but I had a feeling it had something to do with this bar. How everyone treated him. How he seemed like the big man on campus.

What aren't you telling me? "Uh, I'll have whatever you're having."

He grinned. "Sure about that?"

I shrugged. "What else is there?"

The woman clicked her tongue. "We got burgers, spicy wings, chicken sandwiches, and hot dogs. Anything trip your trigger?"

"Oh, a hot dog sounds nice."

"Great. Anything on it?"

A man walked up to us. "You should get one with what you want, then get one with everything. Trust me, it won't disappoint."

My eyes panned over to the gruff-looking man that had come to stand beside the waitress. He slapped her butt and she squealed, then swatted at his chest playfully, as if it hadn't offended her at all. My eyes widened as Max chuckled. The man wore a faded leather jacket with patches on every joint I could see. He had tattoos creeping up the side of his neck, trying to intrude upon his jawline. He had a scar clear across his left eye, almost slicing it in half. And the dastardly grin he had on his face made my toes curl.

Not in a good way, either.

"Oh-okay, then. One hot dog with ketchup, mustard, and chili, and one with everything."

The waitress scribbled it down. "Fries? Onion rings?"

The man put his hand on my shoulder. "Always do the onion rings here."

Max growled. "Off. Now."

The man jerked his hand away as if he'd touched a hot stove, and my eyes widened even further. I had no idea what in the world I had just stepped into, and I didn't know how to feel about it. I mean, I was used to house parties my mother threw and holiday parties in banquet halls my father hosted for our families. Decorated cakes and champagne flutes and impeccably bright colors on the walls. This place was so far from my reality. So far from what I had been raised in.

I couldn't stop myself from staring at it all.

"Oh! And just to let you two know, we got dessert now. A nice slice of chocolate cake with ice cream. Let me know if you want some."

The waitress's voice ripped me from my trance. "I will, thank you."

Max nodded. "That'll be all. You too, Granger."

The gruff man harrumphed to himself before walking away, but not before slapping the waitress on her tuckus again. I shook my head slowly as men came and went in my view. Tall men. Short men. Fat men and muscular men. Men with tattoos running up and down their arms. Men with tattoos on their faces. Men with chains dangling from their jeans and leather jackets of all shapes, colors, and shines.

And the women.

The women were mesmerizing.

There was another waitress walking around, but she was dressed completely differently. She had on baggy black jeans with a chain slid through the belt loops, barely holding thcm up on her hips while her tight top fell off her shoulder. Almost as if she had cut the neck open herself. Her exposed shoulder was covered in a brightly colored geometric tattoo that disappeared underneath her shirt. And when she turned to look at me, the scar on her chin caught my eye.

"Her ex," Max said.

I whipped my head around to face him. "What?"

"The scar. On her chin. Her ex gave her that scar."

My jaw dropped open. "Wait, seriously?"

He snickered. "Don't feel sorry for her. Man's eating through a tube for the rest of his life for it."

I paused. "How do you know that?"

He shrugged. "She likes bragging about it."

"Wait, *she* did that to him?"

"Trust me, the girls in here can hold their own. Even the ones who walk around in heels. Don't let them fool you for a second."

I didn't know whether to feel horrified or proud.

"It's pretty chaotic in here."

Max slid his foot against mine under the table. "Yep. Gets pretty wild some nights."

"But it's fun."

"You think so?"

I nodded. "Yeah. I mean, that guy kept slapping her on the butt and she didn't think anything of it. Is it always like that? So… carefree like that?"

He chuckled. "Pretty much. The girls draw their own lines with the guys, and they have permission to rectify a situation any way they see fit if it's crossed."

"Permission from who?"

He shrugged. "The crew."

I paused. "I don't get it."

"My crew owns this bar. When I said this was our clubhouse, I wasn't kidding. The crew, as a collective, owns this place. We keep it running with the money we make, and it works for us."

"Is it ever open to the public?"

"Eh, when we want to open it. Sometimes, we throw parties. Invite people we know. Rake in some money that way. But mostly it's a safe haven for us. A place to come and enjoy drinks, some food, and good company without expectations and shit."

I smiled. "That sounds wonderful."

"Yeah, it's a pretty nice set up."

"Hey! Max! Got a second?"

The foreign voice pulled my attention upward and I saw a gangly man approach the table. He looked like a pipe cleaner with eyes. And he had the most gorgeous woman at his side. She kept sucking on his neck and leaving brown lipstick marks everywhere. Her hands kept traveling over his torso while she whispered in his ear. And each time she did, a goofy grin crossed his face.

It made me wonder what she was saying to him.

"Ralph. Nice to see you. And who's this girl hanging off you?" Max asked.

Pipe Cleaner smiled. "This here's Marcie. Marcie, say hi."

"Hi."

She wasted no time in going back to covering him with kisses after the momentary break to socialize.

Max chuckled. "Well, nice to meet you, Marcie. What can I do for you, Ralph?"

"Just wanted to come by and shake your hand! Been a little while since you've dropped in. We were all beginnin' to think we had to send out a search party or some shit like that."

I snickered. "That might be my fault. Sorry."

Max took my hand over the table. "Never apologize for something like that."

My gaze found his stare and he winked at me. He really liked doing that in here. And I enjoyed how it felt. A flush trickled down my neck as Marcie giggled. I loved how this all felt. How kind and open everyone was. How things didn't seem so taboo here.

So different from how I was raised.

"Hey, maybe the four of us could get together for a date or somethin' sometime."

Pipe Cleaner's voice pulled me from my trance. "I wouldn't mind. Max?"

He shrugged. "We'll think about it. You know how it is with our schedules."

Marcie giggled. "Boy, do I ever."

She gripped the man's chin and pulled his lips

down to hers. The two of them started making out right at our booth, and my eyebrows slowly rose on my forehead. I peeked over at Max and he just watched them with a curious grin on his face and a twinkle in his eye. Was this normal? Did people just make out while others watched?

"All right, you two. Get a room. Can't get your nasty fluids on our food now." Max laughed. "Ah, I can smell the onion rings now."

I pulled my hand back. "Was that our waitress?"

I watched her shove through the two lovebirds with two massive plates of food. The pipe cleaner and his lipstick-riddled girlfriend finally stepped off to the side, seemingly oblivious to everything that was happening. The two hot dogs with onion rings dropped down in front of me, making my mouth water before I reached for my drink.

And when I looked over at Max's plate, I was glad I hadn't ordered what he had.

"I can smell how hot that is," I said.

He rubbed his hands together. "And it's about to be in my stomach. Honey?"

The waitress smiled. "Keep the drinks coming, I got it. You two enjoy, and let me know if you want some of that dessert later to soak up all this fat and alcohol."

"You two got room over here?"

Max held his arms out. "Rupert!"

"And this must be the girl who's got your attention so bad."

Max laughed with joy. "John. Nice to see you out

and about. Here. We'll scoot. You two have a seat with us."

The one named Rupert had such bright red hair I could have never missed him. But the one called John walked with a cane. He had kind of a crooked stature to him, and as he sat down, I heard him grumbling and groaning beneath his breath. While Max and the redhead hugged, I studied the man who sat down beside me, taking in his green eyes, the slope of his nose, and the strength of his jawline.

"Yeah, we look too much alike, don't we?" he asked.

I blinked. "Are you and Max related somehow?"

Max interrupted. "That's my older brother, John."

John stuck out his hand. "And you are…?"

I shook his hand. "Dani. Hey. It's really nice to meet you. I wasn't sure you actually existed."

The redhead snickered. "Doesn't shock me. Hey! Sweetheart!"

The waitress yelled back, "You hold your horses! I'll be there in a second, Fire-dick!"

Everyone in the place roared with laughter. Even Rupert. I wasn't sure why. Didn't she just insult him?

John leaned over to my ear. "Don't worry. You'll get used to it."

I nodded. "Thanks for the update."

"So what's got you out and about today, John? Picking up pain meds? Or you tired of all those spaghetti dinners you choke down every night?" Max asked.

John shrugged. "I don't know. Figured I'd come out

after picking up my vitamins and maybe try to steal your girl in the process."

"Wait, what?" I asked.

Rupert roared with laughter. "Good luck. Max has been after this one for a while."

John grinned. "You don't have to tell me twice. He's practically stopped bringing girls home since this one came into his life."

Max took a pull of his beer. "Not my fault I found the cream of the crop and you're stuck with my sloppy seconds."

John pointed at him. "That only happened twice."

Max chuckled. "And the first time was because the girl was still so drunk that she wandered into your room instead of back to mine."

I held up my hand. "Uh, hi. I'm right here."

Rupert snickered. "Yeah, Max. She's right here."

John bent back down to my ear. "It was three years ago. Don't worry about it."

A guy piped up from behind me. "Oh! Tell her about the one who tracked you down at the club meeting!"

The entire room groaned as I quirked an eyebrow at Max.

"What happened now?" I asked.

He picked up a chicken wing. "I'm gonna need some more booze for that story."

"Because you fucked her anyway? Or because you're sitting with a girl you want to fuck but haven't yet and you're trying to save your chances?" I asked.

Max's eyes connected with mine as the pub

exploded in roaring laughter. People banged their fists on tables and stomped their feet on the floor. Even the bartender--as unfriendly as he was--cracked a smile at my words. Max held the chicken wing in front of his face, seemingly startled at my words. And I couldn't blame him, because I was, too.

Where in the world had those words come from?

"Oh, shit. That was good. Holy fuck," Rupert said through his laughter.

"I have to admit, that was good. Hoo-wee, I've never heard a girl go in on my brother like that."

I kept holding Max's gaze, hoping and praying I hadn't insulted him in any way. As my heart stopped in my chest, I watched him take a massive bite of his chicken wing. He practically stuffed the entire thing into his mouth and slowly pulled it out, removing all the meat with his tongue. An action that made me shiver and my toes curl.

Then he leveled me with another wink, one that settled my nervous gut and helped me relax into the atmosphere of the pub.

36

MAX

I placed money onto the table before I stood. As I reached my hand out for hers, I heard the guys whooping and whistling around me. I grinned as Dani blushed, slipping her soft hand against mine. And as my fingers wrapped against her skin, I led her to the front door.

"Have a nice night, you two!"

"Get it, pillow princess!"

"Don't let him have all the fun now!"

Dani giggled. "He'll have to fight me for it, that's for sure!"

The bar let up a slew of claps and whistles as a growl burst forth from my chest. This girl had been using that kind of language all night. Cursing. Making sexual innuendos. Blushing at me and alluding to things with her eyes that made my gut churn with desire for her. She was scratching on a door she wasn't ready to open. But damn it, I was ready to open it.

"I like your friends. They're a lot nicer than they look."

I grinned. "Yeah? Were you nervous?"

She reached for her helmet. "Yeah, a bit. I mean, when I first saw them. But they're nice. And funny."

"I'm glad you think so."

I watched her undo the strap on her helmet. She kept fumbling with it. She leaned against my bike and tucked the helmet underneath her arm to try and get a good grip on it. She looked so cute during her struggle, trying to get the damn thing unclipped and moving her hair out of the way long enough to slide the helmet over her head. She huffed and grumbled with the cutest little voice I'd ever heard.

"I'm glad you had a good time, beautiful."

She lifted her head. "Huh?"

I wrapped my arm around her quickly, pulling her into my chest. And as her eyes grew wide, I went in for the kill. I crashed my lips against hers as soft thumps and claps could be heard behind me. Not even the walls of the pub could mute their sounds of joy. I knew they were watching. Waiting to see what might happen. And as Dani let me claim her mouth, my body filled with desperation for her.

"I think they *really* like you," I murmured.

She giggled as she pulled back, then finally, the helmet slid down onto her head. I pressed my naked forehead against the visor of her helmet, enjoying her warmth for a few more seconds. What had this girl done to me? This little college girl with no more knowledge of the world than the back of my fucking toilet. It astounded me. I still hadn't figured it out.

I didn't want it to stop, though.

"Come on. Let's get out of here."

"I don't have classes in the morning."

I furrowed my brow as I reached for the button that flipped up her visor.

"What was that?" I asked.

She blushed furiously. "I said, uh, I don't have classes in the morning. I mean, if you want to stay out a bit later. I just mean I can, if you want."

I grinned. "Good to know."

I slid the visor back down over her face and reached for my helmet. Then, a few minutes later, we took off on my bike, with her arms draped around me and her legs squeezing my thighs, we raced through the night. Though we sure as hell weren't heading back to campus.

I knew exactly where I wanted to take her now.

I knew she mentioned that for a reason. I saw it in her eyes. In the flush of her cheeks. I raced through town, taking back alleys that made her squeal and cutting curbs just to feel her cling even tighter to me. I sped down the back country roads of the outskirts of town. And once we coasted into the driveway of my house, I heard her snicker.

"I knew you'd be thinking about sex the second I mentioned something."

I flipped my visor open. "Not sure what you're talking about."

She slid her helmet off. "Uh huh. Sure. You didn't

know at all. Right? You know, since your brother's still at the pub?"

I put down the kickstand. "Hey, you can think whatever you want. But I want another drink. And I can't do that while I'm out and driving with you around on the back of my bike. Come on. I'll fix you another rum and Coke."

We made our way inside and I sat her down at the kitchen table. I set about making us another round of drinks, favoring whiskey in a glass over another beer. I wanted something stronger. Something to sip on instead of gulp down. I sat the drink in front of Dani and watched--maybe a bit too closely--how she wrapped each individual finger around it.

Every movement of her body mesmerized me.

I wasn't sure why.

"You know, all of this is new to me."

Her voice brought me back to reality. "I can tell."

"Does that turn you off at all?"

I grinned. "Am I acting like it does?"

She snickered. "No, I just--maybe that wasn't the right term."

"Take your time. Find the right term."

I watched her take a long pull from her drink before she set it back down, licking her lips and thinking hard on my question.

Mesmerizing me with the movement of her tongue.

"I just meant, me not knowing much of this kind of lifestyle, it doesn't bother you at all?"

I shook my head. "Why would it?"

She shrugged. "I don't know. I guess…"

I waited for her to find her words as her eyes stared off over my shoulder.

"My father's a perfectionist. That's just how he was raised. He's Korean, and in his family, failure is anything other than our most perfect. It's why I'm always striving to get good grades. I mean, I want to get them, yes. But I also don't want to disappoint my father. Which happens more than I'd like it to."

I nodded, but I didn't interject. It looked like she needed to talk.

"And Mom? Well, she's a business owner. She's got her own interior design business. She makes just as much as my father, if not more. And she still found time to raise me, and keep our house put together, and get her own degree, and all sorts of other stuff. They're… two perfect peas in a perfect pod. It's exhausting to keep up with sometimes."

I nodded. "I can imagine."

She snickered. "You must think I'm stupid, complaining about that kind of stuff. I mean, I've got two parents who love me pay for my education, and give me everything I need or could ever want. Who want me to have the best start in life."

"Grass isn't always greener."

"And in some ways, I was fine with that. You know? I was fine with the judgment and Dad constantly critiquing my clothes and Mom constantly wanting me to dress up for dinner parties and Dad going over my research papers in school with a fine-toothed comb. I was okay with all of that because it was supposed to make me better. It's supposed to put me in this world and make me this person they want to be. This person *I* want to be."

"Sure you really want to be that person?"

I shrugged. "I don't know now."

I squeezed her hand. "Dani, look at me."

Her eyes slowly came back to mine and I saw tears lining them. The words coming out of her mouth didn't match the sadness in her eyes. And it killed me inside. Such a beautiful girl, with her entire life ahead of her. Just now finding out she wasn't really happy with it.

I could sympathize with that.

"What do you want *now*, Dani? Right now? This very second?"

Her eyes danced between mine. "Something different."

Something came over me. Whether it was lust, or passion, or a desire to know her more, I ran with it. I tugged her hand toward my body, raising her up from her chair. I captured her in my arms and pressed my lips against hers, tasting the Coke, the rum, and the way she opened up to me. The way her tongue slid against my own set my veins on fire. The way her back bowed to press her body against my own sent my gut churning. I picked her up and walked her out of the kitchen. She wrapped her legs around me and shed her coat, leaving it in a pile on the floor just outside my bedroom. She ripped at her scarf, tossing it to the floor. As I closed the door with my foot, I sucked on her lower lip, causing her to moan down the back of my throat.

As I settled her back against my mattress, I gazed into the depths of her twinkling eyes, needing her to answer me before I went any further.

"Are you sure this is what you want?" I asked.

She answered me by gripping the collar of my jacket to slide it off my shoulders.

"No more talking, Max."

Music to my fucking ears.

37

DANI

I hardly got his coat off before his lips slid down my neck. I felt his teeth raking against my pulse point as my nipples puckered for him. I gripped his shirt and ripped it over his head. As his body kissed down my clothed torso, I felt his hands fiddling with my jeans, undoing the button and sliding down the zipper. Then he fell to his knees on the floor.

I lifted my head and gazed at the man kneeling before me. A powerful man. A strong man. Chiseled with muscles and carved with tattoos. He slid my feet out of my boots and gripped my jeans, pulling them off my body. I giggled as I fisted the sheets, making sure I didn't go flying off the bed with them.

When his eyes found mine once more, my heart stopped in my chest.

"Lie back," he commanded.

I eased myself back down against the mattress, doing exactly as he asked. He picked my foot up, pressing kisses to each of my toes as I jumped and moaned involuntarily. Just the smallest touch of his lips drove me wild. Nothing like his tongue, though. I felt it darting against my skin, his lips nipping at my ankle and calf, all the way up the inside of my leg as my lower lips wet themselves for his viewing pleasure.

"Max," I moaned.

He slid my legs over his shoulders. "When I'm done, you won't have a voice to say my name with."

His tongue fell against my slit and my back arched. My jaw unhinged and my eyes widened as his tongue parted my folds. I gasped with shock. The electricity that overwhelmed my body swirled my head. My body took over, bucking against him wildly. As if it already knew what to do.

As if it had done this kind of thing before.

"Yes. Yes. Max. Oh, my gosh. Max, what are you--?"

He growled as his lips puckered. The suction from them sent my toes curling. My bare heels dug into his muscles, feeling them undulate and roll, working just for me. My breath came in short spurts. My hands flew to his hair. Tugging at him. Gripping him. Giving me leverage to roll hard against his face.

"Come for me, Dani," he growled.

"Oh, shit," I whimpered.

The coil within me popped, and my body shivered. My legs jumped and my toes flexed as I gasped for air. His tongue dove further between my legs, and when I felt something dancing at my entrance, my body collapsed back to the bed, groaning as his finger pierced me for the first time.

"Oh, Max," I moaned.

"So tight. We'll fix that in a minute."

I felt another finger at my entrance as the coil began to wind tight once more. His tongue dug into me, lapping deeply as my body scooted closer to the edge of the bed. Closer to him. And as his fingers filled me--spread me--I rocked against his stubble.

"Oh, yeah. Oh, Max. Just like that. Just like that. Don't stop. Don't stop. Oh, fuck. Please. Please, Max!"

"I love your sounds," he grunted.

"Max!"

I wailed out his name as my back arched off the bed. My eyes rolled back, screwing shut as stars burst behind them. His fingers stretched me. His tongue cleaned me up. And as my entire body locked out, I felt my world spiraling. Falling.

Drowning itself in Max's darkened abyss.

His tongue slowed down and I heaved to catch my breath. Over and over, beads of sweat trickled down the nape of my neck. His fingers moved, and I felt empty. And I didn't want to ever feel empty again.

"Max," I whispered.

"I'm right here, beautiful."

I managed to sit myself up on my elbows and watch while he undressed. His chest, gleaming with colors and tattoos I had never seen, made me lick my lips. I wanted to trace them with my tongue. I didn't even know why. That's just what my tongue wanted to do. My jaw fell open as he stripped himself of his boots. His pants. His boxers. His… everything.

And when my eyes fell to his cock, I swallowed hard.

"Oh, boy."

He chuckled. "Don't worry. I'll take care of you."

He lunged onto the bed and crashed his lips against my own. His hands clawed at my shirt, physically ripping it over my head, ripping everything else away from my body. He ravaged me. Mind, body, and soul. And as his mouth explored my crevices, I felt my legs spread further for him.

"Fill me up. Please," I whispered.

His chuckle shot electricity down between my legs, wetting me further as I felt him reach between us. His arm slid underneath the small of my back, holding me close to him, tilting my pelvis toward him.

"Look at me. Not down there."

My head snapped up. I hadn't even realized I'd been watching. But as he held my gaze, I felt the thick tip of him breach me. Spread me. Fill me up. My legs jumped as my muscles contracted, and he stopped his movements.

"Relax, Dani. I've got you."

The soothing, dulcet sounds of his voice relaxed me against his arm. I threaded my own around his neck, my nails digging into his back. He grunted softly, pressing further into my body. The dull pain made me wince. But he went slow, stopping when he felt me tighten. He didn't force his way through, like I figured he might.

It almost felt like he cared.

When I felt his hips bottom out against my own, I sighed and kissed his neck. Along his shoulder. Even down his arm. He settled my back against the mattress, his hand smoothing my hair away from my eyes. And when he drew back, he inched his way in again.

Watching me as I shivered.

"Oh, my God!"

He grinned. "There it is."

"What--what is that? What are--oh!"

He rolled his hips, sliding against a part of my body that made me jolt. Fire ignited behind my eyes. I felt my legs already locking around his waist. His hips moved slowly. They thrusted upward, stroking that sweet spot that made my damn mouth water. And as I dug my nails into his back, I clung to him. Waiting for him to take me on the ride he promised.

"Hang on tight, gorgeous," he growled.

His hips pulled back and he slammed into me. My head fell back as my voice erupted from my throat. My tits jumped. My body soared. And with each thrust of his body, I leapt for his viewing pleasure. I watched him smile wolfishly. My eyes kept fluttering closed as he pounded into my body. Filling me, and leaving me. Filling me, and leaving me. Making me feel beautiful with the sounds of skin slapping skin.

And the sounds of his headboard battering against the wall.

"Holy fuck, Dani."

"Max," I said hoarsely.

"That's it. Squeeze that cock. Holy shit, woman."

"Yes. Yes. Yes. Yes."

"That's it. Come for me. Come on my cock."

"Max!"

His teeth sank into my neck as he sucked and nibbled. He fucked me through my orgasm, my walls collapsing around him. The world tunneled around me. Colors burst and sizzled in my pinhole vision. But, he didn't stop. He didn't stop his beautiful assault on my body until I erupted again. His fingers fell between my folds. He swirled around my aching clit. I bucked against him wildly, raking my nails up and down his back. His arms. His sides.

"Yes. Yes. Do it again. I know you've got one more for me, Dani."

I tried to catch my breath enough to call out his name, but I couldn't. All I did was cough. And sputter. While that coil wound tighter with every thrust of his hips and every swirl of his fingertips.

"I have to pee," I finally managed.

My eyes fell open and his eyes ignited.

"Oh, no you don't."

"What?"

"You don't have to pee."

"What? I--Max, you have to--Max. I can't--."

"Just let go. Trust me, and let go, Dani."

"But I have to--."

"Do it, Dani!"

His fingers pressed deeply into my body and I caved. My silent wails tried to burst forth as my muscles contracted and released. Something spilled between my legs. Something sprayed, coating Max as he ground against me. Rutting, like the fucking animal he was.

"That's it. Oh, yeah. Give it all to me, Dani. There it is."

I whimpered at his words as my body gave out. Spent, against the mattress, as the wet spot underneath me grew.

"Max," I said hoarsely.

He growled as his spurts of arousal blanketed my walls. I felt them. All of them. Filling me, until they dripped down my ass crack. I saw his muscles twitching. I saw the sweat dripping down his face. And I saw the satisfied smile on his face as he fell beside me, pulling me out of our mess and close against his body.

"I've gotcha. Come here."

My head fell lazily against his arm. He picked up my hand and settled it over his chest. Giving my fingertips a chance to trace his tattoos.

Specifically, the one over his heart.

It was a gorgeous tattoo. There was a sun rising behind a red rose. And the rose was surrounded by this circle of interwoven vines. The entire circle was filled with the light of the sunrise in the background, and I couldn't take my eyes off it.

"Every member has one."

I paused. "Hmm?"

He kissed my forehead. "The tattoo you're tracing. Every member has one."

I nodded. "I love them. They're wonderful."

"At this rate, I'll end up making arrangements to get you inked, too."

I snickered. "There's no way."

I felt his body tighten before he gripped my chin. He tilted my head up to his, our gazes meeting. I saw something flash behind them. Something that sent my stomach fluttering with butterflies.

"Who said you had a say in the matter, Bambi?"

I giggled, before I realized he wasn't joking. "Max, I-I-I… I can't get a tattoo. I mean, come on."

He didn't answer me, though.

"Max, seriously. My parents would--."

"Never have to know."

"I don't think that's how that--."

"Besides. They're not the boss of you."

I bit my bottom lip. "I suppose you're right on that. Technically, I'm the boss of me."

And when he threw his head back with laughter, his next words sent a chill down my spine. A chill I wasn't sure was a good thing. But, wasn't really a bad thing, either.

"Oh no, baby girl. You've got a great deal to learn if you want to stay at my side. And the first thing you learn, right now, is that you're wrong. *You're* not the boss of yourself."

His eyes filled with hunger before he rolled me back over onto my back. Pinning me down with his body as his lips hovered over my own.

"*I* am."

38

MAX

Now, Dani's arms around my waist only felt second-best to the feeling I had this morning. Because waking up with that girl curled up against me left me speechless. And trust me, speechless wasn't a trait. I always had something to say, and I never hesitated to say it. But, gazing down into her sleeping face. Watching the way her eyes fluttered as she tried to wake up, only to curl in deeper and fall back into slumber. It was a sight to behold.

Especially when she let me wake her up fully with my tongue.

We spent the entire day together. Lounging around in bed. Watching television while I massaged her body. She was sore, as I figured she would be. But, massaging her gave me another chance to feel her. Drink her in. Trace her curves with my fingertips. And with wandering hands came interesting places to explore.

I loved the sound of her orgasms filling up my room.

But, the day had come to a close. Night sat heavily upon the town, and I had to get her ass back to campus. So, she clutched me close. Pressing herself against me as I sped back to the dinky little college campus where I had first saw her.

Seems like an eternity ago.

"I had a great time, Max."

She slipped her helmet off with ease this time, and it made me grin.

"Me, too."

She handed it to me. "See you soon? Maybe?"

I slipped my hand into my pocket. "Use it whenever you need it."

I handed her a slip of paper with my number on it. I wasn't sure she got it the first time. When she opened it up, her eyes came to life. I wanted that look to forever be on her face. As if I had given her the greatest treasure life had to offer.

"Thank you. Really."

I nodded. "Might as well have it. Text me when you get upstairs, so I've got yours."

She slipped it into her back pocket. "I will. I promise."

I reached for her and pulled her in for one last kiss. One last parting goodbye before I swatted her pert ass playfully. She giggled as she walked away from me, peering over her shoulder and waving. She really did have a giggly little schoolgirl down in that soul of hers.

She really is something.

I watched her as she walked into her dorm. I didn't move until that door closed behind her. I watched her top-floor window, waiting for the light to come on so I knew she got up there safely. There was always a chance she wouldn't. And I sure as hell didn't want to peel off before I saw that light flicker on.

However, I felt my pocket vibrating, pulling me from my trance.

"What?" I asked.

Benji snickered. "Where the hell are you?"

"At your school. Just outside your dorm. Why?"

"Good. I have to talk to you. Stay out there."

"You don't give the orders around here."

"Stay there. I'm coming down to meet you."

I lifted my head and watched Dani's room light turn on. And not too long after that, I felt my phone vibrate in my hand, signaling that she had obeyed me.

Good girl. "You've got two minutes of my time. Make it quick."

I hung up the phone and opened the message, smiling at the little heart she left me. The words *I made it safe. Thank you for a wonderful time* warmed my heart. And I immediately saved her number in my phone. Then I slipped it back into my pocket and waited for the little asshole that had really been testing my patience lately.

Crossing a line no man ever wanted to cross with me.

With that stunt he'd pulled on Dani at the pool, I had a great deal I wanted to say to him as well. But not just about that. The shit he'd pulled with my father, running to him like a fucking tattle tale, I couldn't let that stand.

This ended now.

I flipped my kickstand down and slid off my bike. I leaned against it, watching the dorm door and waiting for Benji to come out. After two minutes had passed-- clocking them by the second in my head--I reached for my phone.

A voice sounded behind me.

"Oh, no you don't."

I felt something wrap around my neck before a hard force slammed against my jaw. My eyes widened, my presence completely caught off-guard. And that was hard to do most days. My legs buckled and the harness around my neck let go, causing me to plummet to the ground face first, where my cheek crashed against the pavement.

"You're ours tonight, little girl."

I growled. "If you say so."

I turned around and counted the goons around me. Three of them, all staring at me with spit practically dripping from their fucking fangs. I threw both of my boots up, knocking two of them in their balls. And when the third one went to punch me, I wrapped my hands around his forearm and dragged him to the ground, rolling him over before I straddled his body.

The men had black masks over their faces. But, for some reason, a pair of eyes looked familiar. I wailed on the man beneath me, landing punch after punch directly to his face. I felt something snap underneath my knuckles before someone pulled me off, and I whipped around with my arms outstretched, wrapping my hands around the man's neck and closing off his ability to breathe. And when his eyes widened, I wonder where I had seen them before.

Why do I feel like I know you guys?

I took stock of what I could as fists flew and legs kicked. All of them had gold rings stacked on their fingers. Gaudy, disgusting rings that hurt every time a punch connected. Fucking hell, I hated rings. All kinds of rings. Every single fucking ring.

Because they always tore at skin, no matter what direction they came from.

Cheap fighters. Might as well have brass knuckles, assholes.

I slammed my knee into the stomach in front of me, then turned around and clocked my bleeding fist into another stomach in front of me. I watched two men hit the ground before I looked around, searching for the last one. My nostrils flared. My blood pumped through my veins. One more asshole to take down before I dragged them into the woods to beat the ever-loving shit out of them.

"Looking for someone?"

A searing pain ripped through my neck. I felt those damn rings sink into the nape of my neck before tearing back, bringing skin along with them. I growled as I fell to my knees, and someone landed a punch to my gut. As I bent down onto all fours, trying my best to keep myself upright, a boot came sailing into my ribs.

Taking me down for the count.

"Puny fucker."

"Bullshit man."

"You're a piece of shit. I hope you know that."

Their gruff voices rang out in my ears. I felt blood working its way up the back of my throat. I heard people yelling in the distance. Shrieking, way off. As if someone had finally seen what the hell was going on. I saw the light on the ground growing brighter. I felt a hand fist my jacket before pulling me up. And when my head rolled back, I gazed at the two men standing behind me. Upside down.

I don't know who you guys are, but you're dead.

"I love a good session of foreplay. Hope you do, too. Because this is just an appetizer to the main event."

And as the man behind me threaded his fingers together, I watched him hold up his fists, bringing them down with a soaring fury before they smashed into my teeth. I felt something chip and something else popped. And when the man dropped me to the concrete, my body tangled itself up into knots.

The last thing I heard was their laughter as they walked away, drowning out the yells and the cries for help. I thought about Dani. Whether or not she was really okay. And I thought about Benji. Whether or not he had something to do with this. Whether or not he was in on this. And all the ways I might kill him if he was.

All of it, swirling around.

Before my world went black.

39

DANI

I sat there, staring at my phone, waiting for him to text back. I knew he'd seen the text. That little word 'read' underneath the one I sent was taunting me. Staring me in the face and gloating over its own existence. I used to not give a flying crap about stuff like that.

So why did I care this time?

I sighed as I set my phone down. I mean, I hadn't heard his bike take off. I knew he was still here. Was he downstairs doing something? Making his way back up? Did he miss me? Or, maybe I'd left something behind?

I got up from my desk and walked over to the window, determined to see what was going on. What I saw stopped me in my tracks.

"Max!" I exclaimed.

I watched in horror as three men kicked him, slammed their fists into him, leered and jeered and hovered over him. I felt sick to my stomach. I had to do something. I had to get down there and help!

I rushed out of my dorm room and barreled for the stairwell before my senses came back to me.

If you go out there, they might attack you.

Would they really attack a woman?

They attacked Max. They've got balls.

My head swirled as I jumped down the steps two by two until I got all the way to the main floor. I burst through the door as I heaved heavy breaths, trying to keep myself as calm as I could. I rushed over to a small window and saw the three men walking away, all of them wearing black ski masks, faded black jeans and black long-sleeved shirts.

Laughing as they left Max's body on the pavement.

I watched in horror as the men stepped off the curb into the middle of the road. They all jogged toward the SUV sitting on the other side of the road that I hadn't even seen and hopped in the back. Not one of them got into the front seat.

There are four of them.

It took all of my willpower to simply stand there and watch. But the second the SUV peeled away and careened around the corner, I rushed for the dorm door. I heard people gasping the second I slammed through it. I saw people with their phones out, taking pictures and videos. Gawking at the scene. But had any of them called 9-1-1?

"Max! Max, Max. Can you hear me?" I asked.

I ran toward him and fell to my knees, my eyes

darting over his body. His eyes were closed and he was barely breathing. Holy shit, he needed a hospital.

"Max, please. I need you to open your eyes, okay?"

I shook his shoulder softly before he rolled over onto his back.

"Holy. Fuck," he groaned.

"Max, I'm calling 9-1-1, okay? Just--just hold on."

He shook his head. "No. No hospitals."

"What are you, insane? Yes. I'm calling you a--"

My hands slid into my back pockets, but I didn't feel my phone. I checked my bra, my front pockets, even the jacket pockets of the leather I hadn't taken off yet. But, my phone was nowhere to be found.

Shit. It's still on my desk.

"I said no hospitals."

I shook my head. "Max, you probably have broken bones, I'm almost positive you're--"

He growled. "No. Benji will be here any minute. He'll know what to do. How long was I out for?"

I looked around to see if I could find the lanky boy. But he was nowhere to be found. Even the people snapping pictures and taking videos had all darted off. You know, after they got what they needed for their social media feeds. Idiots. I hated social media with a passion. It was nothing but a distraction. A way for us to feel--

"Bambi!"

His gruff voice jolted me from my trance. "Uh, sorry. Yeah, uh, a couple of minutes? You were out before I got to you, though. So, easily double that?"

He grunted, but he didn't say anything.

I gnawed on the inside of my cheek as I looked around, searching for anyone that might've been watching. That might know where in the world Benji was. But, the longer I knelt there, the more I wondered if anyone was coming at all.

"Max, I don't think he's coming. It's just us out here. We're all--"

"He'll show. I promise you that."

"What if he doesn't?"

I gazed into Max's eyes just before he closed them. And the icy electricity that shot through my veins made me swallow. Hard. He was angry. I'd never seen that kind of anger in anyone's eyes before. I wiped at the blood trickling from the corner of his mouth and brushed my fingertip over his bruised nose, watching as he winced.

Lord knows that's broken.

"Max, I don't--"

He snarled. "Shut up so I can think."

I nodded, but I didn't say anything.

I waited there with him. At his side. Kneeling there, trying to figure out what in the world to do. My heart raced, fluttering so hard I thought it might be enough to pull me from the ground and fly me into the clouds. I was hyper-aware of everything. The lights on campus. The lack of protection we had around us. The fact that we were right by one of the main roads that outlined campus. Out there, for anyone passing by to see. I felt exposed, like a raw nerve. I wanted, more than ever, to get Max into the shadows. Out of harm's way.

But how in the world was I supposed to accomplish that?

"Okay, executive decision time," I said.

"No. He'll be--"

"Come on, Max. We're in the middle of lights. Help me get you up. Come on, big boy."

I grabbed his wrists and slowly tugged him upright. I was almost certain that bruise on his head meant he had a concussion. I helped him up to his feet and wrapped his arm around my shoulders. Then, together, we stumbled over to the dorm door. I swiped my card and it opened, but it was hard as hell trying to get that massive, stumbling man through it.

"We'll take the elevator up to my room," I said breathlessly.

I knew Hannah might not appreciate it, but at least there I could clean him up. Again.

And possibly get him out of harm's way in the process.

40

MAX

"No. We aren't going anywhere."

I leaned my body toward the wall and slipped my arm away from Dani's shoulders.

"Max, stop being so damn stubborn. We need to get you upstairs."

I sighed. "Do you have a car?"

"You have to lay down. I think you have a concussion."

"Yeah, I know I do. I think. I have to go home. I have to get home. Where's that car of yours?"

"Max, please."

I glared at her. "Car. Now. Or I'll find it and steal it myself."

Her nostrils flared with frustration. "Fine. Yes. I have a car. I'll take you to it."

"Good. I'll tell you where we're going once we get there."

"Fan-fucking-tastic."

I grinned. "Cursing sounds good in your voice."

She scoffed. "Asshole."

I chuckled. "Pretty much."

She took my hand and tossed my arm back over her shoulder. Then we started the hefty trek across campus. Holy shit, how far away was her car? With every step I took, my head pounded even more. It grew worse by the second, and I knew I needed someone to check it out. But not a doctor in a hospital. Not in a place where the police would be called to investigate shit. No, I needed the doctor the crew had on speed dial.

Once I was in the comfort of my own bedroom.

"Where the hell is this thing?"

Dani sighed. "This was your plan, so you can shut up until we get there. All right?"

"Well, look who's a bit testy tonight."

"I wouldn't be if you'd just accept help."

"This is me accepting help. You're helping me to your car so you can help me get home. See? Help."

She sighed. "You're relentless."

"And you're very cute when you're upset."

I watched that frown turn into the smallest grin and I considered it a win. I also took the lack of nausea as a win. My head really fucking hurt, but it didn't come with anything else. No throbbing. No body aches. No fever. No nausea. The world didn't feel as if it were tilting onto its side, nor did it feel like I was floating around on air.

It'd be nice if I didn't have a concussion, that's for sure.

"Almost there. First level of the parking garage across the street."

I grunted. "Finally. Come on, Bambi."

"I hate you," she murmured.

"Bah. That's not true, and you know it."

I peeked down at her and saw her cheeks and neck flush. Hell, even the tip of her nose reddened quite a bit. I smiled as we started across the street, my eyes still hanging onto her every shred of beauty. Man, this girl was something else. A real firecracker, when put into situations like this.

She was dealing with it better than she probably knew.

I heard a car door unlock before she opened the door for me. And as I splayed out along the microfiber seats of the SUV she dumped me into, my breathing grew ragged. Holy fuck, that was a serious trek. I had beads of sweat dripping down my damn back. I closed my eyes, only for a second. I tried to draw in deep breaths, but they only made me cough. I didn't taste blood, though. And that was a good thing.

At least it isn't broken.

"You've broken a rib, probably. That's why you're struggling to breathe."

I chuckled. "Reading my mind now, are you? And for your information, it's bruised. I'd be tasting blood if it was broken."

"And your lip needs stitches."

"Nothing a Band-Aid can't fix."

"And you need ice packs. Serious ice packs for those bruises."

I snickered. "Should I be paying you for your advice now, Doc?"

She cranked up the car. "No, I'm just stating the obvious in the hopes that you'll pull out of this idiotic stupor you've found yourself in."

I coughed again. "Well, it sounds much better in your voice."

"My concern is that you've punctured your lung or something like that."

"And again, no. I'm not coughing up blood. The blood I'm tasting is from my lip. I'll be fine. Get us out of this damn parking garage, though. We need to head back to my place. All this chit chat is making my head hurt."

"Because you're concussed."

"Dani, damn it. Just do as I'm telling you to do."

She sighed. "Which direction am I turning when--"

I groaned as I sat up. "Just pick one!"

She jumped. "Fine. Don't have to be so pissy about it."

I shook my head as I forced myself upright. The pounding was relentless. The higher my head got above my feet, the more it hurt. And I felt that damn knot behind my head forming into a nice little dragon egg of a lump. But I needed to see where the hell we were going so I could guide her in. I mean, even I had the sense to admit when I wasn't in any condition to drive myself.

And this was one of those times.

She took a left out of the parking garage and made her way off campus. The road shifted from brick campus buildings into trees lined with babbling brooks. My favorite road. I loved this road. It was my favorite place to ride whenever I was by myself. A little slice of heaven dropped right into the middle of Ann Arbor. I leaned against the passenger's seat, keeping my eyes out the windshield as I rested my head. If I could just take a small nap...

Dani patted my upper arm. "No, keep your eyes open. Focus on me."

I looked at her face and registered how terrified she looked. I even felt it in the way she patted me to open my eyes again. Soft, fluttering strokes from her shaking hands. I watched as her eyes darted around, even though we were only going twenty-five miles an hour. So scared. So paranoid. Part of me felt guilty for putting her in this position.

Then again, she didn't have to come after me. All she had to do was stay upstairs in the safety of her own damn dorm room.

Faster, Dani. Come on now.

I needed her to step on it, but with the way she was white-knuckling her steering wheel, I figured I'd cut her some slack. She was very nervous, and I felt bad. Apparently, this head contusion had knocked some guilt into my gut.

You have to get home. And quickly.

"Can you pick up the pace a bit?"

She snarled. "I'm going as fast as I can."

"It's forty on this road."

"And I'm doing--!"

Her eyes fell to the speedometer before I felt the engine revving.

"Sorry," she murmured.

I placed my hand on her thigh. "You're doing great. This road ends at a small highway. Take a right when you get to it."

She nodded. "Can do."

I had to get to my brother. I had to call our doctor. But, more than that, I had to talk to him about what the hell just happened tonight. I was almost certain this was a hit of some sort. With explicit instructions to only rough me up. What if I wasn't the only one with a hit out on me right now? And where the fuck was Benji? Had they gotten him, too?

I have to call Rupert.

Hell, I needed to call the rest of the guys. Check up on them. Make sure this wasn't some rival gang trying to reach out and intimidate us on our own territory.

What if this is your father?

My eyes fell back onto Dani and my mind swirled with what that might mean for her. Had my father sent a team after me because she was still in my life? Because if so, that meant this was personal. Good for the guys, bad for me.

And her.

Very, very bad for her.

"Max?"

I groaned as my eyes slipped open. When the fuck had they closed in the first place?

"Where do I go now?"

I blinked slowly. "What happened?"

She sighed. "I took that right turn onto the small highway. What now?"

Fuck, that felt like ages ago. "Uh, two miles, road to your left called 'Sandy Ridge.' Take a left on it."

"Thanks."

Every time Dani called out my name for another direction, my eyes ripped open, with absolutely no recollection of them ever closing in the first place. Was I slipping in and out of consciousness? Sleeping? Was this a bad thing? Did I need to keep my eyes open?

Fucking hell, this is bad.

"Max?"

I grunted as I opened my eyes yet again. "What?"

"Why no hospitals?"

I groaned. "Where are we?"

"Sitting at a stoplight. Why did those guys jump you?"

"Which stoplight?"

She sighed. "The one you told me about that we'd hit before the left I needed to take. Now, answer my questions."

I paused. "When did I give you those directions?"

"Who are you, Max?"

She turned toward me, her eyes finding mine for the first time since we'd gotten into the car. I craned my head back to look at the stoplight. Still red. Trapping me in this hellhole of questions I had no intention of answering for her.

"Please, Max. Who... who are you?"

I cleared my throat. "When you take the left--"

"No, Max. Now. I want an answer. Something to

go on. Who are the Red Thorns? Is this connected to your motorcycle… whatever?"

I grinned as my eyes fell closed again. "Bambi, I'm the man of your dreams and your worst fucking nightmare. Now, step on the gas pedal. I've got shit to do, and you're standing in the way of it."

Thank you for reading RED THORNS. Don't miss RED ROSE, book 2 in Max and Danika's love story, and be sure to join my SMS list below to don't miss any of my future books!

Get an SMS alert when Rebel releases a new book:
Text REBEL to 77948

If you want to support me, consider leaving a review on Amazon. I'd love it!

ABOUT THE AUTHOR

Rebel Hart is an author of Contemporary and Dark Romance novels. Check out her debut series Diamond In The Rough.

NEVER MISS A NEW RELEASE:
Follow Rebel on Amazon
Follow Rebel on Bookbub

Text REBEL to 77948 to don't miss any of her books (US only) or sign up at www.RebelHart.net to get an email alert when her next book is out.

autorrebelhart@gmail.com

CONNECT WITH REBEL HART:

ALSO BY REBEL HART

For a full list of my books go to:

www.RebelHart.net

Printed in Great Britain
by Amazon